Praise for the works of Cade Haddock Strong

The Schuyler House

...is a story about learning valuable life lessons from painful circumstances, opening one's heart to love and making positive changes in one's life. This story captivated me on so many levels because I was taken on a wild journey with Mattie! The numerous twists and turns in the plot kept me wondering about what was going to happen next. I also entertained insane thoughts of just forgoing sleep so I could continue to read on to satisfy my curiosity. If you enjoy a storyline with unique twists and angst filled situations coupled with a dash of slow burning romance, then this is certainly the story for you!

- The Lesbian Review

Fare Game

The author nails intrigue/thriller and romance in this book...The whistle-blowing storyline is plausible, logical, tense and interesting, the romance believable and sweet, the ending satisfying. With all other elements done well, this one makes a second good book by Haddock Strong. I liked it, and will definitely check out her next offering.

-Pin's Reviews, *goodreads*

This author is new to me but I'll be looking for more of her work because I really liked this story. It's a romantic thriller with two likeable leads, some well-done minor characters and very interesting plot that kept me interested from start to finish

-Emma A., *NetGalley*

My belief is that when readers pick up this book, they will be enamored by a carefully and skillfully plotted story line that's also well written and doesn't sacrifice moral complexity to the demands of a fast-moving narrative. Ms. Haddock Strong does such a great job...

-Diane W., *NetGalley*

The plot has many layers—lust, a whirlwind relationship, intrigue (where is the money going?)—and desperate characters on both sides of the law.

-Ginger O., *NetGalley*

I loved how Haddock Strong gets her readers into the story. Her writing is clear and persuasive, and she manages to explain airline financial irregularities, price-fixing, and whistleblowing without ruffling a single one of my feathers. She introduces them slowly as part of the story, mostly in dialogue, and they become one of the many layers of the story. Likewise, the relationship between Kay and Riley is also layered, their professional and personal lives, their exploration of each other and their difficulties. It is beautifully done. This book is a must for readers like me that need a bit of something on the side of their romance. It gives a good read, good romance as well as some very hot sexy moments. An excellent combination.

-*The Lesbian Review*

JACKPOT

Other Bella Books by Cade Haddock Strong

The Schuyler House
Fare Game

About the Author

Cade spent many years working in the airline industry, and she and her wife have traveled all over the world. When not writing, she loves to be outside, especially skiing, hiking, biking, and playing golf. She grew up in Upstate New York but has lived all over the US and abroad, from the mountains of Vermont and Colorado to the bustling cities of DC, Chicago and Amsterdam.

Find Cade on Instagram @cadehaddockstrong, Twitter @CHaddockStrong, Facebook @CHaddockStrong or her website at cadehaddockstrong.com.

JACKPOT

Cade Haddock Strong

BELLA
BOOKS
2020

Bella Books, Inc.
P.O. Box 10543
Tallahassee, FL 32302

Printed in the United States of America on acid-free paper.

First Bella Books Edition 2020

Editor: Alissa McGowan
Cover Designer: L. J. Hill

ISBN: 978-1-59493-609-8

Acknowledgments

I love writing and I am so thankful to everyone who has supported and encouraged me along the sometimes bumpy, and often exhilarating road to becoming a published author. Thank you to Bella for believing in me and sticking by me on this one. Thank you, readers, for reading!

The friendships I have developed with other authors have meant all the difference to me. They've cheered me on and cheered me up; slogged through my early drafts and celebrated with me when I released my work into the world.

Thank you especially to my beta readers, Celeste Castro, Tagan Shepard, and Sarah Jeffries. This story is a thousand times better because of you. You all rock!

A shout out to Ann Roberts for helping me through an earlier draft of this story. Your patience and persistence kept me going.

Thank you to my editor, Alissa McGowan. Sorry if your red pen ran out of ink. Grammar and I are like oil and vinegar. I hope you get back out on the slopes one of these days.

And most of all, thank you to my wife, Lisa, for reading countless drafts, listening to me ramble about characters, and scenes and random scattered thoughts. There is no way this book or any of my others would have become a reality if it hadn't been for you.

CHAPTER ONE

Conversation at Thirsty's Tavern came to an abrupt halt. All eyes were on the TV. A man in a pin-striped suit gave the audience a toothy smile and said, "Good evening and welcome to Lionball, America's favorite lottery game. Tonight's jackpot is more than five…hundred…million…dollars!"

A big glass machine whirled in the background. It spat out a ping-pong ball and sent it dribbling down a small metal chute. The man swooshed his hand through the air and said, "The first number in tonight's drawing is seventeen."

Five more balls followed. He announced each with equal fanfare, and after the sixth and final one, the winning numbers flashed on the screen. Everyone in Thirsty's let out a collective groan and tossed their red and white slips of paper up into the air.

That is, everyone except Ty. She stood behind the bar and stared down at her ticket. Every single one of her numbers matched.

"Holy shit. I won the jackpot."

Her coworker Zach and the patrons within earshot all snapped to attention.

"You're pulling our leg," Rusty, one of the regulars, said.

Ty shook her head in disbelief.

Rusty leaned over the bar. "Let me see that ticket."

Ty stuffed it into the front pocket of her jeans.

He reached out and grabbed her arm. "Hey, Blondie," he slurred.

Ty hated it when he called her that. She wriggled out of his grip and fell back toward the long shelf of liquor bottles, knocking a few to the ground. This caused more eyes to turn in her direction.

"I said, let me see your ticket," Rusty said.

He was twice her size and drunk, but even sober, Ty didn't trust him. On more than one occasion, she'd seen him pocketing money someone had left on the bar for a tip. When he lurched at her again, she took off toward the back of the bar, sped through the kitchen, and slipped out the rear door.

An alley ran along the back of the bar. If she went left, it dead-ended at a tall chain-link fence. If she went right, it would dump her out on the street in front of Thirsty's. She went left. At five foot seven and in decent shape, she could scale the fence, and if he came after her, she was pretty sure Rusty could not.

Her shirt caught on the top of the fence. She tore it free and jumped to the ground on the opposite side just as Rusty and one of his buddies stepped into the alley. After a quick check of her pockets for her phone, wallet, and the lottery ticket, she took off running. To where, she didn't know.

When she was about three blocks from Thirsty's, she dipped behind a parked car to see if she was being followed. It was a mild Saturday night in Asheville, North Carolina, and the street was full of revelers. Fortunately, Rusty and his pal did not appear to be among them. Ty assessed her situation. She had twenty bucks in her wallet, it was a chilly evening in early spring, she was wearing nothing but a ripped T-shirt, and a drunk asshole wanted to steal the lottery ticket tucked in her pocket. *Winning* lottery ticket. She'd have to wait to celebrate that. Right now, her priority was getting home undetected.

After scanning the crowded street one more time, she took off toward her apartment. It would only take her a minute to grab a few supplies. After that, she'd jump in her car and find a safe place to crash for the night. She was pretty sure Rusty had no idea where she lived, but she didn't want to take any chances, at least not until she was able to get the winning ticket in a secure place. Her apartment was on the top floor of an old house a few blocks off the main drag. A lone streetlight flickered, and the faint sound of Journey's "Don't Stop Believin'" could be heard coming from one of her neighbors.

When a car turned down the street, Ty dove behind a row of hedges seconds before its headlights fell on her. The car door opened, and the sound of some top 40 song and laughter spilled out. Three young women climbed out of the car and made their way toward the hub of bars at the far end of the street. Once they were gone, Ty bolted across the road and bounded up the three flights of stairs to her apartment. She put her key into the lock, stepped inside, and closed the door behind her. The only light came from a floor lamp in the living room.

"Hello," she called out.

There was no answer. Her roommate, Misty, was probably down at Lola's, the one true lesbian bar in downtown Asheville.

Ty didn't waste any time. She stuffed clothes and toiletries into a backpack, emptied the jar of cash she kept hidden under her bed, grabbed her laptop off the kitchen table, and snatched her car keys from the bowl near the front door. She locked the apartment door and crept down the back staircase to the gravel parking lot behind the house. Thankfully, her old Subaru wagon started on the first turn. Unfortunately, its gas gauge hovered just above empty.

Not wanting to risk running out of gas, she pulled into a station just outside of town. The bright lights illuminating its pumps lit up the whole block. Ty pulled a credit card from her wallet, but after a moment's hesitation, tucked it back in place. Better to pay in cash, even if it meant having to go inside and prepay. Her paranoia was off the charts, and there was no reason to leave an electronic trail if she didn't have to. She scurried inside the station's convenience store.

"Nice evening, ain't it?" the attendant asked.

Ty smiled politely and handed him a crumpled twenty-dollar bill. "Sure is."

He slowly keyed in the numbers to activate her pump. "Pretty soon it'll be hotter than the dickens. Spring's my favorite time 'round here. Nice weather, and all the college kids leave for the summer. Not that I mind them. It's just nice and quiet once they're gone."

The guy was probably lonely, and Ty didn't want to be rude, but there was no time for chit chat. "Have a nice evening," she said and pushed through the door before he could utter another word.

While the gas chugged into the tank, Ty twisted her long blond hair into a knot on the top of her head. When the pump shut off, she spun the cap back on her tank, slid behind the wheel, and peeled out of the station. As she drove out of town, her eyes darted between the road, the car's speedometer, and the rearview mirror. The last thing she needed was to attract the attention of the local police.

Twenty minutes later, she slowed when a flashing motel sign came into view. It was one of those seedy roadside joints where you park outside the door to your room. Half the bulbs on the neon sign advertising air-conditioning and free cable TV were either flickering or totally burnt out, and it was impossible to tell if they had *Vacancy* or *No Vacancy*, but she decided to give the place a shot. She was only about fifteen miles outside of Asheville, but she figured that was a safe enough distance, and she was anxious to get off the road.

She paid cash for a room, and rather than park out front, drove her car around back. The room was small, and the décor was dated, but it looked clean. She double locked the door and pushed the dresser up against it. Not exactly Fort Knox, but it would have to do for now.

No one knows you're here.

She sat down on the orange and brown floral bedspread and pulled the lottery ticket out of her pocket. As she stared at the small slip of paper, she wondered if it was all a mistake. Maybe she hadn't won at all. Maybe she'd misread the numbers in the midst of all the chaos at Thirsty's. She typed *Lionball* into her phone, and when the winning numbers came up on the screen, she compared them to those on her ticket. They all matched. She really had won. She should be jumping for joy, but instead, she was scared shitless.

The ringing of her phone startled her. It was her best friend Sarah.

"Hello."

"Ty?" Sarah yelled over the booming music in the background, a strong indication she was at Lola's. "Where the hell are you? I thought you were going to meet me after—"

"Sarah, can you step outside for a sec?"

"What? I can barely hear you. Get your ass down here."

"Sarah, listen. I need your help."

"Huh?"

"I need your help," Ty shouted into the phone. "It's kind of an emergency."

"Oh, my God. Are you okay?"

"Yes, no. Can you get away from the speaker?"

"Okay. Hold on a sec."

Ty heard some rustling and the music got fainter. She thought maybe Sarah had dropped her phone. "Sarah, you there?"

After a brief pause, Sarah said, "Yeah, yeah, I'm here."

"Listen, I'm going to text you an address. Can you come right away?"

"Why? What's going on?"

"I'll explain when you get here."

"But I just met a total hottie and she's eyeing me across the room…"

"Please, Sar. I need you to snap out of it. I'm not kidding around."

"Shit, okay. I've had a few shots of tequila."

"I can tell."

"Text me the address. I'll try and find a taxi."

"Hurry. Oh, and Sarah?"

"Yeah?"

"Make sure no one follows you."

Ty ended the call and frantically looked around the room for the motel's address. It was printed on the phone affixed to the wall near the bed. She texted it to Sarah. Aside from her brother, Reed, there was no one in the world Ty trusted more. They'd been best friends since they were five.

After what felt like an hour, there was a soft knock on the door. Ty peeked around the edge of the heavy curtains covering the window. Sarah stood there, coatless and shivering. Ty dragged the dresser away from the door and disengaged the locks.

"What the hell are you doing holed up in this seedy motel?" Sarah asked as soon as she stepped inside.

Ty reinforced the door. "Have a seat and I'll explain."

Sarah lowered herself into a chair near the door and took in her surroundings. "Okay, I'm all ears."

Once Sarah was seated, Ty dug into the pocket and extracted the small red and white piece of paper with the word *Lionball* etched across the top. She held it up for Sarah to see. "I'm here because of this."

"Is that a lottery ticket?"

"Yes, but not just any lottery ticket. It's the *winning* lottery ticket."

"Are you trying to tell me—"

"Yes."

"No fucking way." Sarah ran a hand through her cropped, bleach-blond hair. "The jackpot was huge, like 500 million or something."

Ty stuffed the ticket back in her pocket. "510 million, to be exact, but I'm probably not the only winner."

Sarah waved a hand across the drab, cramped room. "Then what the hell are you doing in a dump like this? And why aren't you smiling?"

Ty sat down on the bed across from Sarah. "I'm scared out of my mind."

"What? How come? Call me crazy, but if I'd won the jackpot, I'd be jumping up and down on the bed. Scratch that. I'd be running through town naked. You're acting like you just lost the family dog."

Ty relayed the story about Rusty and how she'd ended up at the motel. She tapped her pocket. "I've effectively got 500 million dollars in my pocket, and if anyone finds out where I am…"

"Do you have a gun?"

"No! Are you nuts? Of course I don't have a gun."

"Maybe you should call the police," Sarah suggested.

"I considered that, but it would only bring unwanted attention. The fewer people who know I'm the winner, the better. I should probably lie low for a little while."

"In this shithole?"

"I'm not sure yet. I'm still trying to work out a plan."

"Well so far, I'd say your plan sucks." Sarah pointed at the hotel room door. "All that stands between you and the crazies in the outside world is that stupid dresser."

CHAPTER TWO

Karla Rehn took a deep breath and gazed out at the village in the valley far below.

"Game time," she whispered.

She lifted her right ski pole and then her left over the wand in front of her and twisted them into the snow. When she heard the telltale beep-beep-beep indicating the racecourse was clear and it was her turn to go, she bucked the tails of her skis high into the air and charged out of the starting gate.

The top of the course was steep and slick. Two of the skiers who'd gone before her had crashed and burned, but caution would not be rewarded. Each hundredth of a second mattered. Karla had to go full throttle without losing control. She had to dance on the head of a pin.

The edges of her skis were razor-sharp, and as she shifted her weight from one foot to the other, they carved arcs through the hard-packed surface. She'd inspected every inch of the course before the race and knew the precise line to take. A thick crowd lined the lower part of the course, screaming encouragements and ringing cow bells, but Karla heard nothing. Only the sound of her skis rattling over the crisp snow penetrated her ears as red and blue gates whizzed into her vision and vanished behind her.

When she hit the flats at the bottom of the course, her thighs were burning. She gritted her teeth and weaved through the final few gates, clipping each one with her shoulder. When she cleared the last one, she lowered herself into a tight tuck and sailed over the wide red finish line painted in the snow.

She skidded to a stop inches before slamming into the red mesh fence encircling the finish area, spraying snow in her wake. Her chest heaved as she tried to catch her breath. She ripped off her goggles and swung her head toward the leader board. The crowd cheered. She'd slipped into second place. Only one racer—the venerable Italian—remained at the top of the course. No matter what happened, Karla was guaranteed a spot on the podium.

The jumbotron flashed to the top of the course as the Italian kicked out of the starting gate. Karla rocked back and forth in her ski boots as she watched the final racer masterfully maneuver the first set of gates. At the first split, she and the Italian were neck and neck. Ditto for the second split. When the woman flew across the finish line, Karla pumped her hands in the air. She'd been pushed into third, but instead of being disappointed, she felt like she'd won the lottery. Third place was her best finish in a World Cup giant slalom *ever*. She clicked out of her skis and ran along the perimeter of the finish area high fiving the fans along the edge of the mesh fence.

Her elation was short-lived, however. It was too little, too late. Her eyes moistened as she gathered her skis off the snow. She had skied her last race on the big stage. Her dream of being a full-fledged member of the US Ski Team was over, just like that. As hard as it was, she had no choice but to accept it.

She'd been skiing her heart out on the 'D' Team, the precursor to the official US Ski Team, for three years, but she hadn't been called up. Even though she was only twenty-two, it was time to throw in the towel. Her family didn't have the means to support her skiing for another year. It was as simple as that.

She'd already put such a financial strain on them. She couldn't ask them to continue to support a dream that was becoming increasingly unattainable.

Her father ran out on the snow and pulled her into a big bear hug. "Nice run, Karla. You were so smooth. Your line was perfect."

She wiped a tear from her cheek. "Thanks, Dad."

"I'm really proud of you, kiddo. You gave it everything you had. What a nice way to go out."

Karla forced a smile. She knew her father was disappointed too, but it had been settled. After today's race, they were going to announce that she was walking away from the circuit to focus on the next chapter of her life.

Her father threw an arm over her shoulders and they walked past the crowd and out of the finish area. "You should feel good about ending on a high note."

"I know, Dad. It's just—"

"I know, sweetheart. You've been skiing so well…"

It was true. In the last few months, she'd been on fire. She was so close to being called up. If only she had the money to give it one more year.

When a TV reporter approached and pushed a microphone in her face, Karla held her head high. She had a lot to be thankful for, and if there was one thing her father had instilled in her, it was to be a good sport, no matter what.

"Nice race today, Karla," the reporter said. "It seemed like things really clicked for you."

Karla smiled at the camera. "Yeah, I felt great out there today. The conditions were fantastic." She waved a hand toward the racecourse behind her. "Giant slalom has always been my favorite event."

"Rumor has it this is your last race," the reporter said.

"The rumors are true." Karla nibbled on her bottom lip but stood tall. "I'll be attending the University of Vermont next fall. They have an amazing program," she said, referring to UVM's ski team. She'd been recruited by a number of Division I schools, but UVM had offered her the most money. It was going to be hard to leave her family and move to the east coast, but she knew better than to look a gift horse in the mouth. The NCAA circuit was nothing to scoff at. It was incredibly competitive.

After the awards ceremony, and once she'd changed out of her ski clothes, Karla pulled out her phone. Lots of people had sent her messages congratulating her on the race. She opened the one from her best friend Keats first.

So proud of you! You are a skiing Goddess. A fucking modern-day Nike!

Karla laughed and sent back a slew of smiley face emojis.

Keats responded immediately. *Celebratory drinks on me next time we're together.*

* * *

The next morning, she and her father boarded a flight back to the US, back home to Jackson, Wyoming. She fought back tears as the plane tore down the runway and lifted into the air. Moments after takeoff, the guy in front of her reclined his seat, crushing Karla's long legs against her tray table. His shiny bald head was practically in her lap. She pinched the bridge of her nose and let out a long sigh. The next eight hours were not going to be pleasant.

Karla's father patted her leg. "I'm so proud of you Karla. I'm sorry you have to give up your dream. I wish we could afford to—"

Karla held up her hand. "Shhh, Dad. You and Mom have sacrificed so much for me, given me opportunities most other kids could only dream about. I'm the one who should be sorry. I didn't make the team."

"Nonsense. You train harder than anyone else I know. I know you gave it everything you had. I couldn't have asked for anything more."

"Thanks, Dad. That means a lot."

"If you ask me, Lucy Jane doesn't deserve a spot on the team," Karla's father said. "She's a decent skier, but she's got a rotten attitude. She sucks the morale right out of the team."

Karla didn't disagree. She and Lucy Jane had always been on good terms—they'd even had a brief fling—but she'd be the first to admit that Lucy Jane could be a seriously spoiled rich bitch. Her parents always got her the best coaches, and she always flew first class. Karla eyed the flimsy blue curtain hanging in the front of the coach cabin. Lucy Jane was on the other side of it, probably stretched out in her lie-flat seat while she enjoyed a three-course meal.

"In my opinion," her father said, "her behavior yesterday was utterly despicable. She barely missed the gate and gave up. Just skied off the course...inexcusable."

Karla nodded. Her father had always taught her and her sisters never to quit. In his mind, if she'd skied off the course like that, it would have been more egregious than if she'd robbed a bank.

Karla slipped headphones over her ears and closed her eyes. Not long after she nodded off, the toddler behind her kicked her seat. Her noise-cancelling headphones were no match for the child's wailing.

CHAPTER THREE

A fist pounded against the flimsy hotel room door.

"I know you're in there!" a male voice shouted. "Open the goddam door."

Ty's eyes flew open and she sprang to her feet. *Where the fuck am I?* Her eyes darted around the cramped room. Sunlight bled around the edges of the curtains. *Right, shady roadside motel.*

Sarah rolled off the bed and gave her a wild stare. "Who the hell is—"

Another round of pounding ensued, sending them both scampering back toward the bathroom.

Ty tugged on the small window next to the shower with a trembling hand. It was bolted shut. "Shit! What the fuck should we do?"

"I don't know," Sarah croaked. "Do you think it's Rusty?"

"There's no way he tracked me down," Ty said, although she wasn't totally convinced that was true.

"Well, then who the hell is it?"

"No idea." Ty inched toward the bathroom door. "I'm going to go check."

"Are you fucking nuts? He might have a gun."

"You watch too much TV." Ty tiptoed across the brown shag carpet and lowered her eye to the peephole in the door. A hulk of a man, his face wild with anger, stood on the other side. She didn't recognize him. She jumped back when he raised his fist to pummel the door again.

"Vern," the man howled. "Don't make me break this door down."

Ty grabbed a lamp off the night table and gripped it tightly with her fist. "You've got the wrong room, buddy," she hollered toward the door. "This is room twelve. No one named Vern here."

Ty yanked the lamp from the wall and pulled the curtain back an inch. The man looked down at the number on the door and then glanced down the breezeway flanking the front of the hotel. His gruff voice echoed through the door. "Oh, uh, sorry."

Ty lowered the lamp and watched him retreat.

Sarah stuck her head out of the bathroom. "Is he gone?"

"Yep."

"Jesus, he scared the crap out of me."

"Yeah, no shit," Ty said.

"Do you think we should get out of here?"

Ty shook her head. "No, not yet." She sat down on the bed and kneaded the back of her neck. "I need a minute to think."

"This place totally creeps me out," Sarah said. "It's not safe. You need to get a bodyguard, and you should call a good lawyer."

Ty grunted but didn't respond. Sarah was right, though. She needed to find someone who could help her. Problem was, she was a bartender with $400 in her bank account. She didn't exactly have a high-powered attorney on speed dial.

"Or I know," Sarah said, "how about calling a financial advisor, some type of money manager. They'd know what to do and—"

"Sar, please. Take a deep breath."

Sarah put her hands on her hips and stared at Ty. "I'm trying to help you here."

"I know. I'm sorry. I'm a *tiny* bit on edge."

Ty stood, pulled her laptop out of her backpack and sat down at the small laminated table near the door. She googled *Lionball jackpot* and twirled her hair with her finger as the search results slowly populated the screen.

"The fucking wi-fi in this place sucks."

"Just be happy this rat trap has wi-fi at all." Sarah pulled a chair up next to her and pointed at the screen. "Click on that article from *The Charlotte Observer*."

There were three lucky winners in Saturday's $510 million Lionball drawing. Winning tickets were sold in North Carolina, Florida, and Michigan…

"I guess you'll be sharing that 510 mil with two other people," Sarah said. She gave Ty a friendly punch in the arm. "See, there's nothing to be freaked out about. That ticket in your pocket is only worth…Let's see, 510 million divided by three is…170 million."

"Yeah, mere peanuts." Ty skimmed the rest of the article. "Thankfully, there's no mention of *where* in North Carolina the winning ticket was sold."

"That could buy you a little bit of time."

Ty leaned back in her chair and propped her feet up on the bed. "Shit, I can't get my head around that amount of money. I've always fantasized about winning the lottery—haven't we all? But you never really expect it to happen. It definitely doesn't seem real. I'm sure I'll wake up any second now and realize this is all a dream."

Sarah pinched her cheek. "Nope, not a dream. I promise."

"I wonder if there's like a lottery advisor I can call. Someone who can tell me what to do. Given the way Rusty acted last night, I'm petrified about what will happen when more people find out. Crackpots are going to come out of the woodwork claiming to be long-lost relatives."

"I have no idea what to do either. Believe it or not, I don't have much experience in the lottery winning department."

Ty let out a long sigh. "It's times like these when I really wish my dad was around. He'd know what to do."

Sarah reached over to squeeze her hand. "I'm sorry, sweetie."

Ty gave her a sad smile. "I guess good old Google will have to do."

She turned back to her laptop and typed *lottery winner*. The search didn't yield much advice about how she should proceed, but it did provide some interesting fodder nonetheless, mostly on what not to do—lots of stories about how things had gone south for people after winning a big jackpot. One recent winner had blown all his winnings on gambling in less than a year and ended up living in his car.

"Apparently, it didn't occur to him to buy a house, or shit, even an RV before he went on his gambling binge," Sarah said.

"Apparently, not…Oh, look at this one. This guy and his wife won 200 million and he ended up in prison after he tried to kill her. Evidently, he wasn't too good at sharing."

"Yikes."

"I know. These stories are seriously depressing," Ty said.

"Let's keep reading," Sarah urged. "There've got to be at least a few people whose lives didn't turn to shit after they won."

Ty kept scrolling. A few stories had happy endings, but not many, and some of them were just plain weird. One woman used her winnings to buy rare red wine, a private jet, and a Stradivarius violin even though she didn't drink, was afraid to fly, and had never picked up a violin in her life.

"I wonder how she got it in her head that these would be good things to spend her money on?" Sarah asked.

"Who the hell knows. Looks like one thing is for sure." Ty laughed. "Winning the lottery makes people crazy."

"Sure seems like it," Sarah said. "Promise me you'll stay sane."

"I'll do my best."

"Are you hungry?" Sarah asked.

"Starving."

"Do you think we can order a pizza?"

Ty looked at her watch. It was just after ten a.m. on Sunday morning. "Probably."

While Sarah ordered the pizza, Ty looked back at her laptop. The story about the woman who'd bought the Stradivarius was still up on the screen. A lightbulb went off in her head and she slapped her hand against her forehead.

"Holy shit."

Sarah set down her phone. "What is it?"

"Do you remember Kate Kraft? She was two years ahead of us in school."

Sarah nodded. "I think I remember her. A little nerdy, played the violin."

"Yep, that's her. She and I were polar opposites—I was a three-season athlete and she was in the orchestra—but we got along pretty well. We got paired up for some science project and sort of hit it off."

"Yeah, okay. What does she have to do with anything?" Sarah asked.

"I haven't talked to her in years, but I'm ninety-nine percent sure she's a financial advisor. I think she lives in Chicago."

"You should call her."

"I doubt I still have her number, although, I think we're friends on Facebook." Ty pulled up Kate Kraft's profile. "Looks like she works for a company called Allendale Financial." She opened a new tab and googled the firm. "Ooh, says here that they cater to 'high net-worth individuals,' whatever that means."

"It means their clients are rich as shit...I guess you fit that bill now, huh?"

"Yeah, I guess."

"Well, don't just sit there. Send her a message."

"I haven't talked to her since graduation."

Sarah sighed in exasperation. "Uh, I think this is kind of an emergency."

"Valid point." Ty sent a message to Kate and included her phone number. "What if she doesn't respond?"

"We'll figure out another way to track her down," Sarah said. "At this point, we don't have a lot of other options."

"True." Ty glanced at her phone and willed it to ring. "Fuck, it's almost eleven o'clock."

"So?"

"Checkout is at eleven. I only paid for one night." Ty walked over to the nightstand and counted out sixty bucks from the wad of cash she'd taken from her apartment the night before. "I'm going to walk down to the office and pay for another night."

Sarah looked at the money and then back up at Ty. "You think it's safe for you to leave the room? What if someone sees you?"

Ty peeked out the window. There were only a half a dozen cars parked in front of the motel. She reached for the door. "Let's walk down there together."

CHAPTER FOUR

A few hours later, Ty's phone vibrated on the nightstand. She lurched for it, knocking her paper plate of half-eaten pizza to the floor.

"Hello," she gasped.

"Ty?"

"Yeah."

"It's Kate Kraft. I got your message…Are you okay? You sound like you're out of breath?"

"Yes, I'm fine. Well, actually, I'm not fine." Ty started talking a mile a minute. "I need your help. I didn't know who else to call…I need to talk to someone, someone I can trust."

There was a brief pause before Kate responded. "Um, okay."

"I reached out to you because…This is going to sound crazy…You totally won't believe this, but, there was a big Lionball drawing on Saturday night, and—"

"Yes, I heard about it on the news."

"Well, I was one of the winners. Like, I won the Lionball jackpot. I mean three people won it, but I'm one of them."

"Wow!" Kate replied. "Are you serious?"

"Dead serious, and I'm kind of freaking out. No, not kind of. I am freaking out."

"Take a deep breath, Ty," Kate said with a laugh.

"I'm sorry. I'm just nervous, and it feels really strange to hear the words come out of my mouth."

"Tell her you need advice," Sarah whispered in her ear.

"I'm getting to that," Ty said through clenched teeth and batted her out of the way.

"What was that?" Kate asked.

"Sorry," Ty said into the phone. "I was talking to Sarah. Sarah McLean. She's here with me. You probably remember her from high school?"

"Of course," Kate replied.

"Anyway," Ty said. "I was calling to ask…I need advice, and I thought maybe you could help."

Kate didn't miss a beat. "I'd be happy to help, if I can."

Ty collapsed into one of the chairs near the door. "Thanks, Kate. I feel better already."

"Where's the winning ticket now?" Kate asked.

"In the pocket of my jeans." Instinctively, Ty patted her pants. She hadn't taken them off since she'd won, not even when she and Sarah had passed out on the bed the night before.

Kate's next question was, "Where exactly are you?"

"Hiding out in a fleabag motel outside Asheville, North Carolina—that's where I live now."

"We need to get you and your ticket to a safer place," Kate said. "Not to scare you, but a lot of people would kill…okay, bad choice of words…go out of their way to get their hands on that ticket."

"I know."

"I want you to put the ticket in a safe deposit box, at least temporarily. Do you think you can do that?

"Uh-huh. I'm sure one of the banks in town has them."

"Okay, good, but first, I want you to snap a picture of both sides of the ticket and send them to me."

"I'll do that right now. Hold on." Ty stood and pulled the ticket out of her pocket. She smoothed it on the table and used her phone to take photos of both sides. When she was done, she placed the phone back to her ear.

"Okay, where do you want me to send them?"

Kate gave her an email address and she sent them off.

Ty heard some typing in the background, and a few seconds later Kate said, "Okay, got them. And I see you haven't signed the ticket yet. Hold off doing that. We want to keep our options open. We may decide to establish an LLC or a blind trust before you claim your prize."

Ty didn't know what a blind trust was, but she trusted Kate. "Sure, whatever you say, but it's Sunday. I can't get to a bank until tomorrow. What should I do in the meantime?"

"For lack of a better idea. I'm going to suggest you stay put, assuming no one else knows where you are."

"I'm fairly certain if someone else," Rusty immediately came to her mind, "knew where I was, they would have come after me by now."

"Okay, good. But promise me you'll get to the bank first thing tomorrow morning."

"I will."

"I also think you and I should meet in person," Kate said. "ASAP. We've got to figure out your next steps. The next few days will be critical. Details about the jackpot are already dominating the news cycle. One of the winners, the one in Florida, I think, has already come forward. Speculation about the other two is likely to send newscasters into a frenzy."

"Okay. Whatever you think is best," Ty said, her voice barely above a whisper. She pulled back the curtain on the window, half expecting a sea of TV crews to be camped out in the hotel parking lot.

"You said you're in Asheville, right?" Kate asked.

"Yes."

"Okay. I can be on the first flight there tomorrow morning."

Ty hesitated. "Would it be okay if I came to you instead?"

"Um, sure. I guess so. Although, normally I travel to see clients, not the other way around."

"It's just, I kind of want to get as far away from here as possible." Ty put Kate on speaker, set her phone on the table, and opened Google Maps on her computer. "Hmmm, it looks like it'll take me about eleven hours to drive to Chicago." She peeked at her watch. "If I leave now, I can be—"

"Hold on," Kate said. "I don't want you going anywhere until you've got that lottery ticket in a safe place."

"Oh, right," Ty said. "Forgot about that little detail."

"Are you sure you don't want me to come there?"

"Yeah, I'm sure. I'll go to the bank in the morning and hit the road right after that."

"All right. I'll have my admin book you a room at the Peninsula Hotel. It's right off Michigan Avenue."

Ty had never been to Chicago, but she'd heard of the iconic Michigan Avenue. "Okay, thanks Kate."

"Until it's secure, guard that lottery ticket with your life," Kate advised. "And, Ty?"

"Yeah?"

"As a friend, I'd urge you to continue to keep quiet about this, at least until after we have a chance to meet in person. That means under no circumstances should you go out and do anything crazy like embark on a shopping spree or buy everyone a round of drinks at your favorite bar. In short, don't do *anything* to draw attention to yourself. The fewer people who know about this, the better."

"Trust me, I have absolutely zero intention of doing anything like that. I'm not gonna step outside this miserable hotel room until tomorrow morning."

As soon as they ended the call, Ty slumped forward in her chair. "God, I feel so much better after talking to her. She was so calm and confident."

"I guess she's used to dealing with high-stakes situations," Sarah said.

"Yeah, probably."

"So, you're Chicago bound, huh?"

"Yep."

"I'd totally come with you if I wasn't jetting off to Brussels tomorrow." Sarah had recently landed a big new job with an airplane manufacturer outside of Asheville, and her boss was taking her along on a business trip to Europe.

"I'll be fine. I love to drive. And the fact you get to go to Belgium is so kickass. I'd never ask you to blow that trip off." Ty gave Sarah a one-armed hug. "Have I mentioned lately how proud I am of you? Landing a *real* job, and a damn good one at that."

Sarah rested her head on Ty's shoulder for a brief moment. "Thanks. I'm pretty proud of myself too."

Ty stepped back. "I'm starting to think I'll be a bartender for the rest of my life."

"Dare I remind you about the lottery ticket in your pocket?"

Ty chuckled. "Yeah, I guess that's going to change things, huh?"

"Yep, and it's up to you whether they change for the better or the worse. You're like a potter with a fresh ball of clay on her wheel."

Ty rolled her eyes, but she knew Sarah was right. She was at a crossroads in her life. It was both exhilarating and terrifying.

"Are you going to let Misty know you're going out of town?" Sarah asked.

"That would probably be a good idea." After she shot Misty a text, Ty held up her phone. "Do you think I should turn this thing off?"

"It couldn't hurt. I mean, if the media gets hold of your number, they might bombard you with calls."

"Jeez, I hadn't even thought of that. I was more worried about someone being able to track me." Ty promptly powered down her phone and set it facedown on the table. "I'm probably being overly paranoid, but better safe than sorry."

"I heard you mention something about going to the bank," Sarah said.

"Uh-huh. Kate wants me to put the ticket in a safe deposit box. Something I obviously can't do until tomorrow." Ty opened her laptop again. A quick search for safe deposit boxes indicated very few banks still had them. "It looks like we'll have to go to the Asheville Trust branch downtown."

Sarah opened her mouth to say something, but then clamped it shut.

"What is it, Sar?"

"It's just, doesn't Rosie work there?" she asked.

Ty swallowed hard. Hearing her ex's name caused a pit to form in her stomach. It had been two months since Rosie had unceremoniously dumped her, and she wasn't over it, not by a long shot.

"She does work there, but she's *always* at the branch in Hendersonville on Mondays. Trust me, I listened to her bitch about having to drive all the way out there every week."

"Still hurts to think about her, huh?"

"Yeah, but it's okay," Ty said with a shrug. "I don't know why the hell I'm so caught up on her."

"Don't beat yourself up. You met her right after your parents—"

"I know. I just don't get why I can't move on. I mean, she dumped me like yesterday's garbage. I should hate her guts."

"You loved her, Ty. You can't just turn off your feelings about someone, even when they do shitty things to you. It doesn't work that way. And you were so vulnerable when she walked into your life."

Sarah was right, as usual. Ty's emotions had been about as raw as they could be. She'd met Rosie not long after her parents were killed in a fiery car accident and had fallen hard and fast.

Sarah stood and pulled Ty into a hug.

"I don't know what I'd do without you Sarah." Ty's voice was muffled by Sarah's shoulder.

It was true. After her parents had died, she'd completely fallen apart, dropped out of school, and moved to Asheville to be near Sarah, mostly because she didn't know where else to go. Her only other family was her brother, and he and his wife, Quy, had moved to Vietnam *two weeks* after their parents' accident. The move had been planned long before that, but Ty still couldn't believe Reed had left. Left her all alone.

"You're stronger than you think, Ty."

"I don't know about that." Ty climbed up on the bed and started jumping on the mattress. "Enough of this gloom and doom. Let's celebrate. I just won the fucking lottery!"

CHAPTER FIVE

Karla stared at the ceiling. It had taken her and her father seventeen hours to get from the race in Switzerland to the small airport tucked between Jackson and Grand Teton National Park. She hadn't slept a wink the entire trip, and she was exhausted, but now, tucked into the twin bed in her childhood bedroom, sleep evaded her. She didn't need to look at the clock. The brilliant blaze of orange outlining the horizon told her what time it was.

She tugged the covers up around her neck and gazed around the small room. Bronze, silver, and gold medals hung from pegs her father had installed years ago, and the shelves were lined with little skier-topped trophies. They stared down at her, taunting her, reminding her of all her hopes and dreams of being an Olympic skier—and how that aspiration had come to an abrupt end. A tear trickled down her cheek and she wiped it away with the corner of her bedsheet.

Her eyelids drifted closed, and when she opened them again, the sun was high on the horizon. She kicked off the covers and sat on the edge of her bed. Her leg muscles bulged against the fabric of her cutoff sweatpants. She stood and padded to the bathroom, where she combed her fingers through her long, dark hair and stared at her reflection in the small, gold-painted mirror over the sink. Her father always said she had a twinkle in her eye. But not this morning. Her big brown eyes were dull and flat, like when she was coming down with a nasty cold.

When she stepped out of the bathroom, she bumped into her father. She forced a smile, not wanting him to know how defeated she felt. She had to remain positive and focus on her future. A future that was bright, if only she'd allow it to be. She was at a juncture, and it was up to her to decide which path to take. Embrace the opportunity to ski for UVM and earn her nursing degree, or obsess about what could have been. And she should be happy. As much as she loved racing, it was a grueling lifestyle. Now, for the first time in her life, she was free from the relentless schedule of training and punishing workouts, travel and races. Free to ski wherever and whenever she wanted, and free to go out and party. Have a social life for once.

Her mother made her eggs and toast, and when she was done eating, she got dressed and drove to Outdoor Sports, a ski and bike shop in downtown Jackson. She'd worked there on and off over the years, and she wanted to talk to Zoe, the store's owner, about getting back on the schedule. Until it was time to leave for Vermont in late August, Karla planned to work at Outdoor Sports and help her father run his summer dryland training camp for ski racers. Between the two jobs, she'd be able to save up enough to give her a little spending money when she headed off to college.

Zoe greeted her with a hug when she walked in the store. "Karla. It's so good to see you." She gestured toward a small TV mounted on the wall over the cash register. "Everybody at the shop watched your race in Switzerland. Third place. Wow."

Karla smiled broadly. "Thanks, Zoe."

Zoe patted her on the back. "So, you're headed off to UVM in the fall?"

"Yep, time to get me a college degree." Karla didn't want to get into why she wasn't going back to ski with the US team. She shifted gears. "I'd love to pick up a few shifts. I mean, assuming you could use the help."

Zoe let out a long whistle. "Could I ever. The season has been insanely busy, and a kid just quit on me. To be honest, it would be nice to have someone like you around, someone I know I can rely on."

"Great. When do you want me to start?"

"Is Thursday too soon? The town is going to be full of spring-breakers this weekend and we're gonna be swamped."

Karla laughed. "Let me guess, busloads of college kids from Texas."

"Yep. We've got more than two hundred sets of rental skis reserved, and knowing my luck, they'll all show up at once."

"Thursday works for me," Karla said. "I'll be here then."

* * *

The next morning, there was a faint knock on her bedroom door. The sun was barely up, but it had been another sleepless night, and she was awake.

"Want to go up to the mountain?" her father asked through the door. "They got ten inches last night."

Karla swung her feet onto the floor. "Sure."

Sleep could wait. She wasn't about to pass up a powder day, and even though it was nearing the end of the ski season, she'd heard the conditions up at Jackson Hole were epic. She hadn't been up there since she'd been home at Christmas, but the mountain had received a record snowfall so far that year.

"Okay," her dad said. "I'll put on some coffee and meet you downstairs. Elin and your mom are coming too."

Elin was one of Karla's older sisters. She and her husband Dan lived in Jackson and coached skiing alongside her father.

It was still snowing pretty hard when they clipped into their skis. They caught the very first tram up to Rendezvous Peak, the highest point at the ski area. Karla's face settled into a perpetual smile. She and her family bounced through the fresh, light snow, run after run. The snow eased up midmorning, and by the time they broke for lunch, there were blue skies as far as the eye could see.

"What an amazing morning," Elin said as she tugged off her ski helmet and set it on the table in the lodge. Her cheeks were rosy. "Unfortunately, I'm going to have to call it quits. I've got to pick the twins up at two. They've got dentist appointments before practice."

"I'm gonna throw in the towel too," Karla's dad said. He patted one of his thighs. "These legs aren't as good as they used to be." He looked over at his daughters and smiled. "You girls sure know how to wear out your old dad."

"And mom," her mother added with a smile.

"Whatever," Karla said. Her parents were in their mid-fifties, and they were in better shape than most people Karla knew, which was saying a lot given they lived in a ski town full of uber-athletic outdoorsy people.

"You want to ride back down to town with us, Karla?" Elin asked.

"Nah, I've still got some gas in the tank." She waved a hand toward the bank of windows at the front of the lodge. "And it's turned into such a beautiful day. You guys go ahead. I'll take the bus back."

After lunch, Karla bid her family farewell and skied down to the tram. When she got back to the top of the mountain, she dipped out of bounds—something she knew she shouldn't do alone, especially because she didn't even have a beacon. But there were few fresh tracks left on the mountain, and the backcountry promised to have some sweet pockets of untouched snow.

She squealed like a little kid when she caught air off a boulder and landed in a puff of snow, then tucked into a bunch of trees, expertly guiding her skis around their trunks. The branches of the fir trees were heavy with snow, and when she brushed one with her shoulder, a heap of cold white flakes blasted her face. She laughed and brushed them away with her glove. All thoughts of the outside world evaporated. She was free, floating down the mountainside. It had been so long since she'd let loose.

At the end of the day, even her well-toned thighs were tired. What she needed now was an ice-cold beer. She clicked out of her skis, set them on a rack outside one of the bars at the bottom of the mountain, and went inside. She parked herself on a stool at the bar and waved hello to the bartender, Kathy, a woman she'd known since grade school. Over the next two hours, Kathy made sure her pint was never empty.

Karla was about to get up and head back down into town when a woman—older, maybe late thirties, with hair so blond it was practically white—sat down on the stool next to her. She winked at Karla and summoned the bartender with a little wave. She wasn't really Karla's type, but her features were striking.

The woman's ski coat probably cost three thousand dollars, and a massive diamond hung off her well-manicured ring finger. Old Fashioned in hand, she swiveled on her stool to face Karla. They struck up a conversation, and an hour later, Karla found herself following the woman back to the nearby Four Seasons hotel. As soon as they stepped inside her room, the woman pushed Karla up against the door and kissed her hard on the mouth.

When they broke apart Karla asked, "What about your hus—"

The woman quieted her with another kiss and pushed her back into the room. Within a few minutes, they were both naked. The blond woman dug her nails into Karla's ass and pulled her down the bed. She ran her hands over Karla's thighs and whispered, "You're so strong." She nibbled on one of Karla's nipples and slipped her fingers between her legs. The sex was fast and frenzied and gave Karla the release she needed.

Afterward, she dressed and slipped out of the room. Although her body was humming, she felt dirty. She wasn't in the habit of fucking strangers, and the woman was married, for God's sake. What had she been thinking? It was late, and the bus wasn't running anymore. Certain she had a serious case of sex hair, she ran a hand through her long, dark locks before she approached the bell stand and asked them to call her a taxi.

CHAPTER SIX

Ty and Sarah were standing outside the bank when it opened on Monday morning. As soon as they got inside, Ty's legs went weak. Rosie was just stepping out of her office. She was wearing a dark, perfectly tailored pantsuit and she looked as beautiful as ever. Even after all she'd done, Ty's heart ached at the sight of her.

"What the hell is she doing here?" Sarah whispered.

Ty was too stunned to speak. She turned on her heels and lunged for the door. Sarah caught her by the arm. "Don't bolt. It'll look suspicious."

"Shit, she's walking toward us." Ty looked down at the floor.

"Let me handle this," Sarah said.

"Good morning," Rosie said. "What a surprise to see you two here." She ran her tongue over her lips—her beautiful, full lips. "What brings you in today?"

"I need to open a checking account," Sarah said quickly.

Rosie gestured to an older woman sitting at a desk nearby. "Gladys can help you with that."

Gladys gave them a little wave and gestured them over to her cubicle.

"So you need to open a checking account?" she asked once they were seated.

"Yes, yes we do." Sarah said.

Ty sat perfectly still. Her knuckles were white from clutching the spiralbound notebook in her hand. The winning ticket was tucked inside.

Mercifully, Rosie wandered back toward her office. Once she was out of earshot, Sarah lowered her voice and said, "We need a safe deposit box."

Without missing a beat, Gladys hustled them to the back of the bank. Fifteen minutes later, the lottery ticket was safely tucked in Box 2311.

Rosie approached them as they made their way out of the bank. Her eyebrow inched up ever so slightly. "I trust Gladys was able to help you with everything you needed?"

"Yep, we're all good," Sarah said.

Rosie placed a hand on Ty's arm. "It's nice to see you."

Her touch sent a tingle through Ty's body. She stiffened, determined not to let Rosie see the effect she still had on her. "I'd appreciate it if you wouldn't mention seeing us at the bank this morning."

Rosie looked her straight in the eye and replied, "Of course not. I won't say a word. I promise."

When they walked out of the bank, Ty collapsed against Sarah. She was relieved to have the lottery ticket locked safely away, but Rosie being at the bank had been a stroke of bad luck. Hopefully she'd be true to her word and keep her trap shut.

Sarah walked Ty to her car, which she'd parked a few blocks from the bank just to be safe, and gave her a hug goodbye.

"You be safe," Sarah said. "Call me the second you get to hotel in Chicago."

"I will, I promise." Ty pressed the button to unlock her car. "But won't you still be in the air on your way to Belgium?"

Sarah looked at her watch. "I might be. I'm scheduled to get to Brussels a little after seven a.m. which would be," she paused as she considered the time change, "around midnight Chicago time."

* * *

A roller coaster of emotions—from elation at having won the lottery to anxiety about what that might mean—kept Ty company during the drive to Chicago. She daydreamed about what she could buy with her winnings...

A fire engine red Ferrari, or maybe a Rolls Royce. She could sit in the back and have a gorgeous woman drive her around. Shit, why not buy both, and maybe a Range Rover too.

Maybe a Van Gogh painting? That would be cool.

Definitely a ski house. One in Colorado and maybe one in Italy or France.

A personal chef would be nice. And maybe a personal trainer.

Those Air Jordan sneakers she'd been lusting after.

A private jet or, oooh, maybe her very own helicopter...

A loud honking sound snapped her out of her thoughts. She'd veered into the neighboring lane, and the eighteen-wheeler next to her expressed its displeasure. Her heart pounded in her chest. She'd almost caused a major accident.

"Get your head out of the fucking clouds, Ty," she yelled into the cabin of her car.

She flipped on the radio and tried to think of something else, but it was a lost cause. Thoughts of the lottery consumed her. She bounced between fantasizing about what she could buy and chastising herself for being so materialistic. Having her own helicopter would be pretty cool—and talk about a serious chick magnet—but traveling by helicopter wouldn't be very good for the environment. And owning one wouldn't help anyone, unless she used it as a medevac or to fight wildfires or something.

Finally, somewhere between Kentucky and Indiana, the path forward emerged from her scattered thoughts. This was her chance to get her life back on track and do the one thing she'd wanted to do her whole life: become a nurse.

By the time she got to Chicago that evening, she was a zombie, exhausted and wired at the same time. Her hands ached from clutching the steering wheel with a death grip for so many hours. She'd driven straight through, only stopping for gas and pee breaks, subsisting on cheddar cheese–filled Combos and Red Bull.

She cracked her knuckles and let out a whistle when she turned onto Superior Street. Even though it was way past dark, it was impossible to miss the sparkling, gold-trimmed canopy demarcating the entrance to the Peninsula Hotel. She pulled her rusty old Subaru up to the valet stand and the lone bellman on duty peered at her over the top of his glasses.

"Checking in?" he asked.

The irony was not lost on Ty. Granted, her car was partially held together with duct tape, but she was probably one of the wealthiest people staying at the hotel, or would be as soon as she cashed in her Lionball ticket.

The bellman gestured toward the rear of her car. "May I help you with your luggage, miss?"

Ty stepped out of the car and held up her backpack. "Nope. This is all I have."

As soon as she got to her room, she turned on her phone for the first time since she'd talked to Kate the previous day. It buzzed like mad the second it came to life. The notifications popped up on her screen like kernels of corn in hot oil. Missed calls and missed texts, most of which seemed to be from her roommate.

Sunday 2:50 pm: *Ty, where are you?*

Sunday 4:30 pm: *Are you okay? Call me.*

Sunday 8:10 pm: *Ty??*

Sunday 9:23 pm: *Called Thirsty's. They said you didn't show up for work?? Worried.*

There were dozens more, most from Sunday but also from earlier that day. From the looks of it, Misty had never received the text Ty sent the day before saying she'd be out of town for a bit.

According to the clock on Ty's phone, it was 12:23 a.m. in Chicago, which meant it was 1:23 a.m. in Asheville. Misty would most likely be asleep, but the situation seemed urgent enough to warrant waking her up. Ty brought up Misty's number, but her phone rang before she got a chance to call. It was Sarah. She'd probably just landed in Brussels.

Ty held the phone up to her ear. "Hello."

"Oh my God, Ty," Sarah said. "I'm glad I got you. I just got off the phone with Misty. She tried to call you like a million times. She tried me a few times too, but I was in the air."

"I was about to—"

"She called the cops."

"What?"

"She reported you missing."

"You're fucking kidding me."

"I wish I was. I guess she freaked when you didn't come home for two days. She even called Thirsty's. They said you didn't show up for your shift Sunday night."

Ty sat down on the bed and ran a hand through her long blond hair. "Fuck, fuck, fuck." She let out a long sigh.

"You need to call her. And you better call the cops and get this all sorted out."

As soon as she hung up with Sarah, Ty did just that. She explained to the officer that she was in fact not missing. It had been a big misunderstanding.

When she reached Misty, the poor thing was beside herself. "I thought you'd been kidnapped or something."

Ty hadn't known Misty all that long, and she could be a bit of a drama queen, but she was about the sweetest person Ty had ever met. Heeding Kate's advice, Ty opted not to tell her about winning the Lionball. Instead, she made up some story about having to leave town because of a family emergency and apologized for not leaving Misty a note or something. She didn't even ask if Misty had gotten her text because the answer to that question was obvious.

After she returned a few other messages from worried friends, she opened her laptop and googled *Lionball* to see what the news was reporting about the recent jackpot winners. An article from Asheville's local paper caught her eye: "Local Woman Reported Missing."

ASHEVILLE, NC—An Asheville woman, Margaret "Ty" MacIntyre, is reportedly missing. The 23-year-old is a bartender at Thirsty's Tavern, and according to the Asheville Police Department, she was last seen on Saturday night.

"Ty was working the bar when she disappeared," Zach Monroe, the owner of Thirsty's Tavern, said. "And she didn't show up for work on Sunday evening. In two years, she's never missed a shift, not a single one."

According to one of the regulars at Thirsty's, she ran out of the bar right after the Lionball drawing on Saturday evening.

Her roommate called police when Ms. MacIntyre didn't return home. According to the roommate, "Ty has never vanished like that before."

Authorities are asking anyone with information to contact the Asheville Police Department.

As if that wasn't bad enough, another story in the Asheville newspaper reported that lottery officials had released the names of the retail outlets where the three winning Lionball tickets had been sold, and lo and behold, one of them was a convenience store in Asheville.

Ty slapped her laptop shut. "Fucking fantastic."

She was irritated that Misty had gone to the police— it brought her exactly the sort of attention she was trying to avoid—but knew her roommate hadn't meant to stir the hornet's nest.

News of Ty's disappearance coupled with the report that a winning Lionball ticket had been sold in Asheville must have sent Rusty and the rest of the regulars at Thirsty's into a tailspin. Shit, the whole town of Asheville had probably gone into speculation overdrive. There was nothing like a little hometown gossip.

Ty flopped back on the king-size bed and stared at the ceiling.

Thank fucking God I got the hell out of town.

She sat up and scanned the room for a minibar. Bingo. There was a small wet bar adjacent to the closet. She pulled a beer out of the minifridge, popped the top, and took a long swig. Her phone chirped just as she was throwing back another sip, causing her to choke and cough-spit most of it up. She used the sleeve of her shirt to wipe the suds off her face and snatched up her phone. It was her brother Reed calling on WhatsApp from Vietnam. That was good and bad. Good because she needed to talk to him, but bad because she should have called him before now.

"Hey, Reed."

"Ty, shit, are you okay? I got a call from the Asheville Police."

"Yeah, I'm fine. It was all a big misunderstanding…Although, I gotta say, I'm pretty impressed the Asheville PD was able to track you down in Vietnam."

"Ty, Quy and I were really worried. Stop kidding around and tell me what happened."

Reed was five years older than Ty. They'd always gotten along but had never been super close. Ty chalked it up to their age difference. She'd only been thirteen when he went off to college. She loved her brother, and he was the only immediate family she had left, but he could be such a wet blanket. Sometimes she wanted to shake him and tell him not to take life so seriously. Although, in his defense, he hadn't ridden her ass when she dropped out of college and moved to Asheville. He'd seemed to understand that she needed some time to put herself back together after they buried their parents.

"Are you sitting down?" she asked finally.

"What?" Reed asked.

"I'll tell you what happened, but you better sit down."

"Yes, I'm sitting down. I'm in my office at school. You're kinda freaking me out, Ty."

"Okay, well, I did sort of go missing, but I had a good reason. You know what Lionball is, right? The big lottery here in the States?"

"Yeah, of course."

"Well, there was this big drawing on Saturday night and, well, I actually won."

"Like you won the jackpot?"

"Yes. Well, me and two other people. There was also a winning ticket in Michigan and one in Florida."

"Holy shit, Ty. Wait, are you pulling my chain?"

"No, I'm dead serious. You remember Kate Kraft from high school?"

"Of course I remember her. What does that have to do—"

"I'm in Chicago. That's where she lives. I called her right after I won. We're meeting tomorrow."

"I'm not following you. I didn't think you two were that close in high school."

"We weren't, but she's a financial advisor. With Mom and Dad gone and you so far away, I wasn't sure who else to call."

"Still, that doesn't explain…Why did you leave Asheville?"

Ty gave him a blow by blow of the night she'd won the lottery and explained how Rusty had chased after her. "I was anxious to get out of town."

"I guess that makes sense. Where's the ticket now?"

"I put it in a safe deposit box before I left Asheville."

"Okay, good."

"Aren't you going to ask me how much I won?" That was probably the first question most people would have asked, but not Reed. He and Quy lived a very simple life, and even on their limited income, managed to either save or give away most of what they earned. Ty knew her brother had a nice computer, but aside from that, they bought nothing unless they deemed it an absolute necessity.

"How much did you win?"

"A hundred and seventy mil, give or take."

Reed let out a long whistle. "That's a lot of dough."

"To put it mildly."

"That's quite a gift."

"Yes, it is."

"I hope you'll use it wisely, Ty."

Ty groaned into the phone. Typical Reed. Blatant innuendo. "I'm not going to blow it, Reed."

"I didn't suggest—"

"You didn't have to…Can't you just be happy for me?"

"I am happy for you," Reed said. "I love you, and I want what's best for you."

"I know."

"Let me know how things go with Kate."

"All right, I'll call you tomorrow."

"Okay…Oh, and Ty?"

"Yeah?"

"Be careful. There are a lot of crazies out there."

"I will, don't worry."

CHAPTER SEVEN

A crystal-blue sky greeted Ty when her eyes fluttered open the next morning. She clicked on the TV and fumbled around on the nightstand for her phone. Text messages continued to pour in from concerned friends. She replied to a few and checked the weather. The blue sky was deceiving. It was only thirty-nine degrees outside.

Right. Chicago. Late March. Still cold.

After a quick workout in the hotel gym, she nibbled on a blueberry muffin and skimmed the news headlines on her laptop. Apparently, word in Asheville had traveled fast. The local paper quoted the Asheville police saying Ty was no longer considered missing.

She opened Google Maps and typed in the address for Kate's office. It was only about a mile from the Peninsula, easily walkable, although there was the weather to consider. The warmest thing Ty had with her was a hooded sweatshirt.

Fuck it. I'm no softie. I'm from Upstate New York. It's not like there was a blizzard.

She showered and dressed. The only clean clothes she had were a pair of ratty jeans and a long-sleeved Wonder Woman T-shirt. Probably not typical attire for one of Kate's *high net worth* clients, but it would have to do. She mentally added clothes shopping to her to-do list for later that afternoon. With her hoodie cinched tight around her face and her hands jammed deep inside its fuzzy pockets, she marched up Michigan Avenue. Her outfit proved no match for the wind whipping down the wide boulevard.

As she neared the Chicago River, she spotted the Wrigley Building's gleaming white terra-cotta exterior. When she craned her neck to admire the stunning piece of architecture, the glittering silver tower beside it caught her eye. It was so ostentatious next to its elegant architectural neighbors. All one had to do was look at the giant silver letters that adorned is façade to understand why. T-R-U-M-P. To Ty, those letters represented greed, vanity, and materialism, everything she was determined not to become. They served as a stark warning not to misuse her newfound wealth.

Her body was completely numb when she finally reached Kate's building on the corner of Clark and Madison, an area of the city that, according to Google Maps, was called the Loop. As she rode the elevator up to the seventeenth floor, Ty caught a glimpse of her reflection. Her hair was wild, and her cheeks were bright red. Nice. Running her fingers through her hair didn't do much good.

"Hello. Who hit seventeen?" An irritated female voice asked.

"Oh, sorry," Ty said. "That was me." She slid off the crowded elevator and practically bumped into a tall, curly-haired man coming out of the glass door across the hall. He was cute in a nerdy kind of way. "Sorry," she muttered again.

He smiled at her. "It's okay."

Ty smiled back. "You don't happen to know where Allendale Financial is, do you?"

He gestured toward the glass door he'd just exited. "Yep, it's right here."

Ty blushed. The name was etched across the door in giant block letters. "Oh, um, thanks."

When she stepped into the sleek, sparsely decorated reception area, a perky young woman greeted her with a full set of bright white teeth. "May I help you?"

"I'm here to see Kate Kraft. My name is Ty. I mean…" They probably had her listed under her given name. "Margaret MacIntyre."

The receptionist tapped a few keys on her keyboard. "Ah, yes. I see you listed for ten a.m., Ms. MacIntyre. Why don't you have a seat and I'll let Kate know you're here."

"Okay, thanks."

"May I get you anything to drink while you wait?" the receptionist asked. "Coffee, tea, water?"

"Coffee would be great, thank you."

Ty sipped her coffee and eyed the other people waiting in the reception area. There was an exquisitely dressed woman with coiffed white hair sitting next to the reception desk, and in the far corner, a young man and woman Ty guessed were brother and sister. They had "trust fund" written all over them. She'd encountered her fair share of trust fund kids when she'd been a student in Denver, and they had a discernable look. Nicely dressed, but not overly so, and never with any flashy labels, flawless skin, perfect teeth, a sharp jawline, and good posture.

Ten minutes later, the receptionist led Ty back to a conference room. Its floor-to-ceiling windows looked out over Chicago's skyline—a cluster of low, brick buildings and shiny skyscrapers hugging the shore of Lake Michigan, which was so big it looked more like an ocean than a lake. A lone sailboat braved the chilly waters.

She looked around the conference room. It was incredible to think that here she was, standing in the middle of downtown Chicago. So much had happened in the last seventy-two hours. There hadn't been a minute to stop and let everything sink in. She felt like the same person, but at the same time, her old life back in Asheville was already a distant memory. Suddenly she was a nervous wreck. Her mouth was dry, and she wished she'd asked the receptionist for some water. She licked her lips and lifted her arms to air out her wet pits.

She had her hoodie halfway over her head when she heard the conference room door opening. She flapped her arms wildly to free them from her sweatshirt, and when her head broke free, she smiled and said, "Oh, hi."

Kate bounded into the room, trailed by the curly-haired man Ty had nearly collided with earlier.

"Ty, it's soooo good to see you!"

Kate looked pretty much the same as she had in high school, except she no longer wore glasses, and the cardigan sweater and corduroy skirt she'd sported as a teenager had been replaced with a well-tailored charcoal skirt suit.

Kate gestured toward the man. "This is my colleague, Derek."

Although his hair was a bit unruly, Derek's suit was impeccably pressed, like he'd just slipped it out of the dry-cleaning bag.

Derek extended a hand. "Nice to meet you, Ms. MacIntyre." Derek didn't seem arrogant, but he did come off mildly aloof.

"Please, call me Ty."

Kate skipped any further pleasantries and became all business. She gestured toward the conference table. "Why don't we all take a seat."

Kate's first question was about the whereabouts of the lottery ticket. Once Ty assured her it was safely tucked away in a safe deposit box in Asheville, she went over some formalities and asked Ty to sign a few generic-looking documents.

"All right then," Kate said. "Now that we have the paperwork out of the way..." Her eyes settled on Ty. "As you've already experienced, winning the lottery can be both a blessing and a curse. It will undoubtedly change your life. The shape that change takes is up to you, but," she waved a hand between herself and Derek, "we're here to try and help you navigate the whole process." Kate stood and walked to the wall of windows. With her back to the conference table, she said, "Before we go any further, Ty, I need to be blunt."

Ty sat up straighter in her chair and cleared her throat. "Okay."

Kate turned to face her. "People who become wealthy overnight, by winning the lottery or receiving a large inheritance, for example, tend to be terrible clients. In our experience, they are often, shall I say, *reluctant* to follow our advice, and we generally avoid taking them on. Same with people in the entertainment business. You'd be surprised at how many extremely wealthy people have trouble paying their bills. They ignore our guidance and spend their money irresponsibly."

"Really?" Ty asked.

"Really. And they come running to us when it's all gone, but by then it's too late." Kate paused before adding, "We're only willing to take you on as a client because you and I go way back, but I—"

"I promise I'll follow your advice," Ty replied. "I'll be a model client."

Kate walked back to the conference table and sat down across from Ty. "I have no doubt that you will."

At that point Derek piped in. "As Kate said, we're here to help you, Ty. We'd like to start off by asking you a few questions."

Ty swallowed hard. It felt like she was under a microscope. Even though she was the client, she was way out of her league. After all, Derek and Kate dealt with rich and powerful people all day long.

"Okay," she croaked.

Derek gave her a broad smile. "The first question is pretty easy: Have you given any thought to what you'd like to do with your winnings?"

"Um, I…"

"For example," Derek prodded, "do you have dreams of buying a house, taking an around the world trip, donating to charity, anything like that?"

Ty looked to Kate for support, but her expression was blank.

"The reason we're asking," Kate said, "is because we're going to put together a financial plan for you, and it would help if we knew a little bit about how you plan to spend the money, any big purchases we should consider."

Ty cleared her throat. "I, um, I'm not—"

"We want to hear some of your general thoughts," Kate said. "I realize it probably hasn't fully sunken in, the fact that you are now a multimillionaire."

"No it definitely hasn't," Ty said with a laugh, "but I did have a lot of time to think during the ten-hour drive to Chicago, and well, this probably sounds kind of lame, but I want to get my life back on the right path." Ty twirled her pen in her fingers and stared out the window. "I dropped out of school after my parents died. I thought I'd take a year off, but, well, it's been almost three years now…"

Kate's expression softened and she patted Ty on the arm. "I remember hearing the news. I'm so sorry."

A tear trickled down Ty's cheek. "Thanks. Anyway, when it happened, I was about to finish my junior year in Denver. I was a complete mess. It was like all the wind had been sucked out of my sails, and I was bobbing in the water. And now I've been given this gift, winning the lottery, and I want to make the most of it. I want to go back to school."

"And finish your degree?" Kate asked.

Ty nodded. "Yes, but it's more than that. Before I dropped out, I was on track to graduate magna cum laude with a BS in Nursing. I've dreamed of being a nurse since I was in kindergarten. My great aunt Merce was a nurse—Merce the Nurse—and I worshipped her. As a kid, I was fascinated by her stories. She trained at St. Mary's, the hospital the Mayo brothers started. Anyway, I want to help people like she did."

Kate made a note and then smiled up at Ty. "That's very admirable."

"Being a nurse is all I've ever wanted to do."

"Anything else?" Kate asked. "Any plans to buy a house or a new car, for example?"

"I don't know, maybe."

"Come on, Ty," Kate said. Her expression was stern again. "You're trying to tell me you just won $170 million, and you haven't fantasized a little bit?"

Ty's shoulders stiffened. She hadn't expected to be grilled about her plans for the money. She knew Kate and Derek were just trying to do their job, but still. "I guess a new car would be nice," she muttered. "Mine is on its last legs."

"Is that it?" Derek asked. "No diamond-studded Rolex watches? Maybe a private jet?"

Ty squirmed in her seat and felt her cheeks warm. "No, nothing like that," she bit back. "Listen I know there are lots of horror stories about people winning the lottery and doing all kinds of crazy shit. That's not me. I'm going to be responsible and use the money to help people."

Kate's expression softened. "Ty, please understand, we've seen it all. People have the best intentions, but then...I don't want to see you fall into the same trap so many others do. We have your best interest at heart."

Ty wanted to believe her, and she knew she needed their help, but she wasn't a fucking child. She nibbled on her lip. "I know."

After peppering Ty with a few more questions, Kate closed her notebook and set her pen on the glass table. "Why don't we stop there for today. We can regroup tomorrow and get into the nitty gritty then. Derek and I will have some detailed financial scenarios to review with you."

Ty slumped back in her chair and let out a long sigh. This lottery winning business sure was stressful.

Kate stood and said, "Before you leave, I'd like to introduce you to Mike, our in-house attorney. He'll be able to help you through the process of claiming your prize."

Ty could barely summon the energy to get out of her chair. In the craziness of the last few days, she hadn't even considered the act of actually turning in her winning ticket. It was like she'd expected the ticket to metamorphize into a pile of money. She rocked back and forth in her chair and used the momentum to get to her feet.

Mike was a giant of a man, and he was completely bald.

"Come on in, Ty, and have a seat," he said after Kate had introduced them.

Ty tried to pay attention as he rattled off a bunch of the legal considerations and implications associated with winning the Lionball. She perked up when she heard him say the word *anonymous*.

"In the state of North Carolina," Mike said, "lottery officials are required to release the winner's names to anyone who asks. They won't allow you to claim the prize anonymously."

Ty's heart sank. So much for keeping her winning ticket a secret. "Oh, I didn't know that. I was hoping I could keep my identity from getting out."

Mike flashed her a grin. "Not to worry. I'm fairly confident we can find a way to keep your identity confidential."

Ty sat up in her seat. "Really?"

"Yes. We can set up a limited liability corporation, an LLC, and present it as the winner."

"You make it sound so easy."

"It is. We'll need to designate an agent, such as myself, to claim the prize on behalf of the LLC."

"Perfect."

"Very well," Mike replied. "I'll prepare the necessary paperwork to establish the LLC. After that, we'll reach out to the lottery officials. We've got up to one hundred and eighty days to claim the prize, but I'd like to get the ball rolling as soon as possible."

"Okay. Thanks, Mike."

"What would you like to call it?"

"Call what?"

"The LLC. You can name it whatever you like."

Ty thought for a moment before answering. "Merce the Nurse LLC."

Mike looked at her with raised eyebrows but didn't say anything. He made a note, then took off his glasses and set them on the desk. "One last thing, Ty."

"Yeah?"

"Be careful."

His rich baritone voice echoed off the office walls, causing the hair's on Ty's arm to stand up.

"The less people you tell about winning the Lionball, the better," he said. "It can be hard to know who you can trust.

People you thought were your friends may surprise you, and not in a good way. They might push you to do things you don't want to do. I think your decision to remain anonymous is a wise one, but that doesn't mean someone won't figure out you're the winner."

A few hours later, Mike's words rang true. While Ty was enjoying a room service dinner, her cell phone rang. She cringed when she saw the name on her caller ID. It was her cousin Garth. He only called on the big holidays—Thanksgiving and Christmas. She wanted to ignore the call, but he'd keep calling until she picked up. He could be *very* persistent.

When her parents had died, Garth had showed up right away and offered to help her and Reed in any way that he could. Reed had questioned Garth's motives, suggesting he was more interested in money than anything else. At first, Ty thought her brother was being cynical. Even though Garth didn't have the best track record, she always tried to see the best in people, and she'd happily accepted his help as they sorted through their parents' affairs. It quickly became evident, however, that Reed was right. Garth put on a good show, but his intentions were anything but good.

She snapped up the phone right before it went to voice mail. "Hello."

"Hi, Ty. It's Garth. I was calling to make sure you're okay."

"I'm fine, thanks," she said, wondering what had prompted the call.

"Oh, that's good to hear. Someone from the Asheville PD called the house and…"

Ty contained a groan. While she commended the diligence of the Asheville PD, it was unfortunate that the tentacles of their investigation had reached to Garth. But she shouldn't be surprised. After Reed, he and his mother, Aunt Paisley, were her closest next of kin, and she'd probably listed them as her emergency contacts at some point down the line.

"They said you went missing on Saturday night, and, well, I was worried."

"I wasn't missing. It was a giant misunderstanding."

"I see," he said. There was a long pause before he spoke again. "Did you hear the news?"

"I'm not following you. What news?"

"They're saying someone is Asheville won the big Lionball drawing…"

Ty jumped out of her chair, the hair on her arms standing on end for the second time that day. She tried to keep her voice even. "It's very sweet of you to call, Garth, but really, I'm fine." She took a deep breath and said, "Say hello to your mom for me," before ending the call.

CHAPTER EIGHT

Karla stared down at the woman between her legs. Her long, shiny, jet-black hair glistened in the moonlight, and whatever she was doing with her tongue felt *really* good. Karla didn't even remember the woman's name. Dana, maybe? Or was it Diana? She was the third woman Karla had fucked in as many days. She was becoming a downright slut. Making up for lost time. Sure, there'd been a fling here and there while she'd been on the ski circuit, but nothing more than that. At the ripe old age of twenty-two, she'd never had a real girlfriend, or boyfriend for that matter. Her love life had been stunted, at best. She'd missed out on all the usual growing up stuff. Proms. Dating. Slumber parties. She'd always been too busy flying down a mountain somewhere.

She tried to shut her brain down. What the fuck was wrong with her? Why the hell was she thinking about skiing when she was getting the best head she'd ever had in her life? She pinched her eyes shut and flinched as the throbbing of her clit intensified. She held her breath as the orgasm rolled through her.

When she walked up the steps of her parents' house just before dawn, her father greeted her at the door. He was in his robe and holding a cup of coffee.

"I heard your car come in," he explained. He looked at his watch, though Karla was pretty sure he knew exactly what time it was. "Don't you have to be at work in a few hours?"

She did, but she could do the job in her sleep. It wasn't exactly rocket science. And she was an adult, for God's sake. She grunted a response.

"Where have you been?" he asked.

"None of your business." She pushed past him and marched up the stairs to her bedroom.

After a few hours of sleep, she dragged herself to Outdoor Sports for her shift. Even though she was exhausted, she refused to let Zoe down. When a busload of skiers from Dallas filed into the store for rental skis, she splashed cold water on her face and did her best to snap out of her I-stayed-out-all-night zombie mode. It took everything she had to plant a smile on her face and focus on adjusting the bindings on the tour group's skis to the proper setting.

During a small break in the rush, Karla slipped into the employee break room for a power nap, but as she was dozing off, another busload of skiers arrived. She rallied as best she could and repeatedly cursed herself for not getting to bed earlier the night before. At the end of her shift, she went into the employee locker room to get her backpack and coat, and even though she'd practically sleepwalked through the entire afternoon, she perked up as soon as she glanced at her phone. There was a text from the dark-haired woman—Dana—who gave great head.

I'd like to see you again. I'm at Abbott's. Drinks on me.

Abbott's was the bar where she and Dana had met the night before. It was only a few blocks from Outdoor Sports, and Dana had sent the text a mere five minutes earlier. Even though she was desperate for sleep, Karla couldn't resist the offer. She typed out a quick response.

On my way.

She waved goodbye to Zoe on her way out. "See you tomorrow."

"Thanks for all your help today," Zoe said. "Have a good night."

"You too," Karla yelled over her shoulder as she pushed open the back exit.

"Oh, hey, Karla?"

Karla paused. "Yeah?"

"Don't forget we've got that big sale tomorrow."

"I won't."

"If it's not too much of a bother, could you come in a little early and help me set up?"

"Sure," Karla replied as she stepped outside.

The sun was setting, and the temperature had dropped significantly since lunchtime. She tugged her coat up around her neck and made the short walk to Abbott's.

The bar was already pretty crowded, which wasn't all that surprising. It was five o'clock on a Friday. Steely Dan played over the speakers, and although all the televisions over the bar were on mute, each one displayed the Final Four basketball game being played in Atlanta. Even without the sound, Karla heard the screeching of sneakers on wood. Dana was at the far end of the long wooden bar and had somehow managed to score two barstools. When her steel blue eyes settled on Karla, her chest tightened, and her stomach fluttered. Dana's gaze was intense. It bore into Karla. No one had ever looked at her that way. It made her feel special.

Dana was beautiful, but her features were unique—high cheekbones, oval-shaped eyes, long eyelashes, and a long, narrow nose. She was a few inches taller than Karla, maybe six feet. She was thin but muscular, like a yoga instructor or long-distance runner.

"Manhattan?" Dana asked as soon as Karla approached.

That was the drink that had gotten Karla into trouble the night before. She should have a Coke. But even a beer would probably be a better choice.

"A Heineken for me, please."

"Come on," Dana replied. "It's Friday night. It's time to party."

Karla shrugged and held her hands out. "Oh, what the hell. Make it a Manhattan." It wasn't like she had to do a hard training session or ski in a race the next morning.

"Coming right up," Dana said and signaled the bartender.

Karla set her elbow on the bar and rested her head against her palm. She watched Dana's interactions with the bartender. She had this aura about her. A charisma that was intoxicating. For reasons she didn't fully understand, Karla was incredibly drawn to her. The bartender laughed heartily at one of Dana's jokes while he made the Manhattan.

"Cheers," Dana said once they both had a drink. "It's great to see you again."

"Cheers." Karla tapped her highball against Dana's martini glass. "Although a Manhattan is probably the last thing I need right now. Thanks to you, I could barely keep my eyes open at work today."

Dana gave her a wink. "My deepest apologies. I promise not to keep you out past your bedtime again." She plucked an olive out of her martini and slipped it between her lips.

Karla wanted to kiss her and her groin pulsed. Dana gave her a knowing look. Karla crossed her legs, but it only caused the throbbing to intensify. When she'd walked into the bar, she'd been determined to stay for one drink then go home and get a good night's sleep. But now she knew the evening would end in Dana's bed, like it had the night before.

It meant she'd have to confront her father's disappointed glare when she wandered home in the wee hours of the morning, but right now she didn't care. After so many years of living a structured life, she was entitled to let her hair down a little bit. Plus, soon she'd be off to school and forced to once again live a more regimented lifestyle. This was her one chance to cut loose, and that's exactly what she intended to do.

"So," Dana said, "we kind of skipped over the small talk last night."

Karla blushed and nodded. It was true. The previous night was a bit of a blur, but Karla was pretty sure there hadn't been a lot of talking. She remembered dancing with Dana, and the next thing she knew, they were in bed together.

Dana rested a hand on Karla's thigh. "If these legs are any indication, I'd say you're a professional athlete."

Karla took a sip of her drink and set the glass on the bar. "I am, or rather, I was. I just retired."

Dana laughed. "You look too young to be retired."

Karla took another swig from her glass. "It's kind of a long story."

Dana ran a long, thin finger down her arm. "I have all night."

"Well, I've spent my whole life ski racing…"

"I knew it. A skier. Based on my, uh, limited exposure, you don't have an ounce of fat on you. I mean, last night…Your body is fucking incredible."

"I was on the US Ski Team for a while, but—"

"Oh, wow."

"That phase of my life is over. I'm heading off to school in the fall. To the University of Vermont. I'm going to ski for them while I earn my degree in nursing."

"That's nice, but why would you ever leave Wyoming for Vermont? The skiing can't compare."

"There's some decent skiing on the East Coast," Karla said, more defensively than she intended. "And, well, the truth is, financially, going to UVM makes the most sense." Karla threw back the last of her Manhattan and Dana ordered her another one before she had a chance to protest. New drink in hand she asked, "What about you. What's your story?"

"I'm in cyber security."

"That sounds fascinating."

"It is."

"Do you work for a company in Jackson?"

Dana shook her head. "No, my company is headquartered in in New York City, but the nature of my job allows me to work remotely. I travel a lot, but otherwise, I pretty much get to make my own schedule."

Karla never got around to having dinner, and after a third drink, she was feeling a little tipsy. She followed Dana out of the bar, but they never made it back to her place. They fucked in the backseat of her car.

CHAPTER NINE

Ty met with Kate and Derek again the next day. Before they got down to business, she told them about the phone call from her cousin.

"Unfortunately, that's one of the major drawbacks of being incredibly wealthy," Kate replied. "People come out of the woodwork. You might want to get a new cell phone number."

Derek nodded in agreement. "Kate's right. This cousin of yours is probably just the first of many calls you're destined to get."

Kate pointed to a stack of binders at the far end of the conference table. "Well, Ty, you ready to roll up your sleeves and get to work? We've got a lot to cover with you today."

"Ready as I'll ever be," Ty said.

Derek got up and handed Ty and Kate each a binder.

Kate tapped on her binder with a cherry-red manicured fingernail. "Derek and I put this together to help guide the more in-depth discussion we hope to have with you today. The information in here is very detailed, but we'll walk you through each section. I expect it will take us a few hours to get through everything, so we've arranged to have lunch sent in. I hope you like sushi?"

Ty had never had sushi in her life, but she wasn't about to admit it. "Yep, sushi sounds great. Thanks."

When Ty opened her binder, her eyes glazed over. The first section was titled *Jackpot Payout Option: Lump sum vs. Annuity.* Sounded like a real page turner.

"With a lump sum, the money is all paid out at once," Kate explained. "With an annuity, the money is paid out in annual installments over a period of thirty years."

Ty nodded, trying really hard to follow. "I've heard those terms before."

"Okay good. Now, if you opt to take the lump sum, Lionball will award you the *cash value* of the jackpot."

Ty gave her a blank stare. "Cash value?"

Kate patiently walked her through the concept, using terms like *present value* and *discount rate.* Terms Ty was sure she'd learned in some econ course she'd suffered through in school but couldn't for the life of her remember what they meant. She tried her best to follow along—it was her money they were talking about, after all—but what a snooze fest.

Seemingly sensing her cluelessness, Kate said, "Maybe it would help if I sketched it out." She stood up and walked to a whiteboard on the far wall of the conference room. "The Lionball jackpot was 510 million, and you were one of three winners." She wrote: *$510 / 3 = $170* and tapped the whiteboard with her finger. "Your share is 170 million."

Ty nodded. She could handle simple division and multiplication.

Next, Kate wrote *LUMP SUM = $106 million.* "If you take the money in one lump sum, you'll get about 106 million, the amount the lottery officials estimate is the *present value* of 170 million."

"Okay. God, I cannot even imagine trying to figure this all out on my own."

"For your reference, the lottery officials use a discount rate of about 3.4 percent," Derek added.

Ty nodded again and acted like she knew what that meant.

Kate picked up the marker again and wrote *ANNUITY = $170 million*. "If, instead, you opt for the annuity, you'd get the full 170 million, but it would be paid out to you in annual installments over a thirty-year period."

Ty felt like she was having an out-of-body experience. She was sitting there discussing these massive amounts of money, money that was about to be hers. It still didn't seem possible.

Kate sat back down at the conference table and gave Ty's shoulder a light squeeze. "You doing okay? I know this is a lot to swallow."

"Yeah, I'm okay," Ty replied. "Overwhelmed but hanging in there."

Kate gestured to Derek. He cleared his throat and took a sip of water. "Now we're going to discuss our recommendation." He walked to the whiteboard and tapped the area where Kate had written *LUMP SUM = $106 million*. "It's our recommendation that you take the lump sum."

"Um, okay," Ty replied. "Why?"

"Well, if you take the lump sum of 106 million, it will *all* get paid out to you at *once* and we can invest the money for you. All we have to do is invest the 106 million so it returns more than 3.4 percent a year—the discount rate used by the lottery officials—and eventually, the 106 million will grow to exceed the annuity payout of 170 million. You'll be ahead of the game."

"Does that all make sense Ty?" Kate asked.

Ty squinted at the numbers on the whiteboard and ran a hand through her hair. "I think so."

Derek drew some charts on the whiteboard before continuing. "There are some tax disadvantages associated with taking the lump sum. But don't worry. We'll devise an investment strategy and tax management plan for you that will more than offset these tax consequences." Derek paused and looked toward the doorway of the conference room.

Another perky admin held up two big white paper bags, which Ty assumed contained their sushi lunch.

"Why don't we take a quick break to eat," Kate suggested.

The admin set three trays on the table, each containing a few pieces of fish nestled on a ball of rice, which Kate referred to as nigiri. Before she dug in, Ty observed how Kate and Derek held their chopsticks. She took a deep breath and gave it a try. It wasn't pretty, but she managed to scoop/shovel a tuna nigiri into her mouth without dropping it. It was slimier than she expected, but she managed to get it down without gagging. She'd just wrestled a second piece of tuna into her mouth when Kate asked, "Are you free for dinner?"

Ty nodded and tried to swallow the mound of food in her mouth, which triggered a massive coughing fit. She grabbed her bottle of water and washed the fish down her throat.

"Are you okay?" Kate asked.

"Uh-huh," Ty coughed. "It went down the wrong way." After another chug of water, she set down her chopsticks. She decided not to tempt fate and left the rest of her nigiri untouched.

After lunch, Kate and Derek went over various investment vehicles, most of which Ty had never heard of because bartenders with barely two nickels to rub together didn't typically discuss these types of things.

"Our goal is to make sure your money is well protected but also has the opportunity to grow," Kate explained. "Assuming you live within your means and don't go on a wild spending spree, you should be set for life and then some."

At some point Ty's eyes must have rolled into the back of her head because Kate asked, "Clear as mud?"

"Yeah, sorry," Ty replied with a laugh. "It's just so much information at once. Who knew this lottery winning business would be so complicated."

"Why don't you go back to the hotel and rest for a bit," Kate suggested. "We'll swing by around seven to pick you up for dinner."

As Ty walked back to the Peninsula, she gazed in the windows of all the high-end stores lining Michigan Avenue. It dawned on her that the Denver hoodie and Converse high-tops she was sporting probably wouldn't be suitable attire for dinner. She was standing in front of a store called Burberry. It wasn't a name she recognized, but the mannequins in the window were elegantly dressed, so she pulled on the big, heavy metal door and stepped inside. Her nostrils were accosted by the strong scent of leather and lavender. The saleswoman behind the counter gave Ty a wide-eyed stare and quickly busied herself organizing an already perfectly organized display on a nearby table. Ty suppressed a chuckle. She felt like Julia Roberts in *Pretty Woman*. She grabbed a blouse off a rack near the front door and carried it to the checkout counter without even trying it on.

"I'll take this."

The saleswoman scurried over and rang her up. "The total comes to $429.54. How would you like to pay for that?"

Ty's eyes almost popped out of her head. Had she inadvertently picked up a shirt with gold buttons? Lacking the gumption to just walk out of the store, she dug around in the outside pocket of her backpack for her well-worn vinyl wallet and handed the woman her Visa card, praying that the charge wouldn't be declined. She may have a $170 million lottery ticket tucked away in a safe deposit box in Asheville, but her credit card company didn't know that yet.

When she got back to her room, she tried on the shirt. She had to suck in her chest to get the buttons fastened, and once she did, her boobs threatened to break free. One deep breath could spell wardrobe malfunction, but it would have to do. She didn't have anything else to wear to dinner, and buying the too-tight shirt had pushed her credit card to the brink.

* * *

Ty was sound asleep when her cell phone rang early the next morning. She didn't have to look at the caller ID to know who it was. Sarah had her own distinct ring. It was barely light outside, and she fumbled for the switch on the bedside lamp.

"You do realize Chicago is seven hours behind Brussels?" Ty asked when she answered the call.

Sarah skipped the preamble. "You're not going to fucking believe this," she said. "I just talked to my roommate. Rusty was arrested last night. Apparently, he tried to drive his truck through the front door of the bank."

Ty sat up in bed. "Huh? What bank?"

"The bank in downtown Asheville. You know, the one where your lottery ticket is hidden away."

"But how did he know…" Ty kicked off the covers and set her feet on the floor. "Rosie. That fucking bitch. She promised me she wouldn't say a word. I bet she told Rusty I came into the bank…God fucking dammit." Ty pounded her fist on her thigh. "Ouch."

"You okay?"

"Yeah, just mad as shit. I can't believe I trusted her."

"Thank God you're in Chicago," Sarah said.

"I know, but too bad my lottery ticket isn't here with me."

"Well, according to my roommate, Rusty's Ford F150 suffered a lot more damage than the bank. As soon as he hit the front doors, it set off all sorts of alarms. The police were there in minutes. Apparently, he put up quite a fight."

"He was probably drunk."

"Probably, but look at the bright side: Now he's behind bars. You no longer have to worry about him chasing you down."

"True, but there's no telling who the hell else Rosie told. For all we know, half of Asheville might know I rented a safe deposit box a mere thirty-six hours after the Lionball drawing."

"I think you should stay in Chicago for a while, Ty."

Ty stared out the window of her hotel room. A sliver of orange hugged the horizon, casting a glow over the lake. "I think you're right. I need to go. I have to call Kate and tell her what happened."

Even though it was still early, Ty was pretty sure Kate would be up. At dinner the night before, they'd gotten talking about running, a sport they both enjoyed. Kate said she ran along Lake Michigan most mornings before work.

Kate picked up on the first ring. "Well hello there, early bird."

"Morning. Listen, I'm sorry to bother you, but I just got a call from Sarah, Sarah McLean." Ty gave her a brief synopsis of what had happened.

"Oh, wow."

"Yeah, wow is right."

"I know you'd only planned to stay in Chicago a few days, Ty, but given the circumstances, I think you should stay here until you and Mike are ready to claim the prize."

"I couldn't agree more."

CHAPTER TEN

Karla clocked out after her shift at Outdoor Sports and power walked across the gravel lot behind the store. She was meeting Dana for drinks, and even though they'd spent nearly every night together for the past two weeks, Karla was downright giddy about seeing her. She couldn't get enough of Dana. Being with her was exhilarating. She had a wild side and was a fucking animal in bed. Although they'd only known each other for a short time, Karla was already all in. She'd never been in love before, but she was pretty sure she was beginning to stumble in that direction.

As luck would have it, Karla walked into the bar at the same time as the rich older woman she'd screwed at the Four Seasons.

"Can I buy you a drink?" the woman asked.

"I'm meeting someone," she said and brushed past Ms. Four Seasons.

Dana waved at her from the bar and Karla hurried over. When Dana's warm lips brushed against her cheek, it sent a shock of electricity through Karla's body.

Once they had their drinks, Dana said, "Tomorrow is supposed to be beautiful. I'm thinking about going snowshoeing. Come with me."

"Gosh, I'd love to," Karla said, "but I can't. I have to work."

"Oh, come on. Call in sick. You need to learn to live a little, Karla."

Karla fidgeted with the corner of the paper napkin under her drink. "I wish I could. I really do, but Zoe's been so good to me, and she's already short-staffed. If I didn't show, it would put her in a real bind."

Dana gave her a little pout. "Think about me, snowshoeing through the fresh snow under crystal-blue skies, all by myself."

It pained Karla to let her down. "It's tempting, trust me. I just—"

"It's settled then."

"Okay," Karla said.

A smile lit up Dana's beautiful face. "Oh, goodie," she said. "Trust me, snowshoeing will be waaaay more fun than work."

Karla had no doubt that it would be, and she should be happy. Dana wanted to spend the day with her. Calling in sick wouldn't be that big a deal. The mountain would be closing any day now for the season, and Outdoor Sports probably wouldn't be all that busy. Surely Zoe could manage without her.

* * *

The weather forecasters were right. The following day was picture perfect. A crisp twenty-five degrees, but there wasn't a cloud in the sky. Karla smiled as she followed Dana over the fluffy snow across a huge meadow and into a forest of Lodgepole pines. After zig-zagging between the trees, they came to a river that was mostly frozen over and covered in snow. Its bank was lined with spruce trees, and a large patch of Aspens dotted the gently sloping mountainside in the distance, their bare branches swaying in the breeze. It was breathtakingly beautiful. Karla couldn't think of any place she'd rather be, and she pushed away the lingering guilt about having called in sick to work.

Dana pulled off her pack and sat on a fallen tree. A small bead of sweat glistened on her forehead. "I could use a break. How about you?"

Although they'd been snowshoeing for over an hour, Karla didn't feel the slightest bit winded or tired, but she knew she was in better shape than ninety-nine percent of the population. "Yeah, a break would be nice. I could use some water."

Dana produced a water bottle and a small leather pouch from her pack. She handed the water to Karla and pulled a tightly rolled joint from her pouch.

"You up for a hit?"

Karla's eyes went wide. "What is that?"

Dana brought her thumb and pointer finger together and held them in front of her lips. She pretended to inhale. "Weed. I've got some great stuff."

Karla had never smoked pot in her life. Heck, she'd never even taken a puff from a cigarette. "I'm good, but thanks. But where did you get that? Isn't marijuana illegal?"

Dana's laugh echoed through the otherwise silent forest. "Not in Colorado, which is where I got this stash."

"Last I checked, we're in Wyoming, not Colorado."

"Whatever. You need to lighten up." Dana lit the joint, took a long drag, and held it out for Karla.

Karla held up her hand. "No thank you."

"Suit yourself, but you're missing out," Dana said and brought the joint back to her own lips. They sat in silence as she puffed away. When she was done, she snuffed out the joint on a nearby rock, tucked the stub into a metal tin, and slipped it back into her leather pouch.

They spent the next two hours marching through the snow, only stopping occasionally to take a sip of water or enjoy the view. Dana surprised Karla with her knowledge of all things nature. She could identify nearly every species of tree they passed, and she was able to identify the breed of a bird from its call. Karla was impressed.

"Where did you learn all of this," she asked.

"I've always been somewhat of a science geek," Dana said. She waved her hands across the backdrop of snow-covered fir trees. "I love it out here. No matter the season, it's so beautiful and peaceful."

"Well, thanks for bestowing your knowledge on me," Karla said.

Dana gave her a soft smile. "My pleasure."

When they got back to the parking lot, Dana said, "Awesome day, huh?"

"It sure was. Beyond awesome."

"Worth blowing off work?"

"Totally."

"You up for grabbing a drink?" Dana asked as they drove back toward town.

"I'd love to, but I promised my parents I'd be home for dinner tonight." Karla hadn't been home much since she'd met Dana, and her parents had made no secret of their disapproval. Sometimes it was like they forgot she was no longer a child. But she was living at their house, and that meant she had to live by their rules. Family dinner was a big deal in the Rehn household.

"Come on, one drink."

Karla wanted to say yes, but she knew she was already skating on thin ice with her parents. "I can't. I'm sorry. Maybe tomorrow?"

"Yeah, maybe."

The following evening, Karla hurried to Abbott's as soon as she got off work. She and Dana had made plans to meet for a drink, but when she got to the bar, there was no sign of her. Karla's phone said it was ten past six. Maybe Dana was just running late. She plunked herself down on a barstool and ordered a beer. When she reached the bottom of the bottle, there was still no sign of Dana. She sent her a text. A response came back a few seconds later.

Sorry, work emergency. I'm not going to make it.

Karla stuffed the phone back in the pocket of her jeans and slumped forward on the bar. Dana's job in cyber security was no doubt super important. It made sense that emergencies would arise, but would it have killed her to give Karla a heads up? She threw some bills on the bar and drove home.

* * *

Dana blew her off two more times over the coming week, but in both instances she at least had the decency to let Karla know ahead of time.

When they did finally see each other, it was late on a Sunday night. They had one drink at Abbott's and went back to Dana's. They were barely in the front door when she practically ripped Karla's clothes off. Any effort to try to slow her down proved futile. Karla was slightly irked, but she rolled with it, and after her third orgasm, any annoyance she'd felt had all but vanished.

CHAPTER ELEVEN

While Kate and the gang at Allendale Financial worked out all the logistics—established Merce the Nurse LLC, opened bank and brokerage accounts, and contacted the lottery officials—Ty hunkered down in Chicago. She explored the city, contacted her old academic advisor in Denver, and re-enrolled in school. By the third week in April, a plan was firmly in place. She and Mike, the in-house attorney at Kate's firm, would travel to Asheville, retrieve the lottery ticket from the safe deposit box, and officially claim her prize. They'd spend a grand total of one night in Asheville, and from there, Ty would fly straight to Denver to begin the next chapter of her life. She should be in Colorado in time for the summer session and could start working toward finishing her nursing degree.

"It is almost May, right?" Ty asked Mike as they climbed into the back of a black Lincoln MKZ in downtown Chicago. It had been drizzling all afternoon and temperatures barely reached the forties.

"Ha," Mike said. "Same way every year. It feels like summer will never arrive, and when it does, it's wonderful, but if you blink, you might miss it."

Ty's stomach was in knots when they boarded their United flight to Asheville. Part of her was excited. Soon, she'd be a very, very wealthy woman. But part of her was scared shitless. Scared about what might await her in Asheville even though Mike had repeatedly assured her that her identity would remain anonymous. She was also anxious about how she'd handle suddenly being insanely rich. She'd told everyone—Kate, Sarah, her brother—that she'd be sensible and would give most of the money away, but what if she *did* go crazy like so many lottery winners before her?

Everything had been arranged for Mike to claim the Lionball prize on Ty's behalf, or technically on the LLC's behalf. Based on Kate and Derek's advice, Ty had opted to take the lump sum payout—a cool 106 million bucks. Once the money was deposited into her bank account, it would be divided across multiple investments based on an interim financial plan they'd developed for her.

When they landed in Asheville, they hurried through the airport to a waiting car. With his bald head and bulky frame, Mike looked like a WrestleMania contestant, and for that, Ty was grateful. He made her feel safe.

When they pulled up outside the Grove Park Inn, Ty clutched her backpack. They'd chosen the hotel because it was outside of town and she didn't know anyone who worked there, but her friends sometimes went there for special events—anniversaries, birthdays, stuff like that. After they'd each checked in and dropped their luggage in their respective rooms, they met downstairs for dinner. Although the Inn had a beautiful terrace, Mike had arranged for them to eat in a private room.

Over dinner they went over some final paperwork and reviewed the plan for the next day.

Mike was scheduled to meet the state lottery officials at the Asheville Savings Bank at ten a.m. the next morning. Among the mound of paperwork she'd filled out over the last few weeks was a power of attorney granting Mike access to her safe deposit box. He'd spoken to Gladys—the woman at the bank who was normally in charge of administering the boxes—and scheduled an appointment with her. The idea was to avoid having to interact with Rosie. She wouldn't know Mike from Adam, so there was no reason for her to suspect he was there to open the box that Ty had rented.

"How long do you think it'll take?" Ty asked.

"Once I have the ticket, the lottery folks will have to validate it. I sign a few documents claiming the prize on behalf of the LLC and that'll be it. It should take thirty minutes, tops. After that, I'd expect the funds—your share of the jackpot after taxes—to be in your bank account within five business days."

"Okay," Ty croaked. Before they left Chicago, he'd explained that taxes on lottery winnings over a certain amount are generally withheld automatically. Based on Kate and Derek's estimates, her payout would be in the neighborhood of $73 million—the $106 million lump sum minus a hefty chunk to the taxman.

"Wow, I can't even imagine what it's going to be like to see all those zeros in my bank account balance."

Mike chuckled. "I'm sure Kate warned you that the government will probably be back for more, so the final amount will probably be a little lower."

"Yeah, she warned me." Ty winked. "I *suppose* I'll manage to get by."

* * *

The following afternoon, Ty met Sarah for a late lunch at one of the brewpubs downtown. By now, the news had reported that an LLC had come forward to claim the Lionball prize in North Carolina. Ty felt safer going out in public now because she assumed the spotlight would finally be off of her. Her theory was that when people learned an LLC had claimed the prize, they'd jump to the conclusion that a company or a group of people who'd pooled their money had the winning ticket. Most people in town would never think that little old Ty, the bartender from Thirsty's, would have the wherewithal to set up an LLC.

Thankfully, it appeared her theory was right. Hardly anyone glanced at her as she slid into the seat across from Sarah.

After they placed their orders, Sarah asked, "So, it's a done deal, huh?"

"Yep. Claiming the prize was amazingly simple. Everything went according to plan."

Sarah laughed. "You don't look any different."

"Ha, maybe that's because I don't actually have the money yet. Check back with me in five to seven business days. I'll have manicured hands, platinum blond hair, and pearly white teeth."

"All kidding aside," Sarah said, reaching out for Ty's hand. "You deserve all this, you know that? You're a really good soul. I know you've had a rough go of it with what happened to your parents and everything, but—"

"Oh, stop." Ty dabbed her eyes. "You're going to make me cry."

"Just promise me you won't take it for granted."

"I won't. I promise."

CHAPTER TWELVE

The tires of Karla's bike skidded in the dirt as she rounded a switchback on the narrow single-track. Her best friend Keats was home from college, and they were taking a spin on their favorite mountain biking trail.

"You go, girl," she hollered when Keats jumped a log that lay across the trail.

Karla scaled the same log and followed Keats up a short but steep incline. When the trail leveled out, Keats stopped and climbed off her bike.

Karla pulled up beside her and gave her a high five. "That was fucking awesome. Wanna do the loop again?"

Keats grinned. "Definitely. But I need a quick breather. My thighs are on fire."

Karla got off her bike and leaned it against a nearby tree. "Apple?" she asked as she reached around to the pockets on the back of her bike jersey.

"Sure."

After Karla polished the two red fruits on the legs of her baggy black bike shorts, she tossed one to Keats.

She snapped it out of the air and crunched her teeth into it, sending a trickle of juice down her chin. When she finished chewing, Keats asked, "You think there's any decent mountain biking in Vermont?"

Karla cocked her head and shrugged one shoulder. "Dunno. Guess I'll find out soon enough though."

"You still feel good about your decision to go to UVM?"

Karla hedged. "I guess." She'd lived in Wyoming almost her entire life, and although she was reluctant to admit it to anyone, she was having some serious second thoughts about choosing UVM. Burlington was so far away from Dana and her family, and when she stepped on campus, she wouldn't know a single soul. The doubt was compounded by her nagging regret at having had to walk away from the US Ski Team. "Although when it comes down to it, it doesn't matter how I feel about it. The decision is made, and it's not like I had a lot of choice. I mean, with the money and all."

"Yeah, I know. Sorry, kid."

"Ah, it's okay. I'm lucky they want me. Their ski program is fucking amazing."

"They're the lucky ones. You are one of the best skiers in the country."

"*Was* one of the best."

"Hey, come on. It's not like you to be such a Debbie Downer."

"I'm sorry." Karla cracked a smile. "I need to make an appointment for an attitude adjustment."

"Does Dana know you're leaving in the fall?"

"Yeah, she knows."

"You think you two will continue something after you move? Like do the long-distance thing."

Karla pulled a packet of energy gel from her jersey and ripped it open. "Gosh, I hope so. I mean, we haven't been seeing each other all that long—what, only about a month—but I'm pretty whipped."

"I've noticed." Keats picked a twig off the ground and snapped it with her fingers. "Don't take this the wrong way, but it seems like you got *really* into her, *really* fast."

Karla's muscles tensed. "What do you mean? No, I haven't."

"Um, yes, you kind of have, and well, you're my best friend. I don't want to see you get hurt."

"I appreciate your concern, but I'm not going to get hurt."

"You said she's blown you off a bunch lately."

"A few times. It's no big deal. She's got this big important job in cyber security."

"Okay, whatever you say. Just remember, you're important too, and you deserve to be with someone who treats you with respect."

"She treats me with respect," Karla bit back.

"Okay, okay. I'm just looking out for you."

The line of questioning grated on Karla's nerves. She pulled her water bottle out of the cage on her bike and squirted water into her mouth. "Enough of this sitting around shit. Let's get back on our bikes. You ready?"

Keats stood up and stretched her arms over her head. "Next time I agree to go mountain biking with a top-notch athlete, smack me upside the head, okay?"

Karla didn't respond. She threw a leg over her bike, clipped into her pedals, and took off. "Last one to the end buys lunch," she yelled over her shoulder as she disappeared into the trees.

When she approached the most challenging section of the loop, she braked lightly. The last time around, she'd walked her bike over the narrow plank that spanned the river, gushing with water from the spring melt. She unclipped her right foot and set it on the ground. Why was she being such a wimp? She'd never been one to shy away from risk. After all, she'd spent most her life speeding down a mountain in nothing but a polyester one-piece race suit. She eyed the water churning around a series of boulders in the middle of the river and said, "Fuck it."

Keats pulled up beside her just as she was twisting the cleat of her bike shoe back into her pedal. "Karla, don't. It's too—"

Karla didn't hear the rest of what she said. She pushed down on her pedal and zoomed toward the plank. Speed was key. Any hesitation would cause her tires to wobble. There was no room for error. A crash into the river ten feet below would be devastating.

The plank vibrated when her front tire hit it. She crouched over the seat and leaned forward to maintain her momentum, keeping her body as quiet as possible. Adrenalin coursed through her as she sailed toward the opposite bank. *Easy peasy.* About ten feet from the end of the flimsy bridge, an uneven joint between two boards bounced her bike to the right. She yanked her handlebars to steady herself but overcorrected, causing her front tire to slip off the plank. Pain seared through her body when she smashed into one of the massive rocks below. Everything went dark.

* * *

Karla opened one eye, but it fell immediately shut. She tried again. Left eye open. Right eye open. Where was she? It was so bright. Both eyes slid closed again.

"Karla," a voice said.

"Yeah," she croaked without opening her eyes.

A warm hand curled around her forearm. "Karla," the voice said again. "It's me, Keats."

Karla forced her eyes open. Keats's bloodshot eyes were staring down at her. "Where am I?"

"The hospital. You crashed."

"Was it bad?"

Keats bit into her bottom lip and nodded. "You just got out of surgery. It's your left leg. You broke it pretty badly. If you hadn't been wearing a helmet, you'd probably be dead."

"Oh," Karla replied, and her eyes drifted closed again.

When she opened her eyes again, Keats was still at her bedside. "Will I be able to ski again?" Karla asked.

Keats looked down at the floor and then back up at her. "I don't know. You'll have to ask the doctor."

"Okay."

"She should be back soon to check on you."

"What about Dana? Does she—"

"Yeah. I called her," Keats said. "She came for a little while, but she had to leave. Some work emergency."

"How long have I been here?"

"A day and a half. Your parents were here all night. They went for something to eat."

"Are they mad?"

Keats shook her head. "No, just scared. We've all been scared, hoping you'd wake up and be okay."

"I'm sorry," Karla said. "Riding across the river was really dumb."

Keats nodded. "Yes, it was."

* * *

Karla's father sat down on one of the overstuffed chairs in the living room of their house. The lines on his tan face were more pronounced than usual. He wiggled his chin, causing his jaw to crack. She propped herself up on the couch, the one she'd been camped out on since coming home from the hospital. She was still in no condition to climb the stairs up to her bedroom.

"We need to talk," her father said.

"I know."

"Your mother told me UVM is off the table."

Karla looked down at the colorful wool blanket covering her mangled leg. "Uh-huh. I talked to the ski coach this morning."

"And?"

"He was understanding, but I've already deferred admission twice, and you heard the doctor." Karla's lip trembled and tears welled up in her eyes. "My racing career is probably over." The doctor thought she'd heal well enough to ski again, but not to race, at least not at the level she had previously, and not at the level she'd need to at UVM.

"You threw away a very good opportunity," her father said.

Tears streamed down her cheek and she wiped them away with the sleeve of her sweatshirt. "I know. I'm sorry," she sobbed.

"I don't know what's gotten into you lately, but I hope this," he waved toward her legs, "scares some sense back into you."

"Maybe I'll heal well enough—"

"Goddammit, Karla. It's time to get real."

She scowled at him and started to lash out but bit her lip and hung her head. She knew he was right, and it stung, a lot. She'd derailed whatever was left of her racing career. Even if she made a miraculous recovery, it would take her months to get back in shape, and all that time away from the snow would set her so far back. The coaches at UVM and the other top ski programs had a deep pool of talent to pull from.

Karla's mother walked into the room with a steaming mug of tea. She set it down on the coffee table next to Karla and placed a hand on her husband's shoulder. "Jake, don't be so hard on her."

Karla's dad started to protest, but a stern look from her mother caused him to back down. He leaned back in his chair and crossed his legs. "I'm worried about you Karla, that's all."

"I'm a little worried about me too, Dad. Walking away from the circuit…I'm taking it harder than I've been willing to admit. Skiing is all I've ever known and…" She started to cry again.

Her mother sat down on the end of the couch and rubbed her good leg.

Karla blew her nose and took a sip of her tea. "I've been doing some thinking."

It was true. That was about all she'd been doing for the last few days. Thinking. When she'd first gotten home from the hospital, she'd been plain old angry. Angry at herself and angry at the world. But she'd always been a fighter, and she knew she needed to buckle up and get her shit together.

"What about, honey?" her mother asked.

Karla wrapped her hands around the mug of tea. "About what I'd like to do. About the next chapter of my life." A small smile crossed her face. "I mean once I can walk again."

"I'm all ears," her father said.

Karla set her mug back on the table and looked from her mother to her father. "I still want to be a nurse. There's no question about that, but now, with everything that's happened, I'm thinking maybe Denver. They have a good program, and I'd be closer to home."

"Your father has a cousin there," her mother said.

"I know, I thought I'd reach out to her. See how she likes the program. Maybe she can help me find a place to live down there." Karla had only met her father's cousin Val a handful of times, but it would be nice to know at least one other person on campus.

"You'll have to take out loans," her father said. "We don't—"

"I know."

"All right. Well, you better get the ball rolling."

"I'll make some calls this afternoon." Karla paused before adding, "I know I messed up, royally. I promise I'll do better."

CHAPTER THIRTEEN

Ty stared at the screen for a long time, her mouth agape. Over the last few days, she'd been checking the bank account for Merce the Nurse LLC approximately twenty times a day. The balance was always the same. $1000—the amount Kate's firm had deposited to establish the account for her. But this time when she refreshed the page, the balance was $73,244,700.07. The seven cents made her laugh. So precise. Once she started laughing, she couldn't stop. She rolled around on the bed in her hotel room giggling and gasping for air. It hadn't seemed real until now. She flutter-kicked her feet on the mattress and screamed into a pillow.

She needed to do something special. Something to celebrate. But what? She was all alone in a room at the Ritz in downtown Denver. Sarah was flying in the next day to help her find a place to live while she was in school, but she wanted to do something now. She jumped off the bed and grabbed the in-room dining menu. There was a Taittinger Comtes de Champagne listed for $480. She ordered two bottles. So what if it was only eleven a.m.

After she hung up the phone, she stripped off her clothes and wandered into the bathroom. She was damp with sweat, and her heart was thumping in her chest. She stepped into the shower, pushed the lever all the way toward the blue dot on the left, and turned on the water. When the blast of cold water hit her body, she recoiled into the glass wall of the shower. As painful as it was, she forced herself to stand back under the spray. She needed to shock some sense into her brain and calm the fuck down.

After polishing off one of the bottles of Champagne, she passed out on the bed. When she woke up again, the sun was low on the horizon. She snatched up her computer and checked the LLC bank account again. Almost all the money was gone. The account balance now hovered around $250K. A month ago, she would have run down Main Street naked if she'd had a bank account with six digits, but now the figure looked sort of puny. Kate and Derek had warned her that the lottery winnings would be transferred out of the checking account soon after they were deposited. She just hadn't expected it to happen that quickly. They'd left her with $250K—a number Kate had chosen because it was covered under FDIC deposit insurance—so she could buy a car and get settled in Denver.

* * *

When Sarah landed the next morning, she and Ty went straight to the Tesla dealer. As soon as they walked into the showroom, Ty made a beeline for a midnight blue Model S and climbed into the driver's seat.

Sarah slid into the passenger seat. "Is this really the car you want?"

Ty smoothed her hands over the soft leather steering wheel and ran a finger over the top of the large screen in the center console. "Uh-huh. Megan Rapinoe drives a Tesla. They're so cool."

"But not very practical for snowy Colorado."

"Is so. They're AWD. It'll kick ass in the snow."

When a salesman sauntered over, Ty said, "I'll take it."

"Aren't you going to try and negotiate a little?" Sarah whispered.

Ty waved her off. "I've never been good at haggling."

An hour later they pulled off the lot in the shiny new car.

"Fuck, this thing has so much power," Ty said as she zipped north on the side streets of Denver. Both of their heads fell back against the seat each time she accelerated from a traffic light. She cranked up the radio and weaved in and out of traffic until a hand clamped onto her forearm.

"Jeez, Ty," Sarah said through clenched teeth. "Slow the hell down."

Ty eased off the accelerator. "Ah, you're no fun."

"I'd just like to live to see another day."

Ty slowed the car on a tree-lined street and pointed out the window toward a well-kept white craftsman-style house with a small front porch. "This must be the place."

When they stepped out of the car, a woman waved at them from the sidewalk. She was a real estate agent Ty had contacted a few days earlier to help her find a house to rent. Ty's first instinct had been to buy, but Kate had advised against it, at least for the time being. Ty didn't know exactly how long she'd be in Denver. It all depended on what she decided to do after she earned her degree. Still, she wanted to find some place decent to live. When she'd been in school the first time around, she'd shared a dump of an apartment near campus with three roommates. Now that she could afford something nicer, she wanted a single-family house.

The agent had suggested they look in a neighborhood called Whittier. Ty had never heard of it, but a Google search revealed it was a tree-lined residential neighborhood with mostly craftsman style homes built in the early 1900s. That and it was diverse, close to school, had a lot of parks, and was popular among young professionals.

The agent showed them three houses that were for rent, but Ty chose the first one they saw. The white one with the front porch. She was a sucker for front porches, and the house was vacant so she could move in right away. Better yet, the place came mostly furnished.

After she signed the lease, she said to Sarah, "Let's go to the mall."

Sarah looked at her like she had two heads. "I thought going to the mall gave you hives."

"Well, it used to, but come on! It'll be fun. Plus, there's an Apple store and I need a new computer for school."

"Who are you? Using the word 'fun' and 'mall' in the same sentence."

At the Apple store, Ty bought a desktop, a laptop, and the latest iPhone. She offered to buy one for Sarah too, but she insisted she was happy with the one she had. From there they went to Lululemon and Runner's World. "I need new exercise clothes," Ty explained.

"Let me guess, you're fresh out of ridiculously expensive silk scarves?" Sarah quipped when Ty led/dragged her into Hermes.

Sarah's mood quickly deteriorated and she rolled her eyes when Ty wandered toward Louis Vuitton. "Ty, really?"

"Don't take away all my fun. I just want to look around."

Sarah gestured toward a small sitting area near the front of the store. "Fine. I'll wait here." Her eyes went wide when Ty returned thirty minutes later with two giant shopping bags. Ty had planned to hit Bed, Bath & Beyond next so she could load up on more practical things like linens and towels and stuff, but she was pretty sure Sarah had reached her breaking point and Ty didn't want to push her luck.

CHAPTER FOURTEEN

On Sarah's last night in town, she and Ty went out to Patty's Place, a lesbian bar near Ty's new house in Whittier.

"Shit, this place is packed," Ty said when they stepped inside. Women stood two deep along the long wooden bar and all of the tables scattered around the dance floor were occupied.

"You want a beer?" Sarah asked.

"Sure, although that might be easier said than done." Ty dug in her pocket for her credit card. "And I'm buying."

"The hell you are. You haven't let me pay for anything the entire time I've been here. Just because you're now a gazillionaire doesn't mean I can't buy you a beer."

Before Ty could protest, Sarah ducked into the crowd. She was only five foot two and Ty lost sight of her spikey blond head in a matter of seconds. While she waited, she leaned up against a nearby pole and scanned the sea of women. They came in all different shapes and sizes, but they all had this outdoorsy, wholesome look about them.

Maybe there's someone out there for me.

Sarah reappeared a few minutes later and held up two Sierra Nevada Pale Ales. "Ta da!"

Ty took one of the beers. "Wow, that was fast."

"Being small has its benefits." Sarah held up her beer. "To your new life in Denver."

Ty tapped her bottle against Sarah's and took a long swig. "I still have a lot to figure out, but I'm so pumped to finally finish my nursing degree."

Sarah squeezed her shoulder. "You should be really proud of yourself, Ty. I know I am. Most people with your kind of dough would be sitting on a beach somewhere sipping an umbrella drink."

"That's not me, you know that. Plus, I've vowed to use my lottery winnings to help people and that's a promise I intend to keep." Ty took another swig of her beer and nudged Sarah with her hip. "I'm going miss you, you know that?"

Ty's chest tightened. She was excited about the next chapter of her life, but she was scared. Scared to be so far away from Sarah. Scared to stand on her own two feet. Sure, she and Sarah could talk and text all the time and hopefully visit each other a lot, but it wouldn't be the same. She wouldn't be able to run to Sarah when she needed a hug or a shoulder to lean on.

"I'm gonna miss the shit out of you too, Ty monster," Sarah said.

Ty didn't want to get all sappy on Sarah's last night in Denver. She was about to suggest they dance when one of the women at the table in front of them nudged her leg.

"We're heading out if you guys want our table," the woman said. "We came to hear our neighbor DJ, but her set just ended." She let out a chuckle. "It's way past our bedtime."

"Oh, wow, yeah, that would be great. Thanks," Ty replied.

The woman pointed to the one empty chair at their table. "You'd better sit down before we stand up, otherwise, someone else will commandeer the table."

Ty sat down and thanked the women again. They looked to be in their mid- to late-forties, and the one nearest Ty had a heart-shaped birthmark on her cheek.

Both women stood and the one with the birthmark said, "Have a good night."

* * *

After dropping Sarah at the airport early the next morning, Ty made her way up to campus. She'd made appointments to meet with some of her old professors, including Professor Cooper, who'd been her advisor before she'd dropped out of school nearly three years earlier. He'd reached out to her a couple of times since her parents died and encouraged her to return to school, telling her the nursing profession needed a bright young woman like her. Ty had been flattered that he'd taken an interest in her, and she was thankful that there'd be one familiar face on campus. Almost all the students who'd been at the university when she'd been there before would have graduated by now.

When she was done meeting with Dr. Cooper, she walked over to the campus bookstore to pick up some of the books she needed for her first round of summer classes. In the past, whenever she went to the bookstore, she'd test all the fountain pens on those little pads of paper they put out, but she'd ever been able to buy more than the bare necessities. Today, she loaded up her basket not only with fountain pens, but notebooks and a smattering of other office supplies, too.

When she got in line to check out, the woman in front of her said, "Would you mind holding my spot? I just realized I forgot one thing."

"Sure," Ty said. "No problem." The woman looked familiar, but she couldn't place her. It wasn't until the woman got back in line that Ty figured out where she recognized her from. She was the woman from Patty's Place, the woman with the heart shaped birthmark.

Ty twirled her hair. The woman probably wouldn't even remember her, but it would be polite to at least say hello. She worked up the courage to tap the woman on the shoulder. "Um, hi, I think we've met before." The woman gave her a blank stare.

"I was at Patty's Place last night and you and your, uh, friend gave us your table."

A smile crossed the woman's face. "Oh, yeah. I remember. Your friend had spikey bleach-blond hair. I was there with my wife Teresa."

"Yep, that's right."

The woman extended her hand. "My name is Val, by the way."

"Nice to officially meet you, Val. I'm Ty."

Val nodded toward the pile of nursing textbooks in Ty's basket. "Are you a student here?"

"Well, I was...I dropped out for a while, but I'm starting back and taking classes this summer. What about you?"

"I'm taking a few prerequisites before I start the Accelerated Bachelor of Nursing program in August."

Ty was familiar with the program. It was for students who already had a bachelor's degree in another field but wanted to earn another one in nursing. "Good for you. I hear that program is seriously intense."

"Yeah, I'm somewhat overwhelmed by the prereqs, so I'm terrified about the accelerated program itself."

"You'll do fine."

"I sure hope you're right," she replied, and then asked, "Hey, I was just about to grab a cup of coffee, care to join me?"

"Sure."

Coffees in hand, they found a place to sit outside in the courtyard.

"So, are you and your wife from the Denver area?" Ty asked.

"No, we recently moved here from Atlanta," Val said. "Teresa was offered a job in Denver and we jumped at the chance to move. We liked Atlanta, but we didn't love it. Even though we lived there for over a decade, it never really felt like home." Val paused to take a sip of her coffee. "Plus, traffic was a nightmare and it only seemed to get worse by the day."

"What did you do in Atlanta?" Ty asked.

"I was a teacher. Eighth grade math."

"Wow, that's hard core."

"It was rewarding, but after twenty years, I was totally burned out. I briefly considered getting a teaching job in Denver, but Teresa pushed me to follow my heart. I've always wanted to be a nurse, so it seemed like a good time to take the plunge!"

"Wow, good for you. It takes guts to make a career change like that."

Val smiled. "Thanks, I'm petrified and excited at the same time. No way I would have done it without Teresa's support." Val shifted gears. "What about you, are you from the area?"

"No," Ty said. "I grew up in Upstate New York. I came out here to go to college, and um, I've been living in Asheville for the last few years. It's kind of a long story," Ty kicked a small stone near her feet, "but like I said, I dropped out of school for a while and I just moved back to Denver. I've got about one more year till I finish up my BS in nursing."

Val seemed to sense that Ty's backstory was a subject she'd rather avoid, and she didn't prod. "Well, good for you for coming back to finish up. That takes guts too."

Ty stared down at the cup of coffee in her hands. "Thanks. I'm pretty excited to be back."

After talking about the classes that they were each taking over the summer, Val asked, "Was that woman with you at Patty's Place your girlfriend?"

Ty chuckled. She considered Sarah to be more like a sister. "No. Sarah's my best friend. She was visiting for a few days to help me get settled in."

Val looked at her watch. "Oh, shoot. I'm sorry, I've got to go. I have a meeting with one of my professors." She stood and gave Ty's arm a gentle squeeze. "It was wonderful to meet you, Ty. I hope I see you again soon."

Ty shook her hand. "You too, Val. I enjoyed talking to you."

Ty meant it too. Val was so easygoing, and she was happy to have made a new friend in Denver.

CHAPTER FIFTEEN

A week later, Ty spotted Val walking across campus. She was with a woman on crutches. A very beautiful woman. Ty waved and walked toward them.

"Hiya, Ty," Val said. "Good to see you again." She motioned toward the woman on crutches. "This is Karla."

Karla's rich, dark brown eyes fell on Ty and she extended her hand. "It's nice to meet you, Ty." Her voice was deliciously raspy.

Ty's mouth went dry. She opened her mouth to say something, but nothing came out. Karla was possibly the most striking woman she'd ever seen in her life.

Val came to her rescue. "Karla's in Denver for a few days while she looks for an apartment. Soon, she'll be starting up classes here too."

Ty snapped out of her Karla-induced haze. "Nice to, uh, meet you, Karla."

Val tapped one of Karla's crutches and said, "Karla had planned to go to school in Vermont, but these babies threw a wrench in her plans."

"Oh, gosh, what happened?" Ty asked and glanced down at Karla's legs. She was wearing shorts, and all of her weight was on her "good" leg, accentuating her colossal thigh muscles. If she were to reach out and touch Karla's leg, Ty knew it would be as solid as a rock.

"I got a little cocky on a mountain bike ride." Karla wiggled the toes that stuck out of the dark gray industrial-looking boot encasing her left leg. "Doc says I've gotta wear this thing for eight weeks. It's only been three weeks since my crash and I'm already going insane." Karla reached up to wipe a strand of her long brown hair away from her face, causing her arm muscles to flex in the process.

Ty gasped and took a step backward, nearly tripping over her own foot. "Oh, gosh, I can imagine. I'd be going crazy too. I'm no good at sitting still."

Karla laughed. "Yeah, same. This dumb boot makes it impossible to do anything. I'm living with my parents in Jackson, and I think they're happy to have me out of the house for a few days. I've been crawling up the walls"

"Jackson, Wyoming?" Ty asked.

"Yes. That's where I'm from."

"Cool," Ty replied.

"I'm actually glad I ran into you, Ty," Val said. "Teresa and I are having a Pride party at our house next weekend and we'd love it if you could come."

Karla smiled. "I'll be there too. It would be great if you came. Aside from Val and Teresa, I don't know a single person in Denver."

Ty wanted to say, "I'm single," but she didn't think that was what Karla meant. She exchanged contact information with Val and watched as she and Karla continued across campus. Next weekend could not come fast enough.

* * *

As luck would have it, Val and Teresa lived only a few blocks from the house Ty had rented in Whittier. Like hers, theirs was a craftsman with a front porch, but it was desperate for a coat of paint and there was grass growing on sections of the roof. A big rainbow flag billowed in the wind and music could be heard coming from the back yard. Out of nervousness, Ty double-checked the address before climbing the steps to the front porch and ringing the bell.

Two wet noses pressed against the glass door. Val appeared a moment later and greeted Ty with a hug. "Glad you could make it. Come on in." She scratched one of the black Labs behind the ears. "This is Apple," she gestured toward the other Lab, "and that's Pear."

Ty followed Val and the dogs through the house toward the backyard. Her eyes immediately settled on the tall brunette on crutches. Karla was talking to a woman who was arranging burgers on a gas grill. Each time a slab of meat hit the grates, flames flared up and the grill emitted a sizzling sound. Although Ty was dying to go say hello to Karla, she was too shy. She pulled a beer from a big plastic tub full of ice and cracked it open.

She smiled into the mouth of her bottle when she saw Karla hobbling in her direction.

"Hey, Ty. It's nice to see you again. I'm Karla Rehn. We met the other day on campus."

Like Ty had forgotten who she was. Fat chance. Her mouth felt like she'd just eaten a spoonful of peanut butter. "Hi. Yes, of course. You were with Val."

Karla nodded and held her gaze.

Ty shifted her feet and looked away. Those eyes, Jesus Christ. She swept her hand across the small yard. "Nice party. Perfect weather." *Go, Ty. What a stimulating conversationalist.*

Val ambled over and rested a hand on Karla's shoulder. "Need another beer?"

Karla held up her bottle. "Nope. I'm good, but thanks."

"So, how do you two know each other?" Ty asked. She wanted to pat herself on the back. She'd managed to put together a full sentence.

"I'm Karla's first cousin, once removed," Val said.

"Oh, wow." Ty turned to Karla. "Are you from Atlanta too?" she asked before catching herself. "Oh, wait, scratch that. You said you were from Jackson, right?" Ty's brain was definitely not shooting on all cylinders, but who could blame her? Karla was fucking sexy as hell. She wore her shorts low on her hips, exposing a sliver of tan skin above her waistband and her large breasts pressed against her cotton T-shirt. Her long, tanned arms were perfectly sculpted and long, dark eyelashes framed her intense brown eyes.

"Yep, I've lived there almost my whole life," Karla said.

Ty blinked a few times and tried to remember what they were talking about. *Jackson, right.*

"I lived in Sweden for a little while when I was a baby," Karla continued, "but my family moved to Wyoming for good when I was three."

"Karla's a mega big-time skier," Val said.

Ty twirled her hair and nodded like some sort of bobble head. "Oh, wow, really? I ski too." She realized she was talking in a really high voice.

Karla let out a cute little laugh. "I'm not sure about the *mega big-time* part, but yeah, I love to ski." She held out her broken leg. "Or at least I did until this happened."

"Great that you two have that in common," Val said. She looked up toward a group of women who'd just walked into the backyard. "If you'll excuse me, I should probably go say hello."

After Val scurried off, Ty asked, "So what took your family to Sweden?"

"My mom's Swedish, and my parents lived there for a few years right after I was born. My mom's whole family lives in Sweden, and I think she wanted to stay there, but she and my dad decided to move back to the US when he was offered the head ski coach position in Jackson. He had a hard time finding work in Sweden, and I think he felt like he couldn't pass up the job. Plus, he grew up outside Jackson and had always dreamed about raising his family there."

"So, I guess you had no choice but to grow up and be a kick-ass skier, huh?"

"Yeah, pretty much," Karla said with a laugh. "As a kid, my whole life revolved around skiing. It could be incredibly intense sometimes, but I adored every minute of it. I was even called up to the US Ski Team a few years back."

"Holy shit! That's amazing." Ty was dumbfounded to be standing there talking to this incredibly beautiful woman who also happened to be a world-class athlete.

"Well, it's not as impressive as it sounds. I was called up to the 'D' or Development team, which is just a steppingstone to reaching *the* US Ski Team. By that I mean, you're not really on the team unless you're on the A or B team. Don't get me wrong; it's a major achievement to be nominated at all, but every kid on the D team dreams about making the A team and being the next Lindsey Vonn or Mikaela Shiffrin. Very few actually make it. I spent a few years on the D team and was never called up, so here I am, gearing up to go to college."

"Wow, that must have been tough," Ty replied. "I mean, to just walk away from the US Ski Team."

"Yeah, it was really tough, especially because I'd basically spent my whole life trying to get there. I desperately wanted to give it one more year, but I'd already put such a strain on my family financially. It was expensive to support my skiing, and neither of my parents makes a ton of money. We were always doing these fundraisers and some of the local businesses sponsored me, but it was never enough."

"I don't understand," Ty said. "Didn't the US Ski Team cover most of your costs?"

Karla snorted out a laugh. "No, not unless you're an elite member of the A Team. In fact, most of us had to *pay* to be on the team."

"Wow, I had no idea."

"Sometimes it's not as glamourous as it sounds."

"Were your teammates surprised when you decided to call it quits?"

"Some of them were. They thought I was crazy to just give up, but unlike me, most of them came from money. They don't get it. They don't understand that some of us are forced to make hard decisions because we don't have unlimited means."

Ty could tell she'd touched on a sensitive topic. "Gosh, I'm sorry."

Karla rested a hand on Ty's shoulder. "Don't be. It's okay, I know I'm lucky. Most kids would kill to even make the D team. I don't take that for granted, especially because my family made so many sacrifices for me."

Karla's gentle touch sent Ty reeling and she blurted out her next question without thinking. "Will you be able to race again, you know, after your leg heals?"

Karla nibbled on her lower lip. A flash of sadness crossed her face, but she supplanted it with a smile. "Doc says I'll be able to ski again, but my racing days are probably over."

Ty felt like a total noob. "Shit, I'm sorry. It's really none of my business."

Karla gave her a soft smile. "Stop apologizing, Ty."

"It's just, I'm sorry," Ty laughed at herself. "Geez, there I go again."

Why was she acting like such a bumbling idiot? Being in the presence of this stunning woman probably had a lot to do with it. The shift in conversation toward money, or the lack of it, was also probably partly to blame. This was the first time she'd really been in a social situation with people she didn't know well since she'd won the lottery. Up until now, the only people she'd interacted with had been Sarah and Kate's team at Allendale Financial, people who all knew about her winning ticket. Even though she was the same person, winning millions of dollars had certainly changed her lot in life, and she hadn't yet grown accustomed to that fact. Far from it.

Karla motioned toward a stone wall along the side of the yard. "Do you mind if we sit for a minute? Standing on these crutches gets old."

"No, not at all," Ty replied.

Once they were seated, Karla propped her booted leg up on a nearby chair. "As Val mentioned the other day, I'd planned to go to the University of Vermont in the fall," she gestured toward her boot, "but, you know, then this happened."

"UVM has one of the best ski teams in the country, don't they?"

Karla nodded. "Probably one of the top three."

"Let me guess, you were going to ski for them?"

Karla gave her a slow nod. "Uh-huh."

Ty looked down at Karla's booted leg. "Yikes. That had to suck. To have to give up that opportunity."

"It did, but it's okay. I have no one to blame but myself, and I'm a firm believer that everything happens for a reason."

Ty's respect for Karla jumped about fifty notches. "Most people, if they'd been through what you have, would be cowering in the corner feeling sorry for themselves. Your attitude is admirable."

Karla shrugged. "Well, if you'd seen me right after the bike accident, you wouldn't have been so impressed. I was a basket case for a little while there. But enough about me, what brought you to the University of Denver? Are you from around here?"

Ty wet her lips and shook her head. "No, I'm from back East. I actually dropped out of school a few years back and I've been living in Asheville, North Carolina, for the last few years, working as a bartender." Ty hesitated while she considered how much to divulge given that she'd only just met Karla. "I just re-enrolled in school. I've got one year left before I finish my undergrad degree."

Karla looked like she was about to say something, but Val reappeared before she got the chance.

"You two are getting acquainted, I see," Val said.

"Yep," Karla said.

"Karla and I are going apartment hunting tomorrow," Val said. "I promised her mom I'd find her something suitable. Since I know you recently went through the process, Ty, do you have any tips?"

"Um, no not really." Ty said. "I rented the first place I saw," she mumbled. "Sorry, I'm afraid I'm not much help."

"No biggie." Val looked down at Karla. "We'll find you something good, kiddo. Don't worry."

"I'm not worried. I know I'm in good hands," Karla said. She reached for her crutches. "Excuse me for a sec. I've got to run to the ladies'."

Once Karla was out of earshot, Val whispered, "You seem pretty smitten with Miss Rehn."

Ty let out a groan. "Is it that obvious?"

Val rolled her eyes. "Uh, yeah."

CHAPTER SIXTEEN

Karla lowered herself onto a bench and set her crutches beside her, although what she really wanted to do was hurl them across the room. For someone who was accustomed to going fast, getting from point A to point B on crutches was downright maddening; and they, along with her booted leg, were a constant reminder of how much her life had changed in the course of a few weeks. She should be working out with the UVM ski team, but instead, she was a fucking invalid. She closed her eyes and let out a low moan.

"Everything okay there?" a voice asked.

Karla opened her eyes. Ty strode over and gave her a broad smile. Her kind blue eyes instantly made Karla feel better. "Yeah, I'm good. Just stopped to catch my breath. That, and have a little pity party for myself."

Ty squeezed her shoulder. "Perfectly understandable. Having a broken leg has got to be a real pain in the ass, especially for someone who's accustomed to flying down a mountain at sixty miles an hour."

Karla huffed out a laugh. "Yeah, it pretty much sucks all around."

Ty pointed to the spot next to Karla on the bench. "Mind if I join you?"

"No, please have a seat. It's nice to see a friendly face after the morning I've had."

Ty sat down and turned to face Karla. "That bad, huh?"

"Yeah, apparently one of the classes I really wanted to take this fall requires a prerequisite. That, and apartments near campus are way more expensive than I expected. I mean, real estate prices in Jackson are pretty insane, but that's because they've been driven up by wealthy out-of-towners. I didn't think Denver would be as bad."

Ty shifted on the bench and looked down at her feet. "From what I've heard, real estate in Denver has taken off in the last few years."

"Anyway," Karla said, "it looks like I don't have a choice. I have to get a roommate, which is fine. I know it's part of college. It's just, I'm a little older than the average freshman and I delusionally thought I'd be able to get my own place."

Ty nodded but didn't say anything.

"What about you?" Karla asked. "Do you have your own place?"

Ty's leg moved up and down like the presser foot on a sewing machine. "Yeah. I, uh, had a little money saved up, so I was able to get my own place."

"Lucky you."

"Yep," Ty said, "but, you know, we'll be so busy with school and stuff, you probably won't even be home all that much."

"Good point."

"And if you ever need a quiet place to study, let me know. The house I'm renting here in Denver has plenty of space."

"That's kind of you to offer," Karla glanced over at Ty and bumped her with her shoulder, "but one you may regret making."

"Ha, I sincerely doubt that. But in all seriousness, I wouldn't have mentioned it if I didn't mean it. Hit me up anytime."

Karla reached for her crutches. "I've got to run. Ha, I guess I should say, I've got to shuffle. It was really nice talking to you."

Ty stood and helped Karla to her feet. "You too." Their hands stayed clasped for a little longer than necessary.

Karla finally drew her hand back. "I'm headed back to Jackson tomorrow," she said, "but I'll be back in August, just before the fall semester starts." She tapped one of her crutches against her booted leg. "And, if I'm lucky, this stupid thing will be gone by then."

Ty gave her a soft smile. "All right, well, I guess I'll see you around."

"Yeah. See ya."

* * *

When Karla got back to Jackson the following evening, she went straight to Dana's house.

Dana greeted her at the door with a deep kiss.

"It's good to see you too," Karla said with a chuckle when she came up for air.

"I missed you," Dana said.

"I missed you too."

Dana pointed to the open laptop on her kitchen table. "I've got to finish up one thing and then I'll show you just how happy I am to have you home."

"Oh, I, um, okay."

Dana gave her a peck on the lips. "Give me a minute, baby."

Karla plunked down on the couch and flipped on the TV. She watched one episode of *Queer Eye*, and then another.

"How's the leg feeling?" Dana asked when she finally emerged from the kitchen an hour and a half later.

"Not too bad. It—"

"Good, because I'm dying to fuck your brains out." Dana sat down on the couch, reached for the remote, and clicked off the TV. "I've missed your amazing body." She tugged Karla's shirt over her head and released her bra.

Karla leaned her head back against the couch while Dana sucked hard on one breast and then the other. She tried not to flinch when Dana climbed on her lap and attacked her mouth with vigor.

After peeling off her own shirt and unbuttoning her shorts, Dana guided Karla's hand inside her waistband. "Touch me," she begged.

The sex was a little rougher than Karla might have liked, especially given her leg, but one thing was for certain, Dana knew how to please her. She came twice before finally collapsing back on the couch.

They both fell asleep, and it was after midnight when Dana stirred and woke her up. Karla peeked at her phone. "Shit, I need to go."

"Stay with me."

"I wish I could, but I can't. I told my parents I'd be home hours ago."

"Text them and tell them you're spending the night."

"I can't, I'm sorry. I need to go home."

* * *

Over the next few weeks, Dana became more attentive. When they'd first met, Karla had gotten the sense that her feelings for Dana were a good bit stronger than Dana's feelings for her, and she wanted to believe that was changing. Wanted to believe that maybe their feelings for one another were now more in sync. That things with Dana were moving to the next level.

Of course, she still had nagging doubt. It could just be that Dana had a little more time on her hands. Maybe it was a slow time of year for the type of cyber security work she did. It was summer after all. Maybe hackers took vacations too. Shut down their computers and took their kids to the beach.

When Karla ran this hacker vacation theory by Dana the following night, she laughed. "I wish, but no. Hackers never rest. They're ever present."

"I asked because lately, I don't know, you seem a little less preoccupied with work. It's nice."

Dana gave her a wink. "Maybe I'm less preoccupied with work because I've got something more interesting to focus on."

Karla blushed and stared down at her hands.

"It's true"—Dana twirled the ice cubes in her glass with her finger—"I like being with you, a lot, Karla and I know you're leaving for Denver soon. I want to spend as much time with you as I can before you go."

Karla's head jerked back slightly. Dana had caught her off guard. "I like being with you a lot too," she said quietly.

Although she didn't fully understand why, she was borderline infatuated with Dana. Even though they'd only been seeing— was that the right word—each other for a little over two months, it was the longest relationship Karla had ever had. If it were up to her, she'd spend every waking minute with Dana. When they were together, conversation was never lacking, and the sex was fantastic, there was no doubt about that, but this was the first time Dana had said anything remotely sentimental.

CHAPTER SEVENTEEN

Ty slammed her textbook shut and sank back into the hard-backed chair. "My brain is going to explode."

It was the end of the first summer session and she and Val had been camped out in the library for the last eight hours.

"Ditto," Val said with a laugh.

"You feel like you're ready for the exam?"

"Better be." Val looked at her watch. "It's starts in approximately twenty-two minutes."

Ty patted Val on the back. "You're an awesome study partner."

"You too, buddy-o-mine. You actually made it fun."

"Right back at you," Ty said as she gathered up her belongings. "Do you and Teresa have anything fun planned for the Fourth of July?"

"Teresa has been making noise about going to see the fireworks, but all I want to do is sleep. What about you?"

"You're going to think I'm nuts, but I'm thinking about driving over to Steamboat Springs. Maybe rent a bike and do some mountain biking. After being cooped up studying, I'm dying to get outside and get some exercise."

"You're right. I think you're crazy. I get that you want to work out, but why drive all the way to Steamboat? That's like what, three or four hours from here?"

"Three, give or take," Ty replied, "but it'll totally be worth it. The ski resort and the surrounding area have some awesome bike trails."

"Suit yourself, but if you change your mind, you're welcome to join us to watch the fireworks."

Ty followed Val down the hall to their classroom. "Thanks. I will." Once they were seated, Ty leaned over and whispered, "Good luck."

When Ty handed in her exam, a sudden burst of energy coursed through her. She hadn't planned to leave for Steamboat until the following morning, but if she went tonight instead, she could get up and go mountain biking first thing in the morning.

Thankfully, the bike shop was still open when she pulled into town. After the salesman showed her the fleet of rental bikes that were available, she made a split-second decision and told him she wanted to buy a bike instead. Thirty minutes later, she walked out of the store with a shiny new blue and yellow Trek bike. Once she added in a new pair of bike shorts, a jersey, a helmet, and bike shoes, the trip to the bike shop had set her back four grand. It took some wrangling—including taking the front tire off the bike—to fit her new toy in the trunk of the Tesla, but she got it to fit.

* * *

As the mountain bike trail neared the top of the gondola, it became steeper and rockier. She pressed the small black gear shift on her handlebar a few times, but nothing happened. The bike was already in granny gear, the lowest of its twenty-seven gears. Her thigh muscles burned but she put her head down and pumped the pedals. The bike inched up the incline so slowly Ty was on the verge of tipping over. She blinked her eyes as sweat dripped into them. She desperately wanted to wipe the perspiration away with one of her bike gloves, but if she let go of the handlebar, even for a second, she'd lose what little momentum she had.

Finally, the trail leveled out and the gondola station and its neighboring lodge came into view. Rows and rows of empty ski racks peppered the dry grass. They looked so out of place on this eighty-degree day. She shifted into a higher gear and her bike bounced over the uneven ground toward them. A gondola swished into the top station and swayed as it slowed to deposit its passengers. Two men with bikes emerged. Unlike Ty, most people rode the gondola to the top of the mountain and rode their bikes down. To some, that was the sensible thing to do, but Ty wanted to *earn* her ride down. It didn't feel right to enjoy the downhill without putting in the work to ride to the top.

She propped her bike up against one of the empty ski racks and took a long swig of water, splashing some across her sweat-stained face. She climbed back on her bike, clipped in, and pedaled to the entrance of the narrow single track that would take her back down to the bottom. It wound through dense birch trees before dumping her out on a wide grassy slope called Rabbit Run—one of the easy "green" ski runs in the winter.

She coasted down a series of broad switchbacks, past the massive, multilevel ski homes that lined the slope. Most of the homes looked closed up for the summer, which was too bad. As much as Ty liked to ski, she'd always preferred the summers in Colorado to the winters. Temperate, blue-sky days and green as far as the eye could see.

Her eye caught a small *For Sale* sign attached to the railing of one of the home's wraparound decks. The sign swung in the breeze, catching the sun on its metal façade. The house stood out from all the others along the slope. Not because it was the biggest, but because it was the smallest, although that wasn't saying much. The average slopeside home probably had seven bedrooms.

She squeezed her brakes and her bike slowed to a stop. Up until this moment, she hadn't intended to buy a ski house, but now, every bone in her body told her she must have this place. She heard Karla's voice echoing in her head, bemoaning all the wealthy out-of-towners who had snapped up second homes and driven up housing costs, making it impossible for the locals to afford anything decent. She also heard Kate's stern voice, warning her to take baby steps and not spend her money irresponsibly. It was just a ski house. It wasn't like she was buying a hundred-foot yacht.

When she got back to her hotel, she called Kate, who reluctantly put her in touch with a local realtor, a guy named Scotty Lane. Apparently, one of Kate's clients had a house in the area, and Scotty came highly recommended. Ty was grateful for Kate's introduction because she knew she didn't fit the part of someone in the market for a multi-million-dollar ski house. Most of Scotty's clients were probably dripping in diamonds and clad in Moncler parkas with rabbit fur collars.

* * *

The next morning, she spotted a handsome, well-dressed, thirty-something man in the lobby of her hotel and walked toward him. "You must be Scotty."

He gave her a toothy smile. "That I am." He reached out to shake her hand. "And you must be Ty."

"Nice to meet you."

He gestured toward the front door of the hotel. "My car is right outside."

Ty liked him instantly. He was polished but not pretentious.

"This place has been on the market for a while," Scotty said as they pulled into the driveway of the house Ty had spotted the day before. "It's a little quirky, and even though the listing says it has five bedrooms, it only has four functional bedrooms—way too few for most people in this price range."

Ty had done her research. She knew the house was listed for $4.2 million. "Does that mean there could be some wiggle room on the price?" She stood up taller. Maybe she did have a little haggle in her after all.

She got another toothy grin. "There might be." If Scotty questioned whether she could afford such a house, he didn't let on. He snapped into salesman mode. "As I'm sure you are aware, the house is ski in/ski out," he said, referring to the ability to ski right out your back door and access the slopes. "It has a chef-quality kitchen, a home gym, and a heated driveway."

"What makes this place quirky?" Ty asked as he unlocked the front door.

He gave her a sideways glance. "You'll see."

The second they stepped inside, she was head over heels in love with the place. There was no question, she *had* to have it. The walls of the vast foyer were covered in bright contemporary art, and a small gurgling fountain sat in the corner. From the front door, she could see straight through to the ski slopes on the opposite side.

"I want it," Ty said. "I don't even need see the rest of it. Where do I sign?"

Scotty laughed. "Let's at least have a look around."

Ty's enthusiasm for the house only intensified as Scotty gave her the full tour. The foyer opened into a long, open rectangular room with an entire wall of windows overlooking the slopes and the mountains beyond. To the right was the kitchen. It had a huge island and all stainless-steel appliances, including a giant wine fridge. To the left was a large but cozy living room with a massive stone fireplace. Ty pulled open a sliding glass door and stepped out onto the deck that ran along the entire front of the house. A hot tub was tucked in the far corner.

"Shall we head upstairs and check out the master bedroom?" Scotty asked when she stepped back inside.

She followed him up a funky wooden staircase that overlooked the living room and kitchen. A large, bookshelf-lined loft greeted them at the top of the stairs and a short hallway led them to the master bedroom. It was spacious but held only a few pieces of contemporary furniture. Like the foyer, its walls were adorned with art, and sun beamed in from the wall of windows facing the slopes.

The master bath had a spa-like shower with multiple showerheads and his and hers (or hers and hers) sink/vanity areas. Off to the side was a walk-in closet that was bigger than Ty's apartment in Asheville. An entire wall of cubbies held thirty or so pairs of high-top sneakers.

"Guess the current owner is into shoes," Ty said. She eyed the collection. "They're all Air Jordan's. Awesome."

"My husband, James, would pitch a fit if he saw these. He's obsessed with Air Jordan's." Scotty laughed. "Although, honestly, James is obsessed with shoes in general. We're going to have to put an addition on the house if he buys one more pair."

"James sounds like a piece of work."

"Oh, he is, and then some. Maybe we can all go out for drinks sometime."

"Sure, that would be great."

Back on the main floor, there were three more bedrooms, two full baths, a powder room, and a spacious laundry room. One of the bedrooms on the main floor had an en suite bath, while the other two shared a Jack and Jill style bathroom. From there, they descended the steps to a big living area/game room on the lower level of the house. It was replete with lot of fun toys: a pool table, a ping-pong table, and a smattering of old pinball and arcade games. Ty smiled when she saw Ms. Pac Man. The icing on the cake was a carved wooden bar lined with stools made from what looked like antlers from some very large creature.

"Cool," Ty remarked. "My brother Reed and I were ping-pong fanatics when we were growing up, but I haven't played in years."

"Check this out," Scotty said as he opened a door off the game room. "Your own private gym!"

Ty laughed. "You sound like the guy on the *Price Is Right*."

Scotty went with it. "And that's not all." He opened another door and flipped on the light. Ty peered inside. It was a massive room full of sports equipment and related accessories. Three walls were lined with racks and racks of skis, mountain bikes, golf clubs, fly-fishing rods, windsurfers, you name it. In the middle of the room, there was a circle of leather benches and a long workbench, presumably for tuning bikes and skis.

"Holy shit."

"The best part is, most of this stuff conveys with the house," he said. "The guy who owns the place is willing to throw in most of the furniture and accoutrements, if you're interested."

"Yeah, definitely. I have like zero furniture and I love the décor of this house."

"Okay, great. Now let's go back upstairs so I can show you one more special feature." He led her back to the living room and pressed a small silver button on the wall to the right of the fireplace. She heard a low clicking sound and the wall slid open.

"Oh, no. Is this some kinky BDSM room?"

He laughed. "No, nothing like that. I promise." He stepped through the opening in the wall.

Ty hesitated before following behind him. She found herself in long, narrow corridor that ran behind the fireplace. It dead-ended at the base of a black metal spiral staircase. The shaft that housed the staircase was windowless, but sun shone through a huge skylight at the top.

Scotty's dress shoes clapped against the metal steps as they wound their way up to what, Ty had no idea. The staircase dumped them on an L-shaped landing that appeared to lead to nowhere.

Scotty reached down and pressed another silver button. "Ta da."

Just as before, the wall in front of them slid open, exposing a room of windows. Ty stepped inside. It was the most wonderful space she'd ever seen. Part solarium, part library. The sun beat through its slanted glass roof. Its wood floor was partially covered with a vibrant red and blue Turkish rug. A few healthy houseplants were scattered about the room, bookshelves lined the walls, and a telescope stood in the corner. Two leather lounge chairs and an ottoman made up the rest of furniture in the room.

"OMG." Ty said. "I was sold on this house when we walked in the front door, but this room is…I don't even have words to describe it. I think I'll call it the *observatory*." As she scanned the room, she could picture herself sitting in one of the lounge chairs and studying or reading for hours. It was incredibly peaceful and bright.

"Apparently, the guy who owns the place is obsessed with stargazing," Scotty said. "I'm sure you know the night sky around here can be incredible. We get so many cloudless crisp nights and there's virtually no light pollution. The stars pop out of the sky."

"This room is amazing during the day. I can't imagine how beautiful it must be at night."

Scotty pointed up. "The glass roof is heated so the snow doesn't accumulate and block your view."

"The guy thought of everything when he built this place, didn't he?"

"He sure did, and speaking of which, check this out." He walked back out to the L-shaped landing and pressed yet another silver button. This time a wall opened to reveal the master bedroom.

"Well, that's handy," Ty said and paused to consider the layout of the house. "But then why the spiral staircase? It's definitely got the 'wow' factor, but it seems redundant since you can access the observatory directly from the master."

"Good point. But if you have people over, you can access this room without having to traipse through your bedroom."

When they got back downstairs to the foyer, Scotty turned to her. "I agree that the house is stunning, but keep in mind that it will only appeal to a very specific buyer, especially because it's on the small side for this market," he warned in his realtor voice. "When you go to sell, it might take a while…"

"I understand, but I don't care. I absolutely must have this house."

"Okay, and for what it's worth, I love the place too."

"What do you think I should offer?" Ty asked.

"Well, as you know, it's listed for $4.2 million…Any idea how much you plan to put down?"

"Put down?"

Scotty loosened his tie slightly. "Down payment, assuming you plan to finance a portion of the—"

"I'm going to pay in cash," Ty blurted out, and Kate's stern face immediately popped into her head. Buying such an expensive house was probably something she should discuss with her financial advisor before moving forward, but she wanted the house—and it was her money, after all.

Scotty gave her another of his toothy smiles. "Wow. Okay, great." He leaned against the wall in the foyer and rubbed his chin. "Maybe we offer three point nine and see how they respond? The fact that you're paying all cash should definitely work to our advantage."

Ty didn't miss a beat. "That seems like a reasonable place to start." Like she had a clue. "Let's do it."

"You got it," Scotty said. "I'll put the offer together as soon as I get back to the office."

He called later that evening to let her know the seller had accepted her cash offer for the house and its assorted furnishings.

Ty skipped around her hotel room. That beautiful house was going to be hers and she didn't care what anyone said, she wanted it.

CHAPTER EIGHTEEN

The metal platform of the leg press wasn't budging. It hung over Karla, taunting her. She glared at her pasty white left leg. It looked emaciated next to her deeply tanned right one.

"Come on, you useless piece of shit," she growled. The platform inched upwards. She gritted her teeth and pushed it to the top. Her leg was shaking, but she wasn't done yet. Three more reps. "No pain, no gain," she mumbled.

After two more reps, her leg was completely spent, and she had to bring her right leg—her good leg—up next to the left one on the platform to finish the final rep. She wanted to punch something. The leg press was set at an embarrassingly low weight, and she still hadn't been able to do ten reps. Pathetic.

She jammed the platform into lock position and used her shirt to wipe the sweat from her face. She was overdoing it, but all those weeks her leg had been held captive in the boot had rendered it a scrawny noodle. She had one goal. Getting her strength back. As soon as she'd returned to Denver, she'd begun working with a physical therapist and supplemented those sessions with long workouts at the gym on campus.

"Karla," a voice called out. She turned. Ty emerged from the sea of weight machines and gave her a little wave. Her face glistened with sweat, and a few loose strands of blond hair stuck to her forehead. She was even prettier than Karla remembered.

"Hi," Ty said. "You're back."

Karla scrambled to her feet. "Yep, I'm back."

"It's good to see you."

"Same."

Ty gestured toward her leg. "And the evil boot is gone."

"Uh-huh. Came off a couple of weeks ago." Karla lifted her left foot off the floor. "Now I need to get this sorry excuse for a leg back in shape."

"Does it hurt at all?"

Karla shook her head. "A little, but not too bad." She waved toward Ty. "Looks like you just finished a workout yourself."

Ty nodded and pulled her T-shirt up to wipe her face, exposing a large section of her smooth, tan stomach.

Karla suppressed a gasp. She was surprised at how toned Ty was. "From the looks of it, you're in pretty good shape."

As soon as the words were out of her mouth, a pang of guilt shot through her. She had a girlfriend, for God's sake. She shouldn't be admiring another woman—even if she did happen to be incredibly charming and hot.

Ty blushed. "I do my best. Maybe we could work out together sometime?"

"I'd like that." Karla hesitated before asking, "Have you had lunch?"

She and Ty had only talked a few times, but Karla didn't know many people in Denver, and she was drawn to the woman. There was something special about her. She was beautiful and nice, but it was more than that: the way she looked at Karla when she spoke, like she was actually listening to what she had to say, and the way her whole face lit up when she smiled.

"Nope, not yet."

"I need to hit the shower but then I was going to grab a bite to eat. Care to join me?"

"Sure, that would be nice."

When they walked out of the gym twenty minutes later, Karla pointed at the food trucks lined up at the curb. "If you like Mexican, Tony's Taco Truck is hard to beat. Val insisted I try his Tabloid Tofu tacos."

"Did you say tabloid?"

"Yeah, because they're *scandalously* good."

Ty groaned out a laugh. "Sounds like I need to try one of those."

Five minutes later, tacos in hand, they settled on the freshly cut grass. The sun was high in the sky and there wasn't a cloud in sight. Karla felt more at peace than she had in a really long time.

Ty let out a contented sigh when she bit into her taco. "Oh, God, this is good."

"I know, right?" Karla reached over, dabbed a dollop of sour cream off Ty's face, and then realizing what she was doing, yanked back her hand. Now it was her turn to blush. That was such an intimate thing to do and she barely knew Ty. She wasn't sure what on earth had possessed her to do it.

Ty touched a finger to her cheek. "Sorry. I can't seem to get this into my mouth fast enough."

"Don't apologize. These things may be delicious, but they're impossible to eat without making a mess. Finger licking is completely acceptable."

Ty peered at Karla as she lifted her taco toward her mouth. "Ah, good to know."

"I'm embarrassed to admit, this is the third time I've had Tony's this week."

"Can't say I blame you."

Karla huffed out a chuckle. "That's one of the good things about not skiing competitively anymore. I can eat whatever I want. I hope I never see another wheatgrass smoothie as long as I live."

"Gross, really? They made you eat stuff like that?"

"Uh-huh. Kale chips were considered a treat, and if someone smuggled chocolate or pizza into the dorms at races, we'd descend on it like vultures after a big kill. It was—"

"Hey, Karla," a high-pitched female voice said.

Karla turned to face the bleach blond woman who was bounding up to them. She was dressed in florescent orange from head to toe and was waving enthusiastically.

"Oh, hey there, Cyndi." Karla waved a hand in Ty's direction. "This is my friend, Ty."

Cyndi extended a hand. "Nice to meet you. I'm Karla's roommate-slash-landlord." She plopped down on the grass next to them and held up a brown paper bag. "Mind if I join you?"

"Not at all," Karla said. The truth was, they were barely a week into the semester and Cyndi was already driving her crazy. She was the sweetest woman; it was just that she was so perky. All. The. Time.

Cyndi pulled some sort of wrap out of the brown bag and gnawed through it as she blathered on about her kids—three little boys who, in Karla's opinion, were complete terrors. While she gave Cyndi immense credit for juggling motherhood and school, the children were in desperate need of more discipline. It was going to be a seriously long year, although Karla shouldn't complain. She had her own "mother-in-law suite" in the basement, and the rent was dirt cheap. In exchange, Karla occasionally babysat for the monsters in human skin.

Cyndi eventually turned to the topic of school, but she mostly gossiped about the other students she'd met so far. Karla had never been big on gossip—not that she was all holier than thou, it just wasn't her thing—and based on her reaction to Cyndi, neither was Ty.

"We should meet for lunch more often," Cyndi suggested.

"Um, sure, that would be great," Ty replied, although Karla was pretty sure she was about as enthused as Karla was about spending more time with Cyndi. They were both just too nice to say otherwise.

CHAPTER NINETEEN

As she made her way back to Steamboat to close on her house, Ty was overwhelmed with feelings of guilt and doubt. She sang along to her favorite Pandora playlist and tried to envision herself curled up with a book in what would soon be her observatory, but the nagging feelings kept bubbling to the surface anyway. It didn't help that not a single person had supported her decision to buy a ski house. Not Sarah, not Reed, not Kate. None of them had come right out and told her not to do it. It was her decision, they all insisted, yet they'd all done little to hide their disapproval. It would have been nice if just one of them had been happy for her. Nice if one of them had uttered "congratulations" or "how exciting."

On more than one occasion, she'd thought about calling Scotty to tell him she couldn't buy the house and wanted to back out of the contract, but she couldn't bring herself to do it. She loved everything about the place. So what if everyone else thought it was too expensive, too big, or that she wouldn't use it enough? Even though she'd have to split her time between Steamboat and Denver because of school, the new house would be the first place she could really call home since her parents had died.

And buying a ski house made sense. Skiing was, after all, one of her all-time, number-one favorite things to do on the whole planet. And sure, $3.9 million was a lot of money, but not in the context of how much she had. It was a drop in the bucket for her, and so far, she'd been almost the epitome of prudent with her money. Why didn't anyone give her credit for that?

As she crested Rabbit Ears Pass and descended toward Steamboat in the valley below, her panic intensified. She gasped for air and the road in front of her became blurry. The bellowing sound of a tractor trailer horn reverberated through the air when her car swayed across the rumble-stripped center line. It scared the crap out of her.

She tapped her breaks, pulled over to the side of the road, and snatched her phone from the center console, to call who, she wasn't sure, but before she got the chance, her phone rang. Ty stabbed the answer button. "Hey, Sar."

"Just calling to wish you good luck. The closing is today, right?"

Ty smiled into the phone. "Yep. It's super nice of you to call. It means a lot to me."

"I can't wait to see the place. Based on the photos, it looks amazing."

Sarah's voice was a little flat, like she didn't really mean what she was saying, but Ty still appreciated that she'd called.

"It is amazing. I'll have you out soon, I promise."

"Rusty's out of jail," Sarah said.

Ty's stomach clenched into a ball. "He is?" she squeaked.

"Uh-huh. I saw him at Thirsty's last night."

"That seems so soon. I mean after what he did."

"I know. He probably knows the judge. Anyway, he asked about you, asked if I knew where'd you run off to."

"Fucking wonderful. I assume you didn't—"

"Of course not."

As Ty continued back down the pass, the bile rose up from her stomach. She pulled over to the side of the road a second time, opened her door, and threw up in the soot-stained snow.

She wiped her mouth with a paper napkin left over from the lunch she'd picked up at the McDonald's drive-through on her way out of Denver and sloshed some water around her mouth. When the nausea passed, she pulled back out on the road and headed straight for Scotty's office.

The closing was over in less than an hour. Because no mortgage was involved, there were only a handful of documents for Ty to sign. Who knew buying a $4 million manse could be so easy? She was anxious to spend her first night at the house. Her house. But Scotty insisted on sending a cleaning crew over first to give the place a scrub down.

"I'm a complete germaphobe," he explained. "A new house should sparkle."

"Can't say I disagree."

"And, James and I want to take you out to celebrate," Scotty said.

* * *

"Do you have sheets and towels and that sort of thing?" James asked when they settled into a bar downtown.

"Well," Ty said. "I have a bed, I know that. The seller left all his furniture behind. That was part of the agreement, but, no, I've been so busy with school and everything that I haven't had time to think about any of that." She grinned. "I did bring my sleeping bag and a pillow though."

"Oh, no, that will not do," James said. "We must rectify this situation *immediately*." He looked at Scotty. "Call Dan at Home Deluxe. Tell him it's an emergency."

Ty laughed. "I don't know about that."

James rested one of his hands on hers. "Oh, honey, but it is."

When Scotty got off the phone with Home Deluxe, he said, "Done. Everything will be at the house by six o'clock. He's also going to bring a box of basics. Toilet paper, dish soap, laundry detergent, oh, and wine."

"Wow, thanks, Scotty. I can't believe he can have it all there that quickly."

Scotty chuckled. "I give Dan *a lot* of business."

"Is there anything else we can do to help?" James asked.

"You've already done more than enough," she replied. "Although, there's one thing...I've got stuff in storage in Upstate New York. I'd like to have it shipped to Steamboat. Any chance you guys could arrange for someone to be at the house to accept the delivery? We're only talking six or seven boxes. To be honest, I'm not really sure what's in them. Probably just my old yearbooks, Christmas decorations, stuff like that."

"No problem at all," Scotty assured her.

Ty inched up her driveway just after dark. The exterior lights had clicked on, giving the house a soft glow, and it looked beautiful. She put the Tesla in park and stared out the window.

"Hi, house," she whispered. "I'm Ty, your new owner. I hope you are as excited as I am."

She pulled a small suitcase out of the trunk and bounded up the front steps. As soon as she pushed open the front door, a series of lights clicked on. Startled, she let out a cry and dropped her suitcase on her foot.

"Ouch, shit," she muttered as she stepped inside and closed the door behind her.

The house was silent aside from the soft gurgling of the fountain in the entryway.

CHAPTER TWENTY

"Sweet catch," Ty said and gave Karla a high five.

Karla twirled the frisbee on her pointer finger. "Thanks."

After they scored, Karla and Ty lined up next to each other in the end zone along with their teammates and Karla launched the frisbee toward the opposing team. The white disk sailed to the opposite end of the field, where Cyndi snatched it out of the air. She pivoted toward one sideline before flinging the frisbee toward one of her teammates.

Just before the frisbee reached its intended target, Ty jumped up and grabbed it. Cyndi let out a low growl. Ty made a short toss to Val and darted across the field to position herself to receive it again.

The woman marking Ty was a pint-sized ball of energy. With her sneakers on, she probably topped out at five feet. Her name was Demi. Ty didn't know if it was her real name or a nickname, like a demitasse, which would have been fitting given that she was about half the size of any of the other women on the field. Demi stuck to Ty like a fly to fly paper. No matter which way Ty zipped, Demi was right there next to her.

Val sent the disk to Karla, and Ty sprinted toward the end zone. The toss from Karla started high, but the disk shuddered in the air and lost altitude. Ty dove for it and clutched it in her hand right before she crashed to the ground. She rolled over on her back and held the frisbee up in the air victoriously. Her teammates gathered around her and gave her celebratory slaps on the back.

On their next possession, Ty dove for the frisbee again, but this time Demi kneed her in the ribs. She fell to the ground and clutched her side.

"It's not a contact sport," she growled through her teeth.

"Get over it," Demi said.

Ty pinched her eyes shut and took a few gasps of air. When she opened her eyes, Karla was kneeling beside her, a concerned look on her face.

"You okay?" she asked.

Ty nodded. "Yeah, I think so."

"I'm all for being competitive, but I hate people who play dirty."

"Me too. It's a recreational game of ultimate, for God's sake. It supposed to be *fun*."

Karla put out a hand. "You think you can stand up?"

Ty curled her hand around Karla's. "Uh-huh."

Karla gently pulled her to her feet. With their hands still intertwined, their eyes locked for the briefest moment.

Ty swallowed hard. "Thanks."

Karla released her hand and stepped back. "My pleasure."

When the game was over, the team huddled in a circle with their arms across each other's backs. Ty had made sure to maneuver herself next to Karla. And she wasn't going to lie, it felt good to be up against Karla's body even if it was only for a brief moment. Ty was so crazy attracted to her, and although she wasn't a hundred percent sure, her gut told her Karla was sort of into her too. Maybe it was wishful thinking on her part, but when they looked at each other, there was this current of electricity that hummed between them. She desperately wanted to ask Karla out. She just had to muster the courage.

"Great game," Val said. She was their de facto coach. They all stomped their feet and threw their arms in the air. Ty loved the comradery.

"Are you coming out for beers?" Ty asked Karla after they'd broken their huddle.

"I wish, but no." She gestured toward Cyndi and her teammates on the opposite side of the field. "I promised Cyndi I'd babysit."

"That's sort of a drag."

"It is, but it's part of the deal. She charges me next to nothing to live in her basement, and in return, I babysit when she's in a pinch."

Ty felt a twinge of guilt. If she hadn't won the lottery, she'd probably be in a similar situation. "From the sound of it, her kids are a handful."

"That's putting it mildly. The trick is to wear them out. I invent these games and make them run all over the yard."

"Genius."

Karla gave her a crooked smile. "Uh-huh."

"How are you getting home?" Ty asked.

"I came with Cyndi and the boys in their minivan."

"I could give you a ride if you want. That way you'd get a little peace and quiet before you have to spend the evening with those little balls of energy."

Karla's face lit up. "Really? That would be great. Let me grab my stuff and let Cyndi know I'll meet them at home." She walked toward the stubby aluminum bleachers and pulled a red and gray Atomic backpack from the heap of bags on the ground. She tugged a neatly folded white T-shirt from an outside pocket and tucked it between her knees.

Ty's lips inched open and her eyes grew wide when Karla pulled the sweat-soaked jersey she was wearing over her head. Ty knew she was staring, but she couldn't tear her eyes away.

Val came up beside her and hip bumped her. "Whatcha looking at?"

Ty quickly diverted her gaze. "Um, nothing."

Val snickered. "My ass."

Karla pulled the clean white tee overhead, uttered something to Cyndi, and walked back toward them. "Ready when you are, Ty."

"You two coming out for beers?" Val asked.

"I am," Ty said, "but I'm going to run Karla home real quick first."

"You're not coming?" Val asked Karla.

Karla shook her head. "Nope. I've got babysitting duty."

Val didn't seem surprised. A little grin crossed her face and she nodded toward Ty. "Well, it sure is nice of this one to drive you home."

Ty was tempted to kick her in the shin. Subtlety was most definitely not one of Val's strong suits. "Catch you in a few. Save a little beer for me," she said as she and Karla turned and started toward the parking lot.

"Holy shit. This is your car?" Karla asked when they approached the Tesla.

Ty let out a nervous laugh. "No, it's on loan from Megan Rapinoe." The quip elicited a laugh from Karla and Ty used the opportunity to change the topic. "How'd your leg feel out there today?"

Karla patted her thigh. "It's feeling great. Not a hundred percent yet, but I'm getting there. I've really been pushing myself in physical therapy and it's paying off. I'm healing even faster than the doctor expected."

"No one watching our game today would have guessed you were on crutches barely three months ago. You're so agile, it's incredible." Ty cringed. God, could she be any more obvious? In an effort to hide her embarrassment, she fiddled with one of the buttons on her steering wheel and changed the radio station.

Karla placed her hand on Ty's arm. "You did pretty well out there yourself today. God, that diving catch you made to score was absolutely incredible."

Ty gave her a sideways glance. "Thanks, but you're the one who deserves the credit for that point. The throw you made into the end zone was epic. Where'd you learn to throw like that?"

"Just tossing the disk around with my family in the backyard. Believe it or not, this was the first time I've ever played ultimate."

"No way. I don't believe you."

"It's true. Growing up, there wasn't time for anything but skiing. I devoted everything I had to that."

"Well, you're an amazing player. I can't wait until we play the Raptors in two weeks. They're the best team in our league, but I bet we can beat them."

Karla drummed her fingers on the armrest. "Unfortunately, I won't be around for the game. I'm going up to Jackson that weekend to see Dana, my—Oh, shit, watch out!"

A kid on a skateboard flew in front of them and the Tesla jerked to a stop. "Shit, that was close," Ty said. "He came out of nowhere."

"That kid lives next door to Cyndi. You should see what he can do on that skateboard. It's insane. I've been begging him to teach me a few of his tricks." Karla pointed to a split-level ranch at the end of the street. "That's Cyndi's house."

Ty pulled into the driveway and leaned over to give Karla a hug goodbye. It was one of those awkward hugs where both heads go to the right and then to the left. Their cheeks grazed when they embraced, and Ty relished at the feel of Karla's soft skin against hers.

Karla stepped out of the car and leaned down to wave goodbye through the open door. "See you around. Thanks for the ride."

"Yeah, see you around," Ty said. When the passenger door clicked shut, she ran her fingers over the spot where Karla's cheek had brushed against hers.

CHAPTER TWENTY-ONE

Ty swept her eyes over the valley below. The trees were a stunning canvas of yellow, orange, and red. She and Karla were standing atop the summit of Mt. Mitchell. Ty plunked herself down on a massive boulder and pulled lunch from her pack.

"Whatcha got there?" Karla asked.

Ty held up the wax paper-wrapped item in her hand. "Peanut butter on a bagel. My go-to meal on hikes."

"Yum. I'm jealous." Karla held up a small tin can. "I've got pork and beans. Zero nutritional value, but it's what Cyndi packed and, ya know, beggars can't be choosers."

"She doesn't strike me as a pork and beans sort of gal. I thought she was a health nut."

"She is," Karla replied. She tapped her spork against the side of the tin. "I bet these have been sitting in her pantry for a decade."

"God, let's hope not." Ty swept her hand across the horizon. "Too bad she had to bail on the hike. This view is magnificent."

"Yeah, too bad."

"I hope her kid is okay," Ty said. Cyndi had been the one to suggest the hike up Mt. Mitchell, but right before they'd hit the trail, her ex-husband had called from her son's baseball game. Apparently, he'd taken a line drive to the face and was being loaded into an ambulance. Understandably, Cyndi had run off to meet them at the hospital, but she'd insisted Ty and Karla go on the hike without her.

The truth was, even though Ty felt bad about Cyndi's kid, she was ecstatic to have a whole day alone with Karla. Even though she hadn't yet gotten up the nerve to ask her out on an official date, the hike together felt like one.

Ty pulled a bag of potato chips from her pack, split apart the two pieces of her bagel, and strategically placed chips over its surface.

Karla laughed.

"What's so funny?" Ty asked.

Karla nodded toward the bagel and her big brown eyes found Ty's. "What is it that you're making there?"

"It gives it a nice crunch."

"You're weird."

"I am not."

"Are so," Karla said, and nudged Ty with her shoulder.

Ty held out her bagel. "You should try it."

Karla held up a hand. "No thanks. It might spoil my mouth-watering meal. Don't want to mess with the pork and beans."

There it was again. The crazy fucking electricity between them. They didn't even need to touch. Did Karla feel it too, or was Ty going insane? If it were up to her, she'd be content to sit up here next to Karla for the rest of the day. Screw the fact that it would be cold and dark in a few hours. She let out a contented sigh and inched toward Karla, bringing them a bit closer than acquaintances might sit. If Karla minded, she didn't show it. They sat together in silence and stared out at the stunning valley that stretched out before their eyes.

After a while, Karla leaned back and stretched like a cat. When she set her hand back down on the rock, her fingertips were within inches of Ty's. Was it intentional?

Whenever they made eye contact, it set off a circus worth of flips in Ty's stomach. Each time, Ty held Karla's gaze longer than necessary. Staring into her rich brown eyes, wondering if Karla felt the fire between them too.

When they finished eating, Karla stood and brushed off her khaki wind pants. "Ready to head back down?"

Ty looked up at her, certain she saw a flicker of desire in Karla's eyes. "Yep."

Karla extended her arms and pulled Ty to her feet, bringing their faces inches apart. A shudder ran through Ty's body. She shifted her gaze to Karla's lips and was just about to lean in and kiss her when Karla bent down to pick her pack up off the ground.

Ty's hiking boots wobbled on the uneven surface. She closed her eyes and took in a long breath before leaning down to get her own pack.

Once they were off the summit, the trail cut back into the trees. They retraced their steps through a series of narrow switchbacks, but as the path leveled out, it was wide enough for them to walk side by side. Occasionally, their fingers or forearms brushed, and each time, it made Ty feel warm all over.

As they walked, they talked.

"Any idea what kind of nurse you want to be?" Ty asked.

"I'm hoping to do something is sports medicine, I'm just not exactly sure what yet."

"Seems like that'd be a perfect fit."

"Yeah, after all the injuries I've had, I feel like I could bring, I don't know, a certain empathy to my job. I know what it's like to devote your whole self to a sport only to be sidelined by injury. The frustration and anger on top of the pain can be a lot to handle, especially for a hard-driving athlete." Karla glanced over at Ty. "Does that make sense?"

"It totally makes sense."

"And to be honest," Karla said, "I miss ski racing and all that came with it—the competition, the exhilaration, the comradery, and even the setbacks. There's something satisfying about dusting yourself off and clawing your way back up again. And, well, I feel like working with top-notch athletes would help fill some of that void. That probably sounds weird."

Ty gave her what she hoped was an encouraging smile. "It doesn't sound weird at all. Skiing was your whole life for so long. That's a pretty big hole to have to fill."

Karla was quiet for a minute before she continued. "I'm not going to lie, the transition to 'normal' life has been a little rocky for me. I go from being sad, to being just plain mad. Mad at myself for not 'making it' to the US Ski Team and mad at myself for breaking my stupid leg. I blew my chances to ski for UVM because I was reckless. There are times when I can't help but wonder if I messed up my life intentionally. One thing is for sure, I self-destructed."

Ty stopped walking again. Karla's big brown eyes were moist with tears. Without thinking, she pulled her into a hug. Karla's arms wrapped tight around Ty's waist. Their bodies pressed together, and it felt wonderful. Ty nestled her face in Karla's long brown hair and breathed in her scent. She didn't want to let go, but she forced herself to step back. She was supposed to be comforting a friend. Now was not the time to be making moves on her.

"You okay?" she asked when Karla slipped from her arms.

"Yeah. I know I shouldn't dwell on the past. There's nothing I can do to change it."

"Easier said than done," Ty said with a laugh.

"Isn't that the truth," Karla said. "Anyway, I'm sorry I dumped all of this on you."

"Hey, no worries. I don't mind at all. Always happy to lend an ear."

A smile overtook Karla's face. "Thank you. It helps a lot to talk about it. You're a good listener."

Ty blushed. "Hey, look at the bright side. If you hadn't busted your leg, we probably would never have met."

The sparkle returned to Karla's eyes. "Very true. Maybe the forces that be brought us together."

"Ha, ha, maybe." Ty knew they were just kidding around, but part of her wondered if it was true. All she wanted to do was be around Karla. Maybe they *were* destined to be a couple. She sure hoped so.

Ty watched as Karla started back down the trail. It may have been her imagination, but Karla seemed to stand taller and hold her head higher than she had all day. It was like her confidence had been topped up.

"But enough about me. What about you?" Karla asked when Ty caught up to her. "What's your big plan after school?"

"Well, for a long time, I thought I wanted to work in a hospital setting," Ty waved a hand in the air, "but my priorities have changed a lot since I was in school the first time around."

"Really, how so?"

"Now I want to work someplace where I can make a difference. Like maybe a community clinic."

"Good for you. Do you think you'll go back East?" Karla asked. "You said you were from Upstate New York, right?"

"Yeah, that's where I grew up, but honestly I don't know where I'll go after I graduate. Guess it depends on where I can find a job."

"Do you still have family in New York?"

Ty stared down at the ground. "No, no immediate family anyway. My brother, Reed, and his wife, Quy, live in Vietnam."

"Oh, wow. That's cool."

"Quy is from there. They're both teachers."

"And what about your parents?"

"They, um…" Ty took in a long breath, "were killed in a car accident three years ago. Drunk driver."

Karla stopped walking and turned to Ty. "Oh, my God. That's awful." She put an arm over Ty's shoulder. "I'm sorry, I shouldn't have—"

"It's okay, you didn't know. That's why I dropped out of school. It was pretty devastating."

"I bet. I can't imagine, but gosh, good for you for coming back to finish your degree. That had to be incredibly difficult."

"Uh-huh," Ty said. "There was a while there when I didn't think I'd ever get my life back on track. I thought I was destined to be a bartender for the rest of my life. Not that there's anything wrong with being a bartender. It's just, I'd dreamed of being a nurse since I was a little girl. It's all I ever wanted to do."

Karla gave her shoulder a little squeeze and pulled her arm away. "It must be difficult, to have your brother living so far away."

Ty missed her touch immediately. She reluctantly turned and continued down the trail. "It is, especially because he's the only real family I have left. I have an aunt and cousin in Upstate New York, but we aren't that close. They're a bit…eccentric." That was the nicest word Ty could think of to describe Aunt Paisley and Garth. Just thinking about her smarmy cousin made the hair on her arm stick up. Thankfully, he hadn't managed to track her down after she'd changed her phone number. "Luckily, I have my best friend Sarah. When I dropped out of school, I moved to Asheville to be near her. Sarah's my rock. She saved me from spiraling completely out of control."

"Are you two, you know, a couple?"

Ty laughed out loud. "No. Sarah's gay, but no. There's never been anything between us. She's more like a sister to me than anything. I'm single." Ty felt a bit silly for adding that bit of information. "I dated a woman, Rosie, for a while, but we broke up a few months before I moved back to Colorado, and there hasn't been anyone since then."

"How long were you and Rosie together?"

"Almost two years…and, well, if I'm totally honest, she dumped me for another woman."

"Oh, gosh. That's terrible."

"Yeah. It pretty much sucked. It took me a while to get over her." Ty hesitated before adding, "I met her not long after my parents died, and I fell pretty hard for her. I was vulnerable, and I kinda latched onto Rosie. That's Sarah's theory, anyway. We weren't the greatest fit, and she didn't treat me that well. That's obvious to me now, although it wasn't at the time. I just…Well, anyway, it was for the best. That we aren't together anymore."

Ty made herself stop there. She was pouring her heart out to this woman she hardly knew. Except it didn't feel that way.

There was such an ease between them, something Ty had rarely felt with another human being. She'd always had a lot of friends, but she let very few people get close to her. And here she was opening up to Karla, letting her in. Karla had this air, like she genuinely cared about what Ty had to say. Being with her was like walking on sunshine.

Karla's lips curled into a small smile. "Well, if you ask me, Rosie wasn't very smart. I mean, if she dumped you."

Ty smiled shyly. She thought she might melt right there on the trail. "Thanks, you're sweet." They walked in silence for a while before Ty asked, "What about you? Anyone special in your life?" She held her breath while she waited for the answer.

Karla hesitated. "Yeah actually there is. Her name is Dana. She lives in Jackson."

Ty's heart sunk and her lungs deflated like a balloon. She forced her lips upward. "Oh, that's nice."

CHAPTER TWENTY-TWO

Karla climbed into the car and tossed her backpack into the passenger seat. Right now, she'd give anything to have her own private helicopter. Driving eight hours back to Denver was about the last thing she wanted to do. She yanked the seat belt across her body and clicked it into place. Snowflakes swirled in the air as she drove out of Jackson.

The long weekend with Dana had been good but not great. They'd spent a lot of time in bed, but when they weren't having sex, there'd been a lot of awkward silences. They'd taken a day hike in Teton National Park and that had been fun. The area outside of Jackson had gotten its first real snowfall for the season, and they'd giggled when they'd made snow angels.

One night they'd gone to Abbott's—the bar where'd they met—and Karla had texted Keats to see if she could join them. When she'd showed up, Dana had been downright rude, and at the end of the night, she'd sulked about how much time Karla had spent talking to Keats. When Karla went off to have breakfast with her parents the next morning, Dana had been equally unenthusiastic. Karla had invited her along, but she'd begged off, saying she had some work thing she needed to do.

When Karla was packing up to leave, Dana had begged her to stay one extra night. It felt good that Dana wanted to spend more time with her, and she'd almost agreed. First, though, she'd asked Dana why she never came to Denver. Big mistake. Dana had made some crack about how it was easier for Karla to blow off class than it was for her to take time away from her job. Even though she hadn't come right out and said it, the implication was clear. Dana was too busy, and important, to spend eight hours driving to and from Denver. Karla had stormed out of the house, and even though Dana had run after her and apologized, Karla was still fuming about it.

She cranked up the radio and sang at the top of her lungs in an effort to shake off the anger. Before long, the signal for Jackson's classic rock station began to crackle. Karla hit the radio's scan button and after it cycled through the frequencies twice without stopping on a decent station, she clicked it off. The only sound was the humming of her tires on the pavement. She was alone with her thoughts.

Her mind drifted to Ty. She was eager to get back to Denver. Eager to see Ty. She liked spending time with her. They were fast becoming good friends, and Ty was funny, smart, and kind. Who wouldn't want to spend time with her? Sure, if circumstances were different, maybe they'd be more than friends. There was no denying the spark between them, and if she had to guess, she'd hedge Ty did want something more. But right now, Karla was steadfast. She wasn't willing to throw in the towel on her relationship with Dana quite yet. Dana was fun and smart too, and they'd been dating for nearly nine months. That had to mean something, didn't it? It was Karla's longest relationship, by a long shot. So, they'd had an argument. Couples who loved each other argued all the time. Karla couldn't just give up and walk away. Relationships took work, and Dana was worth it— wasn't she?

Karla clicked the radio back on and hit the scan button. Her jaw dropped open when "Reelin' in the Years" by Steely Dan blared through her speakers. It had to be a sign. The song was on the playlist at Abbott's, and whenever it came on, she and Dana sang along to it. It was kind of like *their* song.

The *low fuel* light on her dashboard lit up on the outskirts of Denver. She groaned. It was cold and she was exhausted. The last thing she wanted to do was stop. But running out of gas would suck a lot more. She got off the highway and pulled into the first gas station she saw. While the gas chugged into her tank, she skimmed the messages on her phone. Her heart skipped when she saw she had a message from Ty. She tapped it open.

Meeting at Val's for a study session. Join us?

Karla typed a response—*I'm pretty beat. Catch you next time*—but the gas nozzle clicked off before she hit send. She put her phone in her back pocket, hooked the nozzle on the pump, and screwed the cap back on her tank.

When she climbed back in the car, she had a change of heart. Hanging out with Val and Ty was exactly what she needed. It would cheer her up. Help her push aside the argument she'd had with Dana. Plus, the thought of going home, to Cyndi's, was not terribly appealing. Yes, she had her own space in the basement, but the boys would probably still be awake—Cyndi let them stay up way too late—and when they ran around in the living room upstairs, it sounded like a herd of buffalo charging overhead.

She pulled out her phone, erased her message to Ty and typed, *On my way. Be there in twenty.* She ran inside the convenience store at the station, bought a tube of sour cream and onion Pringles and a family sized bag of pretzels as study snacks, and took off toward Val's house.

Val, Ty, and their classmate Dipti were gathered around Val's dining room table when she arrived. Karla's heart swelled when she saw them. In such a short span of time, they'd become such good friends. After the year she'd had—walking away from skiing, breaking her leg, and losing the chance to go to UVM—she couldn't believe how happy she felt. Funny how things had a way of working out. She took the empty seat next to Ty and pulled the snacks from her bag.

"Thought you guys might be hungry."

Ty snapped up the Pringles. "Yum, my favorite." She gave Karla a broad smile. "How'd you know?"

"Lucky guess."

"How was Jackson?" Val asked.

The smile on Ty's face faded ever so slightly.

"It was fine. They've gotten a bunch of snow." Karla bent down and gave one of the dogs a pat on the head. "Is this Apple or Pear? They look so much alike."

"That's Pear," Val said, "but you're not getting off that easy. "How's Dana? What did ya'll do?"

Karla shrugged. "There really isn't too much to tell. We went hiking. That was nice. To be honest, though, I feel like I spent most of the weekend in the car. That drive to Jackson is going to be the death of me." In an effort to shift attention away from her love life, she flipped open her laptop. "I got like zero studying done this weekend. Shall we hit the books?"

CHAPTER TWENTY-THREE

Ty whistled Christmas carols as she roamed the parking garage at the Denver airport looking for a spot. Reed and Quy were due to land any minute. It was the first time Reed had been home for Christmas since their parents had died. He always insisted they couldn't afford the flight to the US from Vietnam. Ty knew there was some truth to that, but she also suspected Reed had used it as an excuse. Christmas had always been their mother's favorite time of year, and the holiday opened the floodgate of emotions. Ty had spent the last few Christmases with Sarah and her family. They'd welcomed her as one of their own, and for that she'd always been thankful, but it wasn't the same. Having Reed home this year meant the world to her. In fact, buying him and Quy plane tickets home was one of the first things she'd done after she'd cashed in her winning lottery ticket.

The international arrivals area was a complete mob scene. A stream of weary looking passengers, most pushing carts piled perilously high with luggage, emerged from behind the automatic sliding door that separated the secure area from the throngs of loved ones waiting on the other side. When Ty finally spotted her brother, she teared up and waved her arms frantically.

"Reed, Quy. Over here."

Reed's face cracked into a broad smile. "Hey, little sis." His strong arms engulfed her in a bear hug. "It's so good to see you."

Once he released her, Quy embraced her warmly.

Ty looked down at the two small suitcases at her brother's side. "Is that all you brought?"

Reed nodded. "We tried to pack lightly."

"I guess it helped that you didn't have to bring any bulky ski clothes." Scotty and James had kindly given Ty some of their old parkas and ski pants for her brother and Quy to wear while they were in Colorado.

"It sure did."

"How was the trip?" Ty asked as they made their way out to the parking garage. "I bet you're beat. That's a seriously long trip."

Reed looked at his watch. "It sure was. We left Vietnam twenty-six hours ago."

"Toss in the thirteen-hour time difference," Ty said, "and that's a recipe that would leave anybody's eyes heavy."

"Actually, I feel pretty good, all things considered," Quy replied. "Thanks to you, we both managed to get a fair amount of sleep."

"Yeah, Ty. We can't thank you enough. It's a true gift to be here, and you went above and beyond," Reed added. "Although, it was totally unnecessary. I hate to think of how much those tickets cost."

Ty had surprised them with business-class plane tickets, a luxury none of them could've dreamed of affording before the Lionball. "It was my pleasure. It's the least I could do."

"Wow, Ty," Reed said when they reached her car. "What is this, a moon car?"

"Ha, ha, very funny. It's a Tesla."

Reed touched a finger to the trunk and yanked it away, like he was afraid the car might electrocute him. "I've actually never seen one. Tesla's aren't big in Vietnam."

Quy snorted out a laugh. "No, they definitely are not."

"What happened to your Subaru?" Reed asked.

Ty shrugged and cocked her head toward the Tesla. "I traded it in for this."

"I see," Reed replied. "Is it any good in the snow?"

Ty threw up her hands. "I haven't really had a chance to test it yet, but it's all-wheel drive."

Reed looked like he was about to say something else, but then thought better of it. He hoisted their luggage into the trunk of the car and slipped into the passenger seat next to Ty. Both he and Quy were snoring within ten minutes of leaving the airport.

"Hello, sleepyhead," Ty said when her brother finally woke up as they were descending the pass into Steamboat. "So much for not having jet lag, eh?"

Reed rubbed his eyes. The leather passenger seat creaked when he turned to check on Quy in the backseat. "She's still out like a light. I'm sorry, Ty. We're pretty lame copilots."

"Don't worry about it. I'm just glad you're here."

Reed squeezed her arm. "I'm glad we're here too. I haven't been home for Christmas since—"

Ty looked over and gave him a sad smile. "I know."

Ty pulled in the parking lot at the grocery store, causing Quy to stir awake.

Her eyes were glossy with sleep as she asked, "Where are we?"

"A few miles from my house," Ty said. "We just need to make a quick pit stop to pick up some stuff for dinner."

Quy shuffled around the store behind Reed and Ty like she was sleep walking. Once they had what they needed, Ty steered the cart toward the checkout counters and unloaded their groceries onto the belt.

Reed pushed ahead of her and pulled out his wallet. "Quy and I will get this."

Ty yanked her wallet out of her back pocket and tried to slip behind her brother, knocking a few packs of gum off the aisle display in the process. "No, it's my treat."

Reed stood his ground. "No. You paid for our airfare. It's the least we can do."

"Come on, Reed. Let me cover it."

"We don't need your charity, Ty."

Ty looked to Quy for support but got only a blank stare in return.

The cashier cleared her throat. "There are people waiting behind you."

Ty relented and let her brother pay.

They drove up to the house in silence and Reed gasped when they pulled into her driveway. "What the hell, Ty? This place is huge." He climbed out of the car and stared up at the house. "I know you sent pictures, but I didn't expect anything quite this extravagant."

Ty cringed. She knew she was about to get a lecture about being too materialistic. Reed and Quy had some very strong opinions about only buying what you need and our duty to give back.

She stood up straight and crossed her arms over her chest. "The slopes are lined with some serious McMansions. This place is small in comparison."

Quy became more alert. "It's beautiful, Ty."

"Thanks, Quy. Come on, I'll give you guys a quick tour."

Once they stepped inside, Reed's eyes moved over the nicely appointed living room and chef-quality kitchen. "This place is over the top."

"And your point is?" Ty asked, trying unsuccessfully to keep the anger out of her voice. She loved her brother, she really did, but sometimes he could be so fucking sanctimonious.

"My point is," Reed said, "you were given a gift. I hope you don't blow it on expensive real estate and fancy cars. There are a lot of people who need—"

"I'm well aware of that. I've told you; I plan to give most of my money away, but I think it was reasonable to buy myself a home."

Quy placed a hand on Reed's shoulder and gave him a look that said, "back off."

"I'm sorry, Ty," Reed said. "I shouldn't have jumped down your throat. I know you have a good soul and you'll do the right thing."

Ty forced a smile. "It's okay." But it wasn't. She was hurt. She'd paid to fly them all the way to the US, hoping they'd have a nice Christmas together, and her brother was being an utter ass.

"You're very generous to let us stay here," Quy said. "Thank you."

Ty bit her lip to hold off the tears. She didn't want to ruin their visit before it even got started. She took a deep breath and asked, "How about that tour I promised?"

As they wandered through the house, Reed and Quy oohed and aahed at all the right places. The sun had set, and it was a clear night. The observatory seemed to win them both over. After Quy excused herself to go unpack, Ty turned to her brother.

"Drink?" she asked, nodding toward the small butler's table in the corner.

"Sure. Thanks, Ty."

She poured them each a glass and handed one to Reed.

"Mmmm, this is good stuff. What is it?"

"Red Breast, a top-notch Irish Whiskey."

Reed took another sip and stared out the windows at the snow-covered ski slopes just beyond the house. "Sorry I was a little hard on you earlier," he said. "I worry about you, that's all."

Ty rested her hand on his shoulder. "I know you do. To be honest, I worry a little about myself sometimes too."

"I don't want you to get too swept up by all the money."

Ty punched him.

Reed rubbed his arm. "Ouch," he feigned.

"Spare me."

Reed got a serious look on his face. "Promise me you'll be careful, Ty."

"I'll do my best. It helps that I have a good support network. I've already made some good friends here and in Denver, and you can rest assured that, if I do anything too crazy, Sarah and Kate Kraft will be on my ass so fast, I won't know what hit me."

* * *

After a morning on the slopes, during which Ty tried and failed to keep up with her brother, she and Reed drove to a large roadside Christmas Tree stand on the far side of town. As soon as she opened the car door, Ty's nose twitched at the sweet smell of evergreens. It triggered a range of emotions. Nostalgia and sorrow for Christmases past, along with hope and happiness for the Christmas she was about to share with her brother and sister-in-law.

"Do you think they have any Douglas firs?" Reed asked as they meandered through the tidy rows of trees perched on crude wooden stands.

"Gosh, I don't know," Ty replied, "but I sure hope so." Growing up, they'd always gone out as a family and cut down a Douglas fir at the Christmas tree farm in the neighboring town.

"Hey, Ty," a male voice said.

Ty looked up and saw Scotty, her realtor, poking through a row of trees. "Hey, Scotty."

Scotty and his husband James stepped out from behind a massive Fraser fir. "Fancy meeting you here."

Ty rested a hand on her brother's shoulder. "This is my brother, Reed. Reed, these are my friends Scotty and James. They're the ones who lent you the ski clothes."

Reed shook their hands and said, "Thanks so much for the snazzy outfits. It saved me a bundle not to have to rent everything, and I've never looked so good."

"Do you guys want to stop by the house tomorrow for a Christmas drink?" Ty asked.

"We'd love to," Scotty replied.

After Scotty and James wandered off, Reed tugged on the limb of a tall, plump tree. "How about this one?" He checked its tag. "It's a Douglas fir."

Ty stood back and examined it. The tree was almost perfectly symmetrical. "Can you turn it so I can see the back?"

Reed did as she asked.

"It's perfect," Ty said. "I don't see any bare areas."

Ty paid for the tree while Reed and one of the stand's employees used hairy brown twine to tie it to the roof of her Tesla.

"Do you want a wreath?" the cashier asked.

Ty eyed the vast array of wreaths tethered to the wire fence behind her. She pointed to a medium-sized one with a simple red velvet bow. "I'll take that one."

Once they got the Christmas tree up in her living room, Reed asked, "Do you have any ornaments?"

Ty jumped to her feet. "Yeah. I can't believe I forgot to tell you. I had the boxes from Mom and Dad's house shipped here. One of them has Christmas lights, plus all the little decorations you and I used to hang on the tree when we were growing up."

Reed stood and brushed little green needles off his pants. "Really?"

"Uh-huh. Our Christmas stockings are in there too. The ones Mom needlepointed for us."

Reed's eyes lit up and then his shoulders slumped. "Do you think it'll be hard to see all of that old stuff?"

Ty pulled him into a hug. "Probably," she said when she stepped back, "but I bet they'll bring back lots of good memories, and it'd be a shame not to use them. I think Mom would be sad if we just left them rotting in a box."

"Where are the boxes?" Reed asked.

"Down in my basement." Ty started for the stairs. "Let's go haul them up."

When they got back upstairs, Ty pulled out a stocking she'd bought for Quy in Denver. She held it up. "I didn't want you to feel left out."

"That was very sweet of you, Ty. Thank you."

"You think those still work?" Ty asked when Reed pulled a giant ball of white lights out of one of the boxes.

"Only one way to find out." He plugged them into the wall and the string came to life. "Sweet."

Quy chuckled. "Good luck getting that giant mess of lights untangled."

Ty laughed. "This is going to be fun to watch."

Reed gave them both a goofy grin. "I bet it would be a lot easier if I had a beer."

Ty got them all beers, and while Reed worked on the lights, she and Quy carefully unpacked all the tiny ornaments and laid them out on the coffee table. Ty started to cry when she unwrapped a tiny felt Santa. Quy leaned over and gently rubbed her back.

Ty blew out a breath. "I'm okay. These are tears of happiness. This is the first time I've been excited about Christmas since Mom and Dad died."

Reed pulled her into one of his big bear hugs.

Ty wiped a tear from her cheek. "How about a fire and some Christmas music?"

Quy clinked her beer bottle against Ty's. "Great idea."

After a few clicks on remotes, flames erupted in the gas fireplace and "White Christmas" streamed from the surround-sound speakers.

Ty hummed along as Bing Crosby sang, "I'm dreaming of a white Christmas." She hoisted her beer. "Merry Christmas."

Reed followed suit. "Merry Christmas, little sis."

Ty sunk into the couch and sipped her beer as she watched Reed wrap the lights around the tree. For the first time in a very long time, she felt like everything was going to be okay.

CHAPTER TWENTY-FOUR

Ty huffed in front of her closet. She was due at Val and Teresa's house for dinner in less than an hour, and everything she owned could be classified as either warm, comfortable, or both. Nothing stood out as being remotely sexy. Karla would be there for dinner too, and although she didn't want to admit it, Ty wanted to look good for her.

Over the Christmas break, Ty had thought about Karla a lot. Wondered what she was doing, if she was having a nice time with her family…and Dana. Why did Karla have to have a girlfriend? This kind, beautiful, strong, funny woman had walked into Ty's life and was totally off limits. Life was not fair.

She and Karla had exchanged a few messages over the break, and of course, Ty had overanalyzed each one. When Karla signed off of one message with an *xoxo*, Ty's heart had about leapt out of her body. Was Karla thinking about her too? Did Karla miss her as much as she missed Karla?

The previous day, when she'd run into Karla on campus—the first time they'd seen each other in over three weeks—Ty had rushed up and given her a hug. Holding Karla in her arms, even for a brief moment, had made one thing abundantly clear. Her feelings for Karla had not dissipated over the holidays. If anything, they'd grown stronger.

As much as she was looking forward to dinner tonight, she was anxious. Whenever she was around Karla, it took willpower of Herculean proportions to hide her feelings. At some point, she had to cave. Give in to the urge to kiss her. But she couldn't, she wouldn't. Not as long as Dana was in the picture.

She kicked one of her crusty old Converse sneakers into the closet and let out a groan. Her emotional tantrum had done nothing to improve the offerings in her closet. She tugged on a pair of jeans and a baggy black wool sweater and padded into the bathroom.

Her long blond hair was still damp, and it hung limply over her shoulders. She rummaged around in the vanity drawers for some hair gel. It was sticky, and it made her hair stiff. After a quick pass with a blow dryer, it looked like she'd stuck her finger in an electrical socket. Fucking fantastic. Her attempt at applying makeup did not go much better. She scrunched up her face and stared at her reflection in the mirror. Mascara clumped on her eyelashes, but it did bring out the blue of her eyes.

According to her phone, it was a balmy thirty-nine degrees outside. The house she rented in Denver was only a few blocks from Val and Teresa's place, and after being cooped up in the house all day studying, a walk would feel good. She pulled two bottles of wine out of the fridge, slipped on her puffy down coat, and stepped out into the crisp evening.

When Teresa and Val's house came into view, she was not at all surprised to see that white Christmas lights still adorned their bushes. They took holiday decorating to a whole new level and they were always a little slow to take things down at the end of each season. Their Halloween decorations had stayed up until they were supplanted with plastic turkeys and colorful corn cobs just before Thanksgiving.

Teresa answered the door and gave Ty a big hug. "Good to see you, Ty. Come on in."

"You too, Teresa. Thanks for having me over." Ty held up the two bottles of wine. "These are for you."

She followed Teresa back into the kitchen. Karla was sitting at the kitchen island. Her dark hair was pulled back in a messy ponytail, her knees poked out of the tears in her jeans, and black cowboy boots rested on the rung of her stool like it was a stirrup. She looked good. Really good. Ty stared a little too long, finally pressing a hand to her cheek to force her head toward the stove, where Val was tending multiple pots.

Val wiped her hands on her apron and gave Ty a knowing look. Obviously, Ty's efforts to mask her attraction needed some improvement.

"Wine?" Val asked.

Ty climbed up on the stool next to Karla. "Yes, please."

A big platter of cheese and crackers sat in the middle of the kitchen island, and she and Karla reached for a piece of cheese at the same time. Their hands touched briefly, sending a warm tingle up Ty's arm.

Karla slowly drew her hand away. "Oh, Ty, I'm sorry. Help yourself. I've already had my fair share of cheese."

Ty smiled shyly and Karla smiled back. There they were again. Holding each other's gaze. The electricity between them was enough to temporarily knock the wind out of Ty.

"Ty?" Karla asked.

"Yeah."

"Everything okay?"

"Uh-huh. I'm just a little out of it. Long day. Sorry."

Val handed her a glass of wine. "This should help."

Not unless you're pouring Love Potion #9.

Ty cleared her throat. "Thanks Val. Whatcha cooking for dinner? Smells wonderful."

"Chicken French."

Ty rubbed her hands together in delight. "Yum. My mom used to make that all the time when I was a kid. It's practically a staple where I grew up."

Teresa opened the back door and their two black Labs bounded into the kitchen. They gave Karla and Ty each a perfunctory sniff and scampered over to the stove.

Val chuckled and gave each dog an affectionate scratch behind the ears. "Sly boys are waiting for me to drop a tasty morsel on the floor." She turned back to the stove and switched off the burner under a large skillet. "Dinner's ready."

They all migrated to the table and Ty made a point not to sit next to Karla. If their legs accidently touched during dinner, she was sure she'd combust. Instead she took the seat opposite Karla, which she quickly decided wasn't any better. Whenever she looked up, Karla's beautiful brown eyes were gazing back at her. Ty tugged at the neck of her sweater, wishing she could take her plate and eat alone in the living room.

"Anyone need more wine?" Val asked.

Ty held up her glass. "I'll take some." She took a big slug before digging into her meal. "Ooh, wow. This is delicious, Val. Even better than what my mom used to make, and trust me, that's saying a lot."

Val grinned. "Thanks, Ty."

"I'll second that," Karla said. "Cyndi really missed out."

"I'm sorry she couldn't make it," Val said.

"Yeah, it's too bad," Karla said. "One of the boys had a hockey tournament in Colorado Springs, and I guess they made it to the finals."

"Oh well," Teresa said. "Means more Chicken French for the rest of us."

Ty held up her glass. "And more wine." She sensed maybe she wasn't the only one who wasn't disappointed Cyndi hadn't made it. Knowing Val, she probably only invited her to be nice. Cyndi was always following them around, and it would have been rude not to include her.

Inevitably, the conversation turned to what everyone had done over the Christmas break. Karla mentioned something about Dana, and Val asked, "How's the long-distance thing working for you guys?"

Karla shifted in her seat and took a sip of water. "Um, pretty well."

"It's got to be tough," Teresa said. "Jackson is what, a good eight-hour drive from here?"

Karla pursed her lips and fiddled with her fork. "Yeah. It's a haul."

It was hard to read the expression on Karla's face. Ty couldn't tell if she was brokenhearted to be so far away from Dana, or if she was apathetic about it.

"When are you going to see her next?" Teresa asked.

Karla set down her fork and leaned back in her chair. "Actually, next weekend. We're meeting up in Vail."

Ty plastered a smile on her face and tried to ignore the twinge in her stomach. "That sounds nice."

"A little romantic getaway?" Val asked.

Karla shook her head. "Oh, no. Nothing like that. We're going with another friend."

The fact that another friend would be tagging along did little to placate Ty's aching heart. She stabbed a piece of chicken and lifted it to her mouth. Mercifully, the conversation shifted away from Karla and Dana.

After dinner, Karla and Ty insisted on doing the dishes and let Val and Teresa relax with the dogs by the fire. As they were finishing up, Karla looked over at her.

"You should come to Vail with us. We've got a three-day weekend because of Martin Luther King Day."

Ty set her drying rag on the counter. The invitation threw her off guard. She rubbed the back of her neck. "Thanks, but I don't want to intrude."

"You wouldn't be intruding at all. My friend Keats will be there too."

"Keats?"

Karla let out a wonderful, rich laugh. "Oh, Keats is her last name. I've always called her that. Anyway, she's super cool and she skis like a maniac. Her dad has a condo in Vail, and he said we could use it for the weekend."

Ty looked down at her feet. She was torn. On the one hand, spending a weekend with Karla was certainly enticing, but Dana would be there, and the prospect of seeing the two of them all cozied up together…She tried to push the image from her head.

Karla slipped a finger under Ty's chin and brought her face up, inches from her own. "It would be really nice to have you along."

Ty ached to kiss her, but they were standing in Val and Teresa's kitchen, and Dana…

"So, will you come?" Karla asked.

Ty's resolve collapsed. "Okay, yes. I'd love to." The words were out of her mouth before she could stop them.

Karla pulled her into a one-armed hug. "Fantastic. It'll be a blast."

Ty reluctantly stepped back from the embrace. It was going to be a very interesting weekend, that was for sure.

CHAPTER TWENTY-FIVE

The week before MLK was a total blur, and it was Friday before Karla knew it. She hummed along to the radio as she drove over to pick up Ty. When her GPS dinged to indicate she'd reached her destination, Karla looked up at the two-story Craftsman house in front of her. It had a large front porch, and the kind of neatly landscaped yard that looked good even in the winter. She double checked the house's address against the one Ty had texted her. This was the right place. She knew Val and Teresa lived nearby, but their house wasn't nearly as big, or as cute, and they had established careers. They weren't your typical struggling college students.

"I love your house," Karla said when Ty opened the front door. "Is the whole thing yours?"

Ty threw a duffel bag over her shoulder and mumbled something Karla couldn't quite make out. Once she'd locked the door behind her, Ty said, "My skis are in the garage. I'll be right back."

Karla watched her dart around the side of the house. Something didn't compute. Ty drove an expensive car, and now, seeing her house, it was obvious she had some dough. It was funny though, because she didn't act like a rich person, at least not like the rich people Karla knew. Maybe Ty was housesitting for someone? That had to be it.

Ty emerged from the garage a moment later with her ski bag. "Okay, all set."

"Mind if we make a quick pit stop at the liquor store before we hit the road?" Karla asked as she pulled away from the curb. "Dana and Keats are making spaghetti and salad for dinner, and I told them we'd pick up some beer and wine."

"Only if you promise to let me buy," Ty said.

"That doesn't seem fair."

"Come on, it's the least I can do. You invited me, after all."

"I invited you because I wanted you to come along." There couldn't be more truth to that statement, and it was something that had tormented Karla all week. At first, she'd told herself she'd invited Ty because she liked to ski, and because why not, the more the merrier. But Karla knew it was more than that. She'd finally admitted to herself that she had feelings for Ty, feelings she shouldn't have. It was something she was having a hard time processing. Inviting Ty for the weekend was probably the last thing she should have done, but she certainly couldn't uninvite her now, and anyway, she didn't want to. She wanted Ty to come to Vail.

It was after five o'clock by the time they got on I-70 and made their way up to the tunnel at Loveland Pass. On a good day, it would take less than two hours to get to Vail, but given it was a Friday before a long weekend, traffic inched along.

"It seems like half of Denver is headed up to the mountains, huh?" Ty asked.

"Sure seems like it," Karla said. "I bet it'll take us at least three hours to get to Keats's condo. She and Dana are lucky. They're coming from the other side of the pass."

"What time are they due to get in?"

The car in front of them came to an abrupt stop and Karla hit the brakes hard to avoid hitting them. She glanced over at Ty. She looked cute in her baggy jeans and furry zip-up fleece jacket.

"Around seven."

"So they'll beat us there."

"Probably."

"You must be excited to see Dana?"

"Super excited," Karla replied with more enthusiasm than she felt. She *was* excited to see Dana, she really was. Just not as much as she normally would be. Karla hoped that would change as soon as she saw her. Being in Dana's presence always made Karla feel alive.

"Have you skied Vail a lot?" Ty asked.

Karla nodded. "Uh-huh. A million times, but I was always racing so I never really got to explore the mountain. What about you?"

"A few times when I was in school the first time around. Lately, though, I've mostly been skiing at Steamboat."

"That's right. You mentioned you spent Christmas break there with your brother."

"Yeah. I have a place, uh, to stay there." Ty tugged the zipper of her fleece up and down a few times. "Is your leg still feeling okay?"

"Great, actually. When I skied over Christmas, it hardly bothered me at all."

Ty looked over and gave her a smile. "That's great, Karla. I know you worked super hard to get back in shape."

Karla smiled back. The way Ty looked at her, it was obvious she really cared. "I did. I know I'll never race at the level I did before, but I'm feeling really strong."

Ty shifted slightly in her seat so she was facing Karla. "You doing any better with the transition, from ski racer to nursing student?"

Karla's heart palpitated under the intensity of Ty's gaze and she had to remind herself to keep her eyes on the road. "Yeah, a little bit better. I'm not as angry, or sad, as I was, and I love being in school. Ultimately, I know being a nurse will fulfill me in a way skiing never did."

"I'm glad it's going better." Ty rested a hand on her arm. "I'm always here if you need to talk."

"I know, thank you." Karla passed the car in front of her before she continued. "I'll tell you one thing: I'm enjoying the freedom. My years on the circuit were intense, crazy intense. Don't get me wrong, I loved it, but now I get to ski wherever and whenever I want, rather than according to someone else's strict schedule."

"Hmmm, I guess I hadn't thought about that. Of course, I've never been a professional athlete, so there's that."

"Ha, you're funny, Ty, you know that?"

Ty gave her a sideways glance. "You're pretty funny yourself."

Karla felt her face get hot. "Anyway, when I was home over Christmas, I kicked back and skied the bumps, trees, powder, whatever I wanted. I cannot tell you how liberating that was."

"Is Dana a big skier?" Ty asked.

"Yep. She never raced like me, but she grew up in Telluride and she's pretty much a beast on the mountain. I mean, we've only skied together a few times, but she was always right on my tail and she'll ski anything. I don't think the word fear is in her vocabulary."

"Sounds like I'll have my work cut out for me to keep up with you on the slopes."

Karla reached over and patted Ty's leg. "I'm sure you'll do just fine."

It was after eight o'clock by the time they pulled up in front of the condo in Vail. A black Jeep Wrangler with Wyoming plates was parked in the driveway.

"Looks like Dana and Keats are here," Karla said.

Ty stretched her arms over her head. "Great, because I'm starving."

Karla paused briefly before turning off the car, partially because she didn't want to leave the cocoon of the warm cabin and step out into the cold night air, but also because she didn't want her conversation with Ty to end. Without thinking, she reached over and squeezed one of Ty's hands. "You're really easy to talk to, Ty."

Ty squeezed her hand back. "So are you."

With great reluctance, Karla pulled her hand back into her lap. She sensed Ty was also in no hurry to get out of the car, but Dana and Keats were waiting for them. They had to go inside.

CHAPTER TWENTY-SIX

Dana met them at the front door and greeted Karla with a kiss and Ty with a handshake. She was tall and slender and had a ballerina-like grace about her.

Keats bounded into the foyer and tackled Karla with a hug. Her short, strawberry blond curls were in striking contrast to Dana's long, straight, jet-black hair. Keats was someone Ty's grandmother would've called "cute as a button."

"Thanks for letting me crash your ski weekend," Ty said.

"The more the merrier," Keats said with a warm smile. "Let me show you your rooms before we have dinner."

Karla and Ty grabbed their bags off the floor and followed Keats past a small open kitchen and a cozy living room with a small stone fireplace. Keats nodded toward Karla when they entered a large bedroom on the first floor. "You and Dana are in here." She looked over her shoulder and winked at Ty. "Thought we'd give the master suite to the happy couple."

When Ty spied the king bed flanking the back wall, she felt a pang of jealousy. Dana got to share that big bed with Karla. God, what she'd give to swap places with her.

Keats pointed up the stairs. "You and I are up there, Ty."

They left Karla to unpack and climbed the narrow wood staircase to the second floor, where there were two smaller bedrooms linked by a shared bath.

"There are towels and shampoo and stuff in the linen closet," Keats said. "Help yourself to whatever you need. Oh, and there's a terrycloth robe in your closet. Use that for the hot tub."

"Thanks, Keats. I'll be down in a few minutes."

Once she was alone, Ty peered out the window of her room. She could see the bright lights of the grooming snowcats creeping up and down the slopes, getting the trails in pristine condition for the next morning. They'd make the snow look like a freshly cut Major League Baseball field.

When she got back downstairs, a fire was raging in the stone fireplace. Karla handed her a glass of white wine. "You're a sauvignon blanc girl, right?"

Ty was touched she'd remembered. "Yes, thank you."

Dana and Keats were busy in the kitchen. Keats pulled a baguette from the oven, while Dana made a salad, pausing occasionally to stir a pot of bubbling sauce and meatballs.

When dinner was ready, they each served themselves a heaping plate of food and settled around the large wooden dining table in an alcove off the kitchen.

"Oh, ow, hot, hot," Keats cried around a mouthful of meatball.

"Doesn't look like we're going to get any fresh snow tonight," Dana said. "In fact, they're saying it's going to be sunny and mild tomorrow."

Keats finally managed to swallow her meatball. "If there won't be any freshies," she said, "then there's no reason to try and catch the first chair in the morning."

Dana nodded. "I totally agree. We might as well sleep in a little. It's supposed to get pretty cold tonight, which means—"

"It'll be totally bulletproof first thing in the morning," Karla finished for her.

They were right. Cold temperatures tonight meant the snow would be rock solid in the morning, at least until the sun had a chance to soften things up a bit.

As dinner progressed, Ty and Karla got into a side conversation about avalanches, and that led to a discussion about climbing Mount Everest.

"Is that something that's on your bucket list?" Karla asked.

"No. I've never had a strong desire to do it. What about you?"

Karla shook her head. "I haven't either. Does that surprise you?"

"Yeah, actually it does. You're so driven, and you like adventure. I guess I'd expect you to want to do something super hardcore like that."

Karla grinned. "I'm full of surprises, huh?"

Ty nodded and smiled back at her. The two of them were in their own little world, and it wasn't until Dana asked if anyone wanted seconds that Ty remembered she and Keats were there.

After dinner, Dana and Karla nestled into one end of the large leather sofa in the living room. As much as it pained Ty to admit it, they looked pretty good together. Dana's frame was a lot leaner than Karla's, and she fit perfectly in the crux of Karla's arm. Ty couldn't help but imagine what it would feel like to be curled up next to Karla like that.

Keats stifled a yawn. "I'm beat. I'm going to head to bed."

Although she wasn't tired, Ty knew she'd feel uncomfortable being left alone with Dana and Karla. "Ditto," she said.

She reluctantly followed Keats upstairs, leaving Dana and Karla to cuddle on the couch. When she climbed into bed, she replayed the evening in her head. Although she'd made a valiant, albeit not totally successful effort to hide it, she wondered whether it was obvious to Keats and Dana that she was crazy into Karla. She hoped not and vowed to try harder to keep her feelings under wraps.

* * *

There wasn't a cloud in the sky when they set off for the gondola the next morning. Given the conditions, they started off with a few groomers. Ty considered herself an expert skier, and Dana and Keats were both very strong skiers as well, but it was instantly obvious that Karla was in a league of her own. Even on the steep black diamond trails, she floated over the snow like a feather in the wind. It was as if she were exerting no effort at all. Her upper body was completely quiet, and her turns were crisp and concise.

They took run after run throughout the morning, the four of them flying down the mountain in a pack. Ty had a perma-grin on her face. In an effort to impress Karla, she was skiing faster than she typically would, but so what. It was exhilarating to ski with a group of women who could seriously rip it up. Heads turned as they whipped by. At one point, a group of teenage boys tried to chase after them, only to be left in the dust.

On one run, a member of the ski patrol waved them down. "You ladies need to slow it down a bit," he warned.

Ty couldn't contain a giggle. She knew he was right, but it was the first time in her life she'd been stopped by ski patrol for skiing too fast.

After they took a break for lunch, Dana suggested they make their way over to a different part of the resort called the Blue Sky Basin. They all headed in that direction and dropped into a vast patch of trees. When Karla stopped about halfway down, Ty pulled up beside her. Dana and Keats were nowhere in sight.

"Everything okay?" Ty asked.

"Yeah, fine. It's so beautiful in the trees. I'd thought I'd stop and take it all in."

Ty lifted her goggles. Massive, snow-cloaked fir trees and bare Aspens surrounded them. The only sound was of birds chirping. Even though they were at one of the largest ski resorts in the world, it felt like they were in the middle of nowhere.

"It really is beautiful."

Karla reached over a brushed a clump of snow off Ty's jacket. "Did you fall?"

"More like tipped over," Ty replied. "It was that or hit a tree head on."

"Sounds like you made the wise choice."

"Keeping up with you is not for the faint of heart." Ty winked. "I'm risking my life here."

"Ha, ha. You're doing great."

"Thanks."

"Well, we should probably go find Dana and Keats."

"Yeah, probably," Ty replied, "although, it's so peaceful in here."

"I know, but patience is not one of Dana's virtues. I don't want to keep them waiting."

Ty slipped her goggles back on and followed Karla out of the woods.

When they clicked out of their skis at the end of the day, Dana suggested happy hour, and everyone nodded enthusiastically.

"I know the perfect place," Keats said. "Follow me."

She led them to a place on the edge of Vail Village. It was dimly lit, and it took Ty's eyes a moment to adjust when they stepped inside. Once she stopped seeing spots, she scanned her surroundings. The walls were covered with saddles, blankets that looked to be Native American, old wagon wheels, and cheesy cowboy signs, but she liked the vibe of the place. From the looks of it, the crowd was more locals than tourists. The place was filling up quickly with other après skiers, but Keats darted toward the large wooden bar and snagged the last open booth.

After downing two beers in quick succession, Ty felt a mild buzz, and apparently, she wasn't alone. Keats started telling stupid knock-knock jokes, giggling each time she delivered the punchline.

"Knock, knock."

"Who's there?" they all asked.

"King Tut."

"King Tut who?"

"King Tut-key fried chicken!"

They all roared with laughter.

"Oh, my, God, that is so bad," Karla said. "Please, knock it off."

"Groan," Dana said.

"All right, all right," Keats said. She raised her pint. "To a kick-ass day."

"I'll drink to that," Ty said. Today had probably been the best day skiing she'd ever had. The conditions had been fantastic, and she couldn't ask for a more fabulous group of women.

"Same here," Dana said as she slid an arm over Karla's shoulder.

Karla stiffened ever so slightly at the contact.

Throughout the day, Ty had sensed a mild tension between the two. It was subtle, hovering just below the surface. They'd been touchy-feely the night before, but that special intimacy lovers share was gone, and Ty had caught Karla staring off into space more than once over the course of the day. Before she had a chance to give it another thought, Keats let out an incredibly loud belch.

She smirked and covered her mouth. "Whoops, sorry."

"Maybe it's time we got something to eat," Karla suggested.

"I'd kill for a pizza." Keats said.

"Maybe we can get them delivered to the condo," Dana replied. "I could use a hot tub, and there's still a ton of beer in the fridge." She nudged Keats. "Not that this one needs anything more to drink."

Keats didn't seem offended. She pulled out her phone and ordered two large pizzas.

The delivery man was pulling up to the condo when they got home, and once they got inside, the pizza was gone within a matter of minutes.

"Guess we were hungry," Dana stated the obvious.

"Hot tub time," Keats hollered. She scurried up the stairs toward her bedroom but stopped halfway and looked back toward the kitchen. "Be advised. House rule: only naked people are allowed in the hot tub."

Ty was glad she'd had a few beers. The thought of seeing Karla naked made her a little uncomfortable, to put it mildly. In fact, there was a strong possibility she might short circuit. When she got to her room, she peeled off her ski clothes and slipped on the terrycloth robe Keats had pointed out the night before. When she got back downstairs, no one else was around. She grabbed a can of IPA from the fridge and slid open the glass door to the deck. A small floodlight at the far end of the house provided the only light.

The sky was crystal clear, and like the night before, she could see the lights of the snowcats creeping up the mountain in the distance. The temperature had dropped significantly since they'd come in off the slopes. It probably wasn't more than twenty degrees outside and plumes of steam hovered over the hot tub. It was hard to tell for sure, but the pool of water looked to be empty.

Ty tiptoed across the snow-covered deck and hung her robe on a nearby peg. Goosebumps covered her body. She dipped a toe in the water. It was hot. She took the steps into the tub one by one, gradually lowering her body into the water until only her head remained above the surface. The scalding water stung at first, but it soothed her sore muscles. She rested her head against the side of the tub and closed her eyes. At the sound of the glass door sliding open, she opened one eye. Even in the darkness, it was easy to discern that the silhouette in the doorway was Karla.

"Hey, you," Karla said as she stepped out onto the deck.

"Oh, hey," Ty replied.

When Karla tugged at the belt on her robe, Ty held her breath and averted her gaze.

Karla poked her toe in the water and yanked it out. "Ouch, it's hot."

"It just stings for a second," Ty mumbled as she stared intently at the water. This was not fair. She was being tested.

Once Karla was finally submerged, she scooted through the water and sat near Ty on the shelf encircling the pool. Although most of her body was submerged, her full breasts bobbed at the water's surface. If Ty reached out, she could touch them, and she wanted to so badly it hurt. She clung to her beer as if it were a life ring and every muscle in her body tensed.

"Um, where's Dana?" Ty asked.

"She's checking the weather forecast for tomorrow. She'll be out in a minute." Karla leaned her head back and looked toward the sky. "What a beautiful evening."

The diversion was welcome and Ty's heart rate slowed a tiny bit. "It sure is. It feels like you could reach out and touch the stars."

Without taking her eyes off the sky, Karla asked, "Did you have fun today?"

"It would've been pretty hard not to."

The glass door slid open again and Dana poked her head out. "Anyone need a beer?"

Ty held up her can. "I'm good, thanks."

"I'd love some water," Karla replied.

When she reemerged a few moments later, Dana shed her robe and sunk into the pool without testing the water.

The three women sat in silence until Keats bolted out of the house buck naked a few minutes later and took up residence next to Ty in the tub.

"Yo, Dana," Keats said. "What's the scoop on the weather for tomorrow?"

"No snow, I'm afraid," Dana said. "A lot like today. Plenty of sunshine."

"Sun is good," Keats said. "And it means we get to sleep in again."

"A big storm is supposed to blow in Monday night," Dana said. She turned to Karla. "Are you sure you can't stay and ski Tuesday? It promises to be an epic powder day."

Karla shook her head. "I can't. We've got to get back to school for class."

Dana shifted her gaze to Ty. "Can you talk some sense into her?"

Ty fluttered the water with her fingers. "Afraid I've got to side with Karla on this one. I'm sorry, but we really need to get back to Denver."

"I'm sure the world will not stop spinning if you miss class," Dana said.

"You never know, it just might," Ty said, biting back an even snarkier retort.

"Please, Dana. Will you let it rest?" Karla asked, the strain in her voice evident.

Ty looked over at Keats, but she just shrugged and said, "You guys want to hear another knock-knock joke?"

CHAPTER TWENTY-SEVEN

When Ty and Karla were packing up the car Monday afternoon, Dana tried one last time to get them to stay. "They're saying we could get seventeen inches."

Karla dropped her boot bag on the foyer floor with a thud. "Dana, we've been through this."

Keats threw an arm over Ty's shoulder. "Thanks for coming. It was awesome to meet you."

"Thank you so much for having me. I had a great time," Ty said. She gave Dana a quick hug goodbye and scooped Karla's boot bag off the floor. "I'll just go put this in the car."

Ten minutes passed before Karla emerged from the house. She climbed in the driver's seat and started the car. "Sorry about that. Dana can be...very persistent."

Ty waved her hand in the air. "No worries."

The drove in silence until they got on I-70.

"I'm really glad you came along this weekend," Karla said.

"Me too. I had a fantastic time. The skiing was fabulous. Keats is hysterical, and it was nice to meet Dana."

The last part wasn't exactly true. Sure, Ty had been curious to see what Dana was like, but seeing her and Karla together had definitely not been nice. In fact, it had been the opposite of nice. It had sucked. And to make matters worse, Ty's feelings for Karla had only intensified over the weekend. Even with Dana in the picture, it had been wonderful to spend so much time with Karla away from school and studying and all of that. Seeing Karla ski, graceful, yet powerful. Watching her interact with Keats. Their banter, the obvious affection and respect they had for each other, the way Karla gave Keats her full attention when she talked. And then there was Karla's laugh. It was soft, and, well, just generally adorable.

Ty shook her head to try and erase the thoughts coursing through her brain. She glanced over at Karla. Bad idea. She was so beautiful that just looking at her caused Ty's heart to ache. She leaned against the passenger side door and let out a long sigh.

"Everything okay over there?" Karla asked.

Ty felt herself blush. "Yeah, I was just thinking about how great the weekend was."

Karla tapped her fingers on the steering wheel and stared out at the road ahead. After a while, she said, "You may, um, have noticed a little bit of tension between me and Dana."

Ty opted to remain quiet rather than admit she had.

"I probably already told you this," Karla said, "but Dana works for a big consulting firm that does cyber security stuff, and anyway, long story short, I guess they've offered her a three-year expat position in Amsterdam."

"Amsterdam, like the Netherlands?"

"Uh-huh."

"Oh, wow. That's big."

Karla huffed out a laugh. "You can say that again. And apparently, she's already told them she'll go. She broke the news to me on Friday night after you and Keats went to bed."

Ty clenched her teeth like the grimacing emoji. "Yikes."

"Yeah, I was pretty upset. To put it mildly."

"Understandably."

"I was so broadsided by it. We've been together for a little over nine months. Ya think she'd have at least consulted me before she signed on."

Ty wasn't sure what to say. "Nine months is a pretty decent amount of time."

"It's the longest relationship I've ever had. Kind of pathetic, huh?"

Ty was a little surprised. Karla was beautiful and smart and funny. One would presume she'd have women, and men, chasing after her all the time. "It's not pathetic at all. I mean, I know skiing was your whole life, until recently. Gah. Sorry. That didn't come out right."

Karla reached over and lightly touched her arm. "It's okay."

Ty hesitated briefly before asking, "Are you guys going to try to keep doing the long-distance thing?"

Karla shrugged. "I honestly don't know yet. I'm going to go up to Jackson the weekend after next. We're going to talk about it, our relationship, then. With school and everything, I certainly don't plan on joining her overseas." A quick flash of anger and hurt crossed her face. "Not that she asked." The way she said the last part made it seem like she was only realizing now that Dana hadn't asked her to come along.

"Geez, Karla, I'm sorry. That really sucks."

"And to make matters worse," Karla said, "she lied to me."

Ty turned in her seat to face her. "What do you mean?"

"Dana was supposed to come to Denver to visit me a few weeks ago, but she backed out at the last minute. Said she had to go to New York. Turns out she actually flew to Amsterdam to meet with the guy who heads up the office over there."

"Ouch," Ty said. "That makes it even worse."

"I know. I can't stand it when people fucking lie. I gave her shit about it, and she said she did it to protect me. Didn't want to rock the boat until she knew she was going for sure."

"That's total bullshit." Ty reached out and squeezed her hand.

"I know. And when I called her on it, she got all defensive. Talked about what a great opportunity this could be for her."

The slightest glimmer of hope stirred inside Ty. If Dana was out of the picture, then maybe...

The car suddenly felt claustrophobic. Ty loosened the scarf around her neck and shifted in her seat. She knew she was a total shit. Karla was obviously upset, and all Ty could do was daydream about the two of them getting together? It was just that she wanted something with Karla so badly, and now there was the tiniest chance that Karla might soon be available.

CHAPTER TWENTY-EIGHT

At the tail end of January, Ty invited Val and Teresa to spend the weekend with her at the house in Steamboat. Karla was going up to Jackson to have her heart-to-heart with Dana, and Ty was afraid she'd be a total basket case if she sat around in Denver. In her heart, she was hoping Karla and Dana broke up. She tried to tell herself it was because she thought Karla deserved better, which was true, but still, she hated herself for rooting against them. She was being selfish.

A ski weekend with Val and Teresa seemed like the perfect distraction, and although she was loath to admit it, Ty was anxious to see if they freaked out when they saw her house. In her fantasy world, someday she'd invite Karla to Steamboat for the weekend, and Val and Teresa's reaction to her house might be a good gauge for how Karla would respond when she saw it.

She made the drive to Steamboat alone because she'd told Val and Teresa that they could bring their dogs, and if they'd all gone in one car, they would have been packed in like a sausage. While she waited for them, she lit the fireplace and puttered around the house. When she heard their car pull in the driveway a little after dark, she hurried outside to greet them.

Teresa and Val climbed out of their car and surveyed the surroundings. Teresa let out a low whistle. "Nice fuckin' digs, Ty."

"Yeah, no shit," Val added. "This place is kick-ass."

Ty broke a small branch off one of the shrubs near her front door and twirled it between her fingers. "Thanks."

The dogs busted out of the backseat of the car and ran up the steps to sniff her.

Ty gave them each a good scratch behind the ears and asked, "Do you guys need a hand unloading the car?"

"Sure," Val said.

Teresa called the dogs off the front porch. "I'm gonna take these beasts for a pee and then I'll come back and help you."

Val handed Ty a bag of groceries and a 12-pack of Miller Lite, threw two duffel bags over her shoulder, and followed Ty into the house. As soon as they stepped into the foyer, Val came to an abrupt stop and dropped both duffels on the stone floor. "Holy shit, this place is amazing." She nodded toward the front windows. "You're right on the slopes."

Ty set the groceries on the kitchen counter. "I can give you guys a tour before dinner if you want?"

"Yes, please," Teresa said as she came in the front door with the dogs.

"Why don't we start with your bedroom?" Ty gestured down the hallway. "Follow me." Teresa, Val, and the two dogs trotted behind Ty as she led them to the largest of her three guest rooms. From there, she led them upstairs, through her bedroom and into the observatory, deciding to wait until after dinner to unveil the secret door and the spiral staircase. Primarily because she wasn't sure how well the dogs would be able to navigate the winding metal steps, but also because Teresa and Val were already sort of wigging out about her house and she didn't want them to have an aneurysm.

It was a clear night and the stars were beginning to populate the night sky. "Screw skiing," Teresa said. "I want to spend the entire weekend in this room."

Ty laughed. "I promise we can come back up here after dinner." She pointed to the small table in the corner. "Perhaps for a nightcap. My friends Scotty and James might stop by later. They're itching to try the limited-edition bourbon I just bought."

"Can we skip dinner and move right to the nightcap?" Teresa asked.

"Suit yourself," Val said. "I'm starving."

"Good," Ty said, "because I bought three *cowboy*-sized steaks."

"I'll *wo*man the grill," Val said.

After a quick pass through the rest of the house, they returned to the kitchen. Teresa got busy making a salad, Val went outside to fire up the grill, and Ty opened a bottle of wine and set out a platter of cheese and crackers. When dinner was ready, they sat down at the large wooden table in the nook flanking her kitchen.

"Oh Val, these steaks are perfectly cooked," Ty said as she cut into her meat.

Conversation over dinner was boisterous. A wave of joy and gratitude flowed through Ty. She was incredibly fortunate to have made two such great friends in Denver. It was fate. She believed that. Something had drawn her and Sarah to Patty's Place that night when she'd first moved back to Denver. The night she'd first met Val and Teresa.

Val opened a fresh bottle of wine and stood to top off everyone's glasses. "So," she said when she sat back down, "what's the story with you and Karla?"

"What do you mean?" Ty asked. "There's no story."

Val cackled. "Shit, girl. You're blushing."

Ty tossed her napkin at Val. "Am not."

"Are so."

"Whatever," Ty said. "She has a girlfriend, in case you hadn't noticed."

"Nice try," Val replied. "You aren't getting off that easy. There's something there. You two have an aura about you."

Ty almost spit out her wine. "An *aura*, huh?"

"Yes, Ty, an aura."

Ty looked at Teresa. "Help me here."

"I think Val is right. The air is electric when you and Karla are in the same room."

"Seriously," Val said with a laugh. "You're like a lovesick puppy when she's around."

"A lovesick puppy, huh? You two are so full of shit."

"You know we're right." Teresa said.

Ty groaned. "Fine, so I have a little crush on her."

"I'd say it's more than that," Val said.

"Shit. You're right. I'm completely and totally head over heels about her." Ty threw back the rest of her wine. "But it doesn't matter. Nothing will happen between us as long as Dana's in the picture."

"Fair enough," Val said, "but I'd love to see you two get together, *someday*."

"Ain't gonna happen," Ty said.

"Speaking of Dana," Val said. "You met her when you guys were in Vail over MLK weekend, right?"

"Uh-huh."

"What was she like?"

Ty kept her voice as neutral as she could. "She was beautiful and nice."

Val didn't let her get away with such a lame answer. "Oh, spare me. You sound like you're talking about some celebrity you bumped into at the ski lodge, not the person who's dating the woman you've been crushing over for months. I bet she was an overbearing bitch. Based on some of the stuff Karla's said about Dana, she doesn't sound like the sweetest person."

"Okay," Ty said, "Dana's very…confident, and maybe a little cold, but she really was nice."

"There's that word again, nice. It's a word you use when you don't have anything good to say about a person."

"Whatever," Ty said. "She seemed really smart and she's a fantastic skier and Karla seems into her."

Ty omitted the part about Dana's impending move to Amsterdam. She figured that little detail was for Karla to tell.

Not only that, she was eager to move on to another topic. After all, the whole idea of the girls' ski weekend was to keep her mind off of Karla. Unfortunately, she could think of little else.

CHAPTER TWENTY-NINE

Karla usually enjoyed spin class. Not today. She double-checked the tension setting on her bike. It was lower than usual. Why did it feel like she was pedaling through quicksand? According to the clock on the wall, they weren't even halfway through the hour-long class. She used a towel to wipe her brow and tried to clear her mind. It was no use.

She stopped pedaling and slipped off the saddle. The toeclips on her bike shoes clacked on the tile as she made for the back door of the spinning studio. It was probably the first time in her life she'd up and quit something before it was over.

She hurried toward the locker room but stopped when she heard someone call her name. She looked up. It was Ty. She had a purple yoga mat tucked under her arm and her muscles glistened with sweat. Seeing her lifted Karla's spirits.

"Hey, Ty."

Ty gave her a broad smile. "Hi, Karla."

"Looks like you're coming from yoga."

"Mm-hmm. It was awesome."

"I keep saying I'm going try yoga one of these days."

"You should come to class with me sometime. I go every Monday and Wednesday."

"Yeah, maybe."

Ty pointed to her shoes. "And it looks like you're coming from spin class."

"Yep." She didn't want to admit she'd walked out before it was over. She dabbed her brow with her towel again. "How was your weekend in Steamboat?"

Ty's face lit up. "It was fantastic. As usual. Val and Teresa kept me in stiches the whole time." Ty shifted her yoga mat from one arm to the other. "Um, how was Jackson?"

Karla looked the floor. "It was fine." Karla left it at that given they were standing in the middle of the gym.

"You headed to the showers?" Ty asked.

"Um, yeah." They walked toward the women's room together and when they got to Ty's locker, Karla paused. "Want to grab dinner?"

Ty set her yoga mat on the bench. "Sure. I'd love to."

After they'd showered, Ty followed Karla to a small restaurant called Zorba's Café. She'd had dinner there with Val and Teresa a few weeks earlier and loved it. It was in a small white house, and a florescent *Open* sign flickered in the window. Given the hour, the dinner crowd was thinning out. The host seated them at a booth made for two. Karla waited until they'd placed their order to break the news.

She took a deep breath and said, "This probably won't come as a giant surprise, but um, Dana and I broke up while I was in Jackson."

Ty reached over and squeezed her hand. "Oh, Karla, I'm so sorry. Are you okay?"

"For the most part. I'm sad but okay. It's for the best."

"Was the breakup pretty mutual?" Ty asked.

Karla thought back to the conversations she'd had with Dana when they'd decided to split. "Yeah, I'd say it was pretty mutual. We talked briefly about trying to continue our relationship with me being here in Denver and her being in Europe, but it was pretty obvious neither of us was too keen on the idea. If I'm brutally honest, I've known for a little while she wasn't 'the one,' if you know what I mean."

Ty gave her a soft smile. "I do."

"And then there's the fact that she lied to me. I've had a hard time getting past that."

"As you should. There was no excuse for that. Before you can really commit to someone, you need to trust them with your whole heart."

Karla leaned back against the hard foam cushion of the booth and blew out a deep breath. "Still, I'm taking it pretty hard. I was pretty into her. Or at least I thought I was. I thought a lot about it on the drive back to Denver. I think maybe I was more into the idea of Dana than Dana herself. Does that make any sense?"

"I think so."

"She was fun to be around, a little wild, and that was addictive. When we met, I was fresh from the womb of ski racing. Up until that point, my life had been so sheltered." Karla fiddled with her silverware. "I'm sorry, I'm rambling. You probably don't want to hear all this."

Ty's bright blue eyes stared back at her. "I'm happy to listen. After all, that's what friends are for, right?"

"Yeah, I guess. You're a good listener. Thank you. Not a lot of people have that trait." Karla could sit there all night and pour her heart out to Ty. "Anyway, I'm a total moron about relationships and stuff."

Ty laughed and tucked her blond hair behind her ears. "We all are."

"I don't know. I always feel like everyone else has it all figured out."

"Well I can tell you I unequivocally do not." Ty took a sip of her water. "Do you think you and Dana will remain friends?"

Karla laughed. "Aren't all lesbians friends with their exes?"

"Ha. I don't know, but I'm definitely not friends with my ex Rosie."

"I hope Dana and I stay friends. Even though she hurt me, I don't hate her. Her career is important."

"You're a bigger person than I am," Ty said. "I don't know if I'd be that quick to forgive."

"I don't know that I've fully forgiven her, but in time, I think I will. On the bright side, my relationship with her caused me to grow up a little."

The waiter arrived with their Caesar salads.

"Shoot, I forgot to tell them I didn't want anchovies on mine," Karla said. She used her fork to pick the small, slimy fish off her lettuce.

"I'll eat those if you don't want them," Ty offered.

"Really?"

"Yeah, I love anchovies."

"You're weird."

Ty grinned back at her, and Karla knew then that everything was going to be all right.

CHAPTER THIRTY

"See, I told you," Ty said as she rolled up her yoga mat. "I knew you'd love it."

"I have no idea why I waited this long to try it," Karla said. "Who knew a few yoga classes would make me feel like a million bucks?"

In the weeks since Karla had returned from Jackson, she and Ty had become practically inseparable. They'd fallen into an easy friendship, but that's all it was, and Ty wanted more. Wanted to be with Karla all the time. For the moment, though, she was content with what they had, or at least she tried to convince herself she was.

And hanging out with a world-class athlete had some serious benefits. Ty was working out harder and more frequently than she ever had in her entire life. Regular exercise had always been important to her, but Karla pushed her to an entirely different level.

"What do you feel like eating tonight?" Ty asked when they reached the locker room.

"I'm thinking tuna," Karla said. "We can make extra so we have some left over for lunch tomorrow."

Spending time with Karla had also made Ty realize frozen pizzas weren't all they were cracked up to be. What had started out as a weekly thing was now a near nightly occurrence. They'd go back to Ty's house after the gym and make dinner with real food like fresh vegetables and fish. It hadn't taken long for Ty to discover that Karla was an incredible cook. The type of cook who rarely used a recipe. One who just added a dash of this or a dash of that.

Everything Ty's mother made when she was growing up had come out of a box, and up to this point, she'd considered spaghetti noodles and butter to be her signature dish. At first, she'd balked at the idea of preparing elaborate meals after a long day at school, but she soon realized that cooking relaxed her, and it was rewarding to dig her fork into a mouthwatering meal knowing she'd played a role in creating it.

Karla was a patient teacher, and Ty did her best to be a dutiful sous chef.

"So, where'd you learn to cook?" Ty asked while she helped Karla make dinner that night. They were coating the tuna steaks with a soy sauce concoction and then pressing them into a plate covered with sesame seeds.

"My dad," Karla said. "He's a total master in the kitchen. Growing up he did most of the cooking for our family. He never had any formal training—he learned everything from his mother—but he'll try anything in the kitchen. If he has a meal somewhere that he likes, he'll try to recreate it at home, no matter how complicated."

"Wow, really?"

"Yeah. Not every meal turns out as it should. He's almost set the kitchen on fire a few times, but that doesn't deter him. He's not one who gives up easily."

"Must be where you got your determination from?"

Karla laughed. "Maybe, although my mom is a tough cookie too. To be totally honest, she wears the pants in the family, always has." She pointed to a dish on the counter. "I'm gonna step outside and grill the asparagus. Think you can finish the tuna on your own?"

"I'll try."

Karla rested a hand on Ty's lower back. "You're doing a great job. Just remember, be gentle so the sesame seeds don't clump on the tuna."

A warmth radiated through Ty's body at Karla's touch. She ached to wrap her arms around her and pull their bodies together but gripped the counter instead. Karla had become increasingly demonstrative, and Ty lived for the moments when Karla's fingers or leg brushed hers. She was pretty sure it wasn't always an accident. Still, she was afraid to take the first step. What if Karla rebuffed her advances? It might shatter their friendship, a friendship Ty cherished.

Karla picked up the platter of asparagus and headed toward the back door. "I'll show you how to sear the tuna when I come back."

Ty eyed the plate with the two tuna steaks they'd already finished and laughed. It was obvious which one she'd done. It looked like a cupcake a three-year-old had decorated with sprinkles.

Over dinner, Karla asked, "Do you have any plans this coming weekend?"

Ty was thinking about going to Steamboat, but she hadn't made up her mind yet. "No, not really."

"Well, I got a text from Keats earlier today. She was supposed to go to Vail this weekend, but now she can't because of work. And, anyway, she asked if I wanted to use the condo this weekend. I was wondering if maybe you'd want to come with me?"

Ty's heart rate picked up. "To Vail?"

"Yeah. I thought it would be fun, you know, if you and I went up together."

Ty tried to play it cool, but it was futile. A giant grin crept across her face. "Sure. That sounds nice." Major understatement. A whole weekend *alone* with Karla sounded fucking awesome.

Karla's shoulders relaxed. "Great. I can't wait."

"Me either."

Like every other night, after they finished eating and washing the dishes, Karla left to go home. Tonight though, Karla lingered in Ty's foyer. Took her time buttoning her coat, like she had a question but couldn't get up the courage to ask it.

They were standing inches apart.

Ty came so close to kissing her.

* * *

The next morning, Ty ordered a dark roast coffee and joined Val at a small table in the campus bookstore.

"I can't believe you drink that stuff black," Val said. "Doesn't it burn a hole in your stomach."

"Milk would ruin the flavor."

"Suit yourself. I like a little coffee with my milk and sugar." Val laughed at her own joke.

Ty leaned back in her chair, closed her eyes, and held the cup of rich Costa Rican roast to her nose. "Ahhhhh."

"Spare me," Val said. "What time is your first class?"

Ty sat up in her chair and set her coffee on the table. "Not until eleven, but I'm meeting Karla at the gym in an hour."

"You two have been spending an *awful* lot of time together lately."

A grin crept across Ty's face. "So? We like hanging out."

"I'm just making an observation."

"We're just friends."

Val leaned forward and looked Ty in the eye. "When are you going to tell her how you feel about her?"

Ty stared into her coffee. "Not any time soon."

"I'm serious, Ty."

"It's only been a month since she broke up with Dana. And what if she doesn't feel the same way about me?"

Val burst out laughing. "It's so freaking obvious you two are crazy about each other. The way you two look at each other, the casual touches. You'd have to be blind not to see it."

"Whatever," Ty said and tried to be all nonchalant, but she prayed Val was right. She and Karla had grown incredibly close, incredibly quickly. Her attraction to Karla was so intense, it had to be two-sided, didn't it?

"You two dance around each other like you're both…" Val stopped mid-sentence. Ty followed her gaze. Karla was walking in their direction.

"Morning," Karla said.

Val snickered. "Ty and I were just talking about you."

"Oh, really?" Karla asked, her gaze moving to Ty.

The blood rushed from her face. "Uh-huh."

"Did Ty tell you we're going to Vail this weekend?" Karla asked.

Val's eyes grew wide, and she got a little smirk on her face. "Um, no. She didn't share that little detail." Then she gave Ty a wink, and said, "Well, I've got to run," and abruptly scurried off.

Karla took the seat she'd just vacated. "So, what were you guys talking about?"

CHAPTER THIRTY-ONE

The city's schools had just let out for Spring Break, and traffic out of Denver was bumper to bumper. Ty and Karla crawled along I-70 on their way to Vail.

"Is it me, or does the air totally reek of pot?" Ty asked.

"It's not you," Karla replied. She pointed out the passenger window at the long row of old warehouses flanking the highway. "All of those buildings have been converted into marijuana grow houses."

"Are you kidding me?"

"No, I'm totally serious."

"I wonder if you can get high driving by them?"

"Ha, I doubt it, but it would make sitting in traffic more tolerable."

"That it would."

Karla picked a piece of lint off her jeans. "Believe it or not, I've never smoked weed in my life."

"I smoked it a bunch when I first moved to Asheville. It was right after—"

"Your parents died."

"Uh-huh. I didn't even like it that much. I smoked it just to smoke it. I haven't touched it in over two years though." Ty laughed. "Which is ironic. I mean, it's legal in Colorado, but I don't know, it just doesn't appeal to me."

Traffic finally started to ease up as they made the climb toward Loveland Pass, and after a pit stop in Silverthorne to pick up some wine and food for dinner, it was after eight o'clock when Ty pulled the Tesla up in front of Keats's condo. Once they got the car unloaded, Karla said, "Um, why don't you take the master and I'll sleep upstairs."

"Don't be silly. I'm technically the guest." Ty picked up her duffel and started up the stairs. "I'll sleep in the same room I stayed in last time. The bed was super comfortable."

When Ty got back downstairs, Karla was struggling to get the cork out of the bottle of red wine they'd bought in Silverthorne. "Want some help?"

Karla chuckled. "Yes, please. I seem to be corkscrew challenged."

The cork made a pop when Ty extracted it from the bottle. "Ta da."

"How'd you do that so easily?"

"I worked as a bartender in Asheville. Opening a bottle of wine was sort of a job requirement."

"I'd forgotten you worked as a bartender. You hardly ever talk about your life in Asheville."

It was true. Ty made an effort not to talk about it. Her mind flashed back to the last night she'd bartended at Thirsty's. The night she'd won the lottery. How would Karla react if she knew about the size of her bank account? "Oh, shit." The bottle of wine slipped out of her hand. It split into a million pieces when it hit the floor, sending red wine splattering in every direction.

"Shit, I'm sorry."

Karla grabbed a dish cloth off the counter and snapped it at Ty's butt. "Is that another skill you learned bartending?"

"Ha ha. If it had been, I probably would've been out of a job pretty quickly."

"Good thing we bought the cheap stuff. It's not like it was a bottle of Oregon's finest."

Ty pulled a broom out of the laundry room and started to sweep up the glass. "Still, I feel bad."

"Don't." Karla looked up and smiled. "I'm suddenly in the mood for beer."

Once the spill was cleaned up, Ty pulled two beers from the fridge and handed one to Karla. "Want me to make a fire?"

"Yeah, that would be great." Karla pulled the foil off the premade veggie lasagna they'd bought. "I'll pop this in the oven and come join you in a sec."

Ty balled up some newspaper and stuffed it into the metal grate in the fireplace. After carefully arranging a few pieces of firewood, she struck a long wooden match and held it to the paper. The newspaper turned black as small red flames spread through it and ignited one of the logs. Once Ty was satisfied the fire would take, she slid the fireplace's metal grate closed and stood up.

Karla had just settled into the couch. She patted the cushion next to her. "Come sit down and relax."

Ty didn't need to be asked twice. She plunked down on the couch. They sat sipping their beers and staring at the flames. Occasionally, Karla's knee brushed against hers. Ty couldn't tell if it was intentional or not. What she did know was, she should have packed a little extra will power for the weekend. It was going to take phenomenal effort to get through the next two days without touching Karla, kissing Karla…

"Nice fire, Ty," Karla said, snapping her from her thoughts.

Ty shook her head, wishing her brain was like an Etch A Sketch. "Uh, thanks. I have Girl Scouts to thank for that."

"You were a Girl Scout?"

"Of course. Weren't you?"

"No. I never had time for stuff like that. If I wasn't skiing, my dad probably had me running steps at the high school football stadium or something."

"Do you ever regret it? Devoting everything to skiing?"

Karla didn't answer right away. "No," she said quietly. "I don't. I mean, I know I missed out on a lot of stuff, but given the choice, I'd do it all over again. I loved everything about it. Training hard and competing."

"I guess I can understand that."

Karla stared back at the fire. "I'd still be doing it if I could."

"Yeah, I know."

Ty couldn't look Karla in the eye. She got up to stoke the fire. Every time they had a discussion that even touched on the subject of money, Ty clammed up. Part of it was guilt. Guilt that she had so much money when Karla had had to give up her dream because of a lack of it. But mostly, guilt that she hadn't fessed up and told Karla she'd won the lottery. About everything else, Ty was an open book with Karla. They shared all of their thoughts and feelings. Failing to mention Lionball—this major life event for Ty—felt dishonest. But then there was the anxiety. Ty harbored a lot of that. Given Karla's feelings about rich people, if she knew the truth, she might go running for the hills. That possibility was terrifying, enough so that it outweighed the guilt she carried.

When Ty sat back down, Karla changed the subject. "Tell me more about your life in Asheville. You never told me, what motivated you to leave and finally go back to school?"

Ty wanted to melt into the couch. How was she going to answer this one? It was like the walls were closing in around her. Not telling Karla about Lionball was one thing, a lie of omission, but being outright dishonest about what prompted her to leave Asheville would be even worse. Just then the timer sounded in the kitchen.

Ty jumped to her feet. *Saved by the bell.* "I'll go pull the lasagna from the oven."

"Have you checked the weather forecast?" she asked when they sat down to eat. She was eager to keep the conversation away from the topic of Asheville.

"Yeah. It's supposed to be sunny tomorrow, but a storm is headed this way. They're calling for a foot tomorrow, maybe more."

"Wow, really? Sweet."

Karla gave her a high five. "Sounds like we might get ourselves a powder day, baby."

When they were done eating, Ty casually asked, "You up for a dip in the hot tub before we go to bed?"

Karla picked up their plates and carried them into the kitchen. Her lips curled into a smile. "Yeah, that would feel amazing."

As Ty rinsed their plates and put them in the dishwasher, she wondered if Karla remembered the house rule: only naked people in the hot tub. She sure hoped so.

"Okay, I'll meet you back down here in five."

Ty's body hummed as she pulled the terrycloth robe out of the closet in her bedroom. She slipped it on and did a little dance. The prospect of another naked hot tub adventure with Karla had her nerves frayed. Last time she'd been bobbing around in the hot tub with Karla, she'd practically exploded, and this time there was no Dana to keep her impulses in check. Which was a very good thing, but also a very scary thing.

When she got back downstairs, Karla was already submerged in the bubbling water. The lights from the house cast a soft glow over the deck. Ty was pretty sure Karla was naked, but the heavy steam coming off the water made it hard to tell for sure. She slipped off her robe and used her toe to test the temperature of the water. She felt Karla's eyes on her, but when she looked up, Karla's gaze darted toward the ski slopes.

Ty tiptoed down the steps into the water and situated herself at what she thought was a reasonable distance from Karla. She was close enough to confirm her suspicions that Karla was naked, but far enough away that their limbs couldn't accidently touch, because if they did, Ty knew that would push her over the edge. She'd jump Karla right then and there. She was human, after all; she had limits.

Ty rested her head against the back of the tub and closed her eyes. Neither she nor Karla spoke. Ty's skin tingled from the combination of scalding water and a naked Karla sitting inches away. Ty wanted to touch her so badly it hurt. She wondered what was running through Karla's head. Was she thinking the same thing?

Ty got a sudden burst of courage and almost told Karla right then. Told her how she felt about her. She opened her mouth, but no words came out. Her bravery proved fleeting. What if Val was wrong? What if Karla didn't feel the same way? Ty couldn't jeopardize their relationship. Even though it was platonic at this point, it meant the world to her. She'd never felt closer to another human being, and they hadn't even known each other that long.

They sat in the bubbling water for another fifteen minutes or so before Karla broke the silence.

"I'm turning into a prune," she said. "I think I'm going to call it a night."

Ty opened her eyes and sat up in the tub. "Um, okay, see you in the morning. Sleep tight."

"You too, Ty."

Once Karla was safely inside, Ty climb out of the tub, pulled on her robe, and went upstairs to bed.

* * *

When they clicked out of their skis at the end of the next day, Ty was so worn out she could barely hoist them up onto her shoulder. She struggled to keep up with Karla as they walked back to the condo, their ski boots crunching on the gravel path.

"You totally kicked my ass," she grumbled.

Karla peered back over her shoulder and gave Ty a broad smile. Aside from her rosy cheeks, one would never guess she'd skied like a maniac for six solid hours. She didn't look even remotely tired. "Just wait until tomorrow. Powder day, remember?"

"That assumes I'm even able to walk tomorrow." Ty paused to loosen the buckles on her boots, nearly dropping her skis in the process. Karla caught them before they hit the ground. Her skis were perched on her right shoulder and she slung Ty's over her left.

"I can carry my own skis," Ty protested.

"Evidently not."

Ty held out her poles. "Can you carry these too?"

Karla laughed and reached out to grab her poles. "Next you're going to ask me to carry you."

"Well, now that you mention it…"

* * *

After a long, hot shower, Ty felt somewhat human again. "What do you feel like doing for dinner?"

"Are you up for going out?" Karla asked.

"I suppose I could muster the energy?"

"You want to go back to that western bar? The place we went to with Keats and Dana?"

"Not really. I liked it, but what would you think about going to the bar at the Four Seasons? My treat."

Karla started to protest, but Ty cut her off. "Come on. It's the least I can do. You've invited me to Vail twice now and given me a free place to stay."

"Okay, but that's very generous. I'm sure the drinks there are wildly overpriced."

"I'm sure they are, but you let me worry about that."

When they walked into the bar at the Four Seasons Hotel, a couple clad in fashion-over-function ski clothes was just vacating a loveseat in front of the massive stone fireplace in the middle of the room.

Ty hurried over. "Are you guys leaving?"

The woman gave Ty a forced smile, exposing perfectly white teeth. "Yes. It's all yours."

"Super, thanks. Have a nice evening."

The couple didn't respond. They were too busy admiring themselves in the mirrors behind the bar.

Seconds after Karla and Ty sat down, a waiter appeared out of nowhere. They each ordered the local IPA on tap, and he handed them a menu with bar snacks.

Once he was gone, Ty scanned the menu. She was glad she'd offered to treat. Hummus and pita was the cheapest thing on the menu and it was twenty-two dollars.

"How hungry are you?" she asked.

"On a scale of one to ten," Karla said, "where one is 'I just finished eating Thanksgiving dinner' and ten is 'I could eat a wild boar,' I'm a 9.8."

When the waiter returned with their pints, Ty ordered an Angus burger medium rare for them to share and a handful of appetizers. She looked up at the waiter. "Do you think that's enough?"

The waiter gave Ty and Karla a quick up and down. "Are you expecting anyone else? Like maybe an NFL linebacker?"

"We're hungry," Karla said.

"Very well," he said. "Would you like me to bring out things one at time or all together?"

"One at a time, please," Ty said. "The burger last."

They'd polished off their beers by the time the waiter returned with their first appetizer, something the menu described as baked artisan mozzarella, but was basically good old-fashioned cheese sticks. Leave it to the Four Seasons to come up with a more pretentious name, presumably so they could charge an arm and a leg for it.

"Another round?" The waiter asked.

Ty looked at Karla and she nodded. "Yes, please."

By the time they finished the last appetizer, tuna tartare with crispy wonton chips, they were both stuffed, and they still had the burger coming.

Ty waved down the waiter. "Apparently our eyes were a little bigger than our stomachs. Is it too late to cancel the burger?"

An annoyed look crossed his face, but he said, "No problem." He eyed their empty beer glasses. "Can I get you ladies anything else to drink?"

Ty turned to Karla. "Are you okay switching to wine?"

"Sure."

Ty pointed to a Sancerre on the menu. "We'll take a bottle of that, please." She snapped the wine list shut before Karla got a glimpse of the price.

By the end of the night, they were both more than a little tipsy. When they stepped outside, big plumy flakes floated through the air and landed in their hair. Ty ran around in the newly fallen snow and tried to catch a few of them with her tongue.

Karla grabbed a handful of snow off the ground and tossed it in the air. "Guess the forecasters were right. It's totally dumping."

Ty came up to her side. "Tomorrow's gonna to be epic." She bumped Karla with her hip. "Promise you won't leave me in the dust?"

Karla squeezed her gloved hand. "I promise."

When they were about halfway back to the condo, they came to a wooden footbridge spanning a small stream. Ice had formed along its banks, but water still gurgled down its middle.

Karla stopped and leaned over the railing. "I love the way the flakes disappear as soon as they hit the water."

Ty joined her at the railing.

When Karla looked up from the stream, her large brown eyes sparkled. She waved her hands in the air. "The snow, it's so beautiful."

Ty brushed the snow from Karla's hair. "So are you."

Karla held her gaze. "I, um, what—"

"I said, you're beautiful."

Karla didn't respond in words. Instead, she leaned forward and placed a gentle kiss on Ty's lips. When Karla began to pull back, Ty slipped a hand behind her neck and deepened the kiss. Karla didn't resist. Just the opposite. She kissed Ty eagerly. When they finally broke apart, Ty cupped Karla's cheeks with her gloved hands and held their faces inches apart.

"I've wanted to do that for a *really* long time," she whispered.

A smile lit up Karla's face. "Me too."

"Be careful, boys," a shrill voice warned seconds before Ty heard small feet scamper across the wooden bridge. She looked down at the two towheaded youngsters who had joined them at the railing. They were cute kids, but their timing sucked.

Karla stepped away from Ty. "We should probably head back to the condo."

Ty was too stunned to move. She ran a gloved finger over her lips, aching to feel Karla's lips against hers again. "Yeah, okay."

Karla waded through the now shin-deep snow on the path, and Ty ran to catch up with her. When they stepped inside the condo, Karla pulled off her coat, wandered into the kitchen, and pulled a glass out of the cupboard.

"I need water. Want some?"

"Yes, please."

After Karla threw back two glasses of water, she walked toward the master bedroom. "I'm beat." She didn't look back at Ty. "I'm going to bed. Goodnight."

Ty stuffed her hands in her pockets. "Can we at least talk about what just happened?"

"Not now. I need to go to sleep."

Ty watched her walk into her room and close the door. "Goodnight," she whispered.

CHAPTER THIRTY-TWO

The alarm on Karla's phone blared at six the next morning. Without opening her eyes, she stabbed the snooze button. Her head hurt, and she just wanted to sleep. She pulled a pillow over her head and rolled into the middle of the king-sized bed. When the alarm went off again nine minutes later, she sat up and opened one eye. All she saw was white. She opened the other eye. Snow swirled outside her window. Now she remembered. It was a powder morning.

She swung her feet onto the floor and staggered across the thick, wall-to-wall carpet to the bathroom. When she flipped on the light, the reflection she saw in the mirror was not pretty. Dark bags accented her bloodshot eyes. She massaged her temples with her index fingers. Why did her head hurt so much?

It took a minute for her brain to kick into gear. Right. Four Seasons. Beer. Wine. The previous night came rushing back. Ty. They'd kissed. She pressed the palms of her hands against the cold stone vanity top and rocked back and forth.

Karla replayed the scene on the bridge, and how'd she'd gone straight to bed when they'd gotten home. Kissing Ty was something she'd ached to do for so long. So why had she panicked after it happened? Was it because, if she hadn't gone straight to sleep, she knew they would have fallen in bed together?

She turned on the faucet and splashed cold water on her face. After dabbing her cheeks dry with a towel, she stared into the mirror. Why was she such an idiot when it came to relationships? She'd fallen so hard for Dana so quickly. It was only after they'd broken up that she'd realized her feelings for Dana hadn't run as deep as she'd thought. If Dana hadn't moved across the Atlantic, would they still be together?

Maybe she was meant to be with Ty. Things with her were so different. They were easy, comfortable. She and Ty were friends, but it was already more than that. They hadn't even known each other all that long, but they shared a bond unlike any Karla had ever had with another person. So what the hell was her problem?

She knew one thing. She and Ty needed to talk. Even though Karla didn't fully understand why she'd acted the way she had after they'd kissed, she owed Ty an apology. Some sort of explanation for the way she'd reacted.

After she got dressed, she went upstairs and knocked on Ty's bedroom door. "You up?" she whispered.

A groggy voice responded. "Yeah. I'll be out in a minute."

Karla went down to the kitchen, started the coffeepot, and checked the snow report.

"Morning," Ty said as she descended the steps dressed in ski clothes.

Karla handed her a mug of coffee. "We got fifteen inches overnight."

"Sweet."

"You want anything to eat before we head out?"

Ty grabbed a banana off the counter. "This will work."

Ten minutes later, they were on the lift up the mountain.

Karla stopped halfway down their third run. She stood at the side of the trail, right along the tree line, and looked up at the sky. It was still snowing lightly, but it looked like the sun was trying to break through.

When Ty stopped next to her, Karla lifted her goggles and blurted, "I'm sorry I ran off to bed last night."

Ty slid around on her skis so she was facing Karla and pulled her goggles up onto her helmet. "It was late, and I know you were tired."

"It was more than that," Karla said. She placed a hand on Ty's arm. "I freaked out a little after we kissed."

"It's okay," Ty said quietly. "Maybe it was a mistake. I don't want it to mess things up between us."

"I don't think it was a mistake." Karla pulled off her glove and ran a finger over Ty's cheek. "I wanted it to happen. I meant what I said last night. I've been dying to kiss you for a while now."

"But then why—"

"I don't know. But I can tell you this, I want something with you. Something more than friendship."

A smile overtook Ty's face. "Really?"

"Uh-huh."

Ty looked her in the eye. "I do too."

"You just have to be a little bit patient with me. I'm still a complete idiot when it comes to relationships."

"We can take it slow."

"That would be good. I've been thinking about it, and that might be partly why I ran off last night. If I hadn't, we'd have ended up sleeping together."

"Possibly."

"I don't want to start something that way. Not with you. This relationship is too important to me."

"It's important to me too," Ty said and leaned forward to place a soft kiss on her lips.

"For the record," Karla said. "Kissing you last night. It was amazing."

Ty gave her a wink, slipped on her goggles, and took off into the powder. "Last one down is a rotten egg," she yelled over her shoulder.

Karla slipped her goggles back in place and took off after her, a smile firmly planted on her face. She was on cloud nine as she bounced down the steep slope through thigh-deep powder. She wished they didn't have to drive back to Denver that afternoon. She wanted Ty to herself for a little bit longer. Tucked away in Vail, away from the hustle and bustle of school and life in Denver.

As soon as they got in the car to head home, it was evident Ty was in no shape to drive. She could barely keep her eyes open. Powder skiing was notoriously difficult, and they'd spent all morning on the mountain.

"I'm happy to drive," Karla offered.

Ty didn't argue. She pulled the car over and they switched drivers. It took Ty all of three minutes to fall asleep.

Karla smiled over at her as she drove back down Loveland Pass. She was beautiful. Her long blond hair poked out of her ski hat, and her cheek was nestled in the palm of her hand. Her delicate eyelids hid her warm blue eyes, but Karla could envision them. Envision what it was like to stare into them. Long, shallow breaths flowed in and out of the small gap between Ty's lips. Lips that Karla had felt on her own. Her core fluttered as she thought back to the kiss they'd shared on the bridge the night before.

Ty's eyes fluttered open. "Hey."

"Hey. Nice nap?"

"Yeah, sorry. I was so sleepy."

"Nothing to apologize for."

Ty sat up and rubbed her eyes. "Did I snore?"

"Only a little."

Ty rummaged around in her backpack and pulled out her water bottle. She took a long swig and held it toward Karla. "Want some?"

"No thanks." Karla twisted the knob to clean the windshield. Although the plows had done a pretty good job clearing the road, the pavement was still covered in a thick brown slush. They would probably go through half a bottle of washer fluid before they got home.

Once the windshield was clean, she glanced back over at Ty. "So I was wondering. Would you have dinner with me tomorrow night?"

Ty beamed. "I'd love to."

The way Ty's face lit up made Karla smile. "Okay, it's a date."

"A real live date?"

"Yep." Karla reached over and placed a hand on Ty's thigh.

"Hey," Ty said with a smile. "Both hands on the wheel. Ten and two."

"I'm sorry. It's just, you're a bit of a distraction."

CHAPTER THIRTY-THREE

Ty pulled on her new cashmere sweater. It had a low scoop neck and it was midnight blue. She was mildly horrified by how much she'd spent on it. It had been an impulse buy. She'd rushed over to the Cherry Creek Shopping Center between classes that afternoon, desperate to find something sexy to wear for her date with Karla.

Her doorbell rang. She took one last look in the mirror and bounded downstairs to open the door. Karla was standing on her doorstep. Ty didn't think she'd ever seen her look so beautiful. Her long, dark, wavy hair hung loosely over her shoulders, and the light makeup she'd applied made her big brown eyes pop. Most notably, she was wearing a dress. It hugged her breasts and left much of her strong legs exposed. The temperature had reached sixty degrees in Denver that day and Karla wasn't wearing a coat.

Karla leaned in and grazed Ty's cheek with her lips. "Hello," she whispered before pulling back. "You look amazing." She stroked Ty's arm. "I love the color of this. Is it new?"

Ty chuckled. "This old thing. I've had it forever."

"Oh, really," Karla said. "Then what's this?" She tugged on a little white tag sticking out of the back of the sweater.

Ty whipped around. "Oh my God. I'll be right back."

Karla called after her, "I can cut it off for you."

"That's okay, I've got it." Ty snatched a pair of scissors out of the drawer in her kitchen and reached back to snip off the tag. She prayed Karla hadn't seen the price. It served her right for having spent so much money on something as frivolous as a sweater. Crap, it was like Reed was speaking in her ear. She tossed the scissors back in the drawer and tried to regroup. She wanted this night to be perfect.

When she walked back toward the front door, Karla was looking at one of the photos Ty had brought from her house in Steamboat to hang in the foyer to make the place feel less like a rental.

"Is this you as a kid?" Karla asked.

The photo she was looking at was of Ty when she was six or seven. She and her brother were standing proudly in front of a massive sandcastle. "Uh-huh."

"Ooooh, you're adorable. I love the pink and green flowered bikini."

Ty nudged her in the arm. "Bite me."

Karla turned to face her. "Ready to go?" She spun Ty in a semicircle. "Just need to make sure we got all the tags."

"Very funny. Okay, okay. Totally busted. I bought a new sweater for our date," Ty admitted as she locked the front door behind them.

"I'm flattered."

"So where are you taking me?" Ty asked once they were in the car.

"This place in the Platt Park neighborhood. Supposedly, it's one of the best sushi and Japanese restaurants in the city...I hope you like sushi. I guess I should have asked."

"I love sushi," Ty said. "Well, to be honest, I've only had it once."

"I had sushi a few times in Japan—when I was there on the ski circuit—and I thought it was delicious so I'm excited to try this place. One of my classmates told me about it. Her sister works there, and she totally scored and got us a table. Apparently, the place books up weeks in advance."

Ty was touched. "I can't believe you were able to pull this all together in such a short amount of time."

Karla gave her a crooked smile. "I wanted to get this night right."

Ty just nodded. Her heart pounded in her chest, and her cheeks ached from smiling pretty much nonstop since Karla had asked her out.

After she expertly parallel parked the car, Karla ran around and opened the door for Ty. She clasped Ty's hand in her own as they walked to the restaurant, their arms swinging in unison between them.

"I'm a little sore today," Karla admitted as they walked. "We skied pretty hard yesterday."

"God, me too," Ty said, "but I've got to say, I can't believe you, athlete extraordinaire, are sore. I thought you were bionic."

"Aren't you the funny one. Powder days spare no one."

The restaurant was totally packed, but Karla and Ty were led to a table right away. It was tucked in the corner and offered a view of the sushi masters performing their craft.

"Your classmate totally hooked you up," Ty said. "I can't believe how busy this place is, on a Monday night no less. It must be fantastic."

Karla gave her a wink. "I hope so. I want to make a good impression on our first date."

A slip of white paper sat in the middle of the table and the waiter explained they needed to check off the items they wanted to order. Ty stared blankly at the long list of options. They had funny names like sashimi, suzuki, and ebi.

"Would you like some help ordering?" Karla asked.

Ty looked up at her. "Yes, please. The last sushi I had was good, but…a little slimy."

Karla explained the difference between nigiri and sashimi and pointed out some of the 'safer' options like salmon, shrimp, and tuna. "But you know what," she said. "You might be better off ordering one of the rolls." She pointed to a section on the paper menu. "The fish is wound up in the rice."

Ty scanned the options. "Oh, I'm going to try the spicy tuna roll."

When the waiter appeared, Karla ordered a bottle of wine and handed him the slip of paper with their selections checked off.

Once their wine had been poured, Karla picked up her glass. "Cheers, Ty."

Ty raised her glass. "Cheers."

Karla got a shy look on her face. "It's nice to be here with you."

Ty's voice cracked as she said, "It's nice to be here with you too."

Karla took a sip of wine and set down her glass. She reached across the table and squeezed Ty's hand. "I hope this is the start of something special."

Ty looked into her eyes. "Me too."

The noise of the restaurant fell away. Karla and Ty got lost in their own little world. They giggled at each other's jokes and gazed into each other's eyes. Ty felt weightless. It was possible she was floating above her chair. They'd officially stepped into the honeymoon stage.

The waiter startled Ty back into the world around them when he returned with their sushi. It was quickly apparent that Karla's chopstick skills far exceeded Ty's. After Ty dropped one of her tuna rolls for the third time, she gave up and picked it up with her fingers.

Karla laughed. "Need some help there?"

Ty nodded. Karla showed her how to hold the chopsticks, but it was no use. The next roll she tried to eat fell to her plate just as she was about to capture it with her mouth.

Karla snared a piece of shrimp off Ty's plate and dangled in front of her mouth. "We can't have you going home hungry," she said as she fed it to Ty.

After they finished dessert, Karla took both Ty's hands in her own. She intertwined their fingers and caressed Ty's hand with her thumb. Her delicate touch made Ty tremble.

When the waiter returned with their bill, Ty reached for her wallet.

Karla snatched the bill. "I've got this. I asked you out, remember?"

Although Ty hadn't seen the bill, it had to be high. It was a nice restaurant, and sushi was expensive. It would put a big dent in Karla's tight budget.

"Can we at least split it?"

"No," Karla said as she handed the waiter her credit card. "Thank you. It was delicious."

They held hands as they walked back to the car and whenever they stopped at a light on the way home. When they got to Ty's house, Karla put her car in park and shifted in her seat to face Ty. The front porch light cast a soft glow over the car. Karla reached up and trailed her fingers over Ty's hairline.

Ty turned to kiss her hand before leaning forward to find her lips. After a few soft kisses, Ty clenched Karla's shirt and pulled them closer together. They shared a long, deep kiss that left Ty breathless. She fell back against her seat.

"Jesus."

Karla let out a heavy sigh and gave her a knowing smile. "Yeah, I know."

After she caught her breath, Ty said, "This taking it slow thing is going to be excruciating."

Karla reached for her hand. "I know, but I really want to try."

"Okay," Ty replied and gave up any thought of inviting her inside.

* * *

Ty stood at edge of the food court while she waited for her lunch to be ready. Invariably, her mind drifted to Karla. To their date. To the kisses they'd shared. They'd officially been together a grand total of three days, and she was already whipped.

"Yo, Ty." The voice was unmistakable. Val was walking toward Ty, waving her arms like a crazy woman.

Ty gave her a hug and asked, "What's up, stranger?"

"Not much. It's been a crazy week. How are you?"

"Not too bad. Not too bad at all."

"You looked like you were a million miles away."

Ty furrowed her brow. "Huh?"

"Just now," Val said. "You were staring off into space, and you had this dreamy look on your face."

"You're a poet, and you didn't even know it."

"Ha, ha." Val nodded down at the orange plastic tray she was carrying. "Care to join me for lunch?"

"Sure. My food should be up in a second."

As if on cue, the bell on the counter at Thai Phoon rang. Ty's chicken satay and steamed dumplings were ready.

"You're coming Saturday night, right?" Val asked as soon as they sat down. She was throwing a birthday party for Teresa at their house.

"Yep. I've got a study group that afternoon so I might be a little late, but I wouldn't miss it for the world. What can I bring?"

"The usual, booze, if you don't mind," Val said. "Oh, and I just saw Karla. Sounds like she'll be there too."

Heat crawled up Ty's neck at the mention of Karla's name. "Yeah, she mentioned she was going."

Val gave her a wicked grin. "Speaking of Karla, how was your little *getaway* to Vail?"

"It was not a *getaway*." She couldn't keep the smile off her face. "We had a…nice time."

"From the look of it, you had more than a nice time."

"What is that supposed to mean?"

"That dreamy look is back with a vengeance." Val set down her sandwich. "Wait, what are you not telling me?"

"What are you talking about?"

"Something happened in Vail, didn't it?"

Ty blushed. "We just maybe might have kissed."

Val let out a long whistle. "Well, it's about damn time."

"And that's not all. We went out on a real live date Monday night." Ty took a swig from her water bottle. "But, we're, um, taking it slow."

Val let out a loud chuckle. "Uh-huh. Let me know how that goes, okay?"

CHAPTER THIRTY-FOUR

The party at Teresa and Val's was is in full swing by the time Ty arrived on Saturday night. Teresa was holding court in the kitchen. Telling some crazy story about her twenty-first birthday that had everyone in stiches. Without missing a beat, she opened the fridge, pulled out a Sierra Nevada Pale Ale, popped the top, and handed it to Ty.

"Thank you," Ty mouthed.

When Teresa finished her story, she gave Ty a hug. "Hey, girl. Glad you could make it."

"Me too. Sorry, I'm a little later than I'd hoped. Happy birthday, by the way."

"Thanks. God, I cannot believe I'm forty-five."

"You don't look a day over thirty, Teresa."

"Aren't you the charmer? Oh, and on that note," Teresa gave her a double wink, "Karla's here."

Apparently, word traveled fast. And what was it with Teresa and Val and the winking? A couple walked up to say their goodbyes and Ty politely excused herself to go in search of Karla.

The family room off the kitchen was packed with more than a dozen women and a few men. Ty recognized a handful of people, but just waved hello. She was on a mission. When she spotted Karla in the back of the room, Ty got all tingly inside. Karla was chatting with their friend Dipti.

"Hey, you," Ty said. She leaned in and gave Karla a hug and then turned to say hello to Dipti.

After a few minutes, Dipti excused herself. "My boyfriend just arrived."

Once she and Karla were alone, Ty touched her lightly on the arm. "Hey you."

Karla's soft brown eyes met hers. "Hey."

Ty ached to kiss her. She brushed her lips against Karla's cheek and whispered, "I've missed you."

Karla nuzzled her neck. "I missed you too."

Ty pulled back and slipped her hand into Karla's. "How long have you been here?"

"About an hour."

"I'd hoped to get here earlier," Ty said, "but my study group went late."

"Well, I'm happy you're here now."

Ty looked back into Karla's eyes. She detected a sadness that wasn't normally there. "You okay?"

Karla shrugged. "Yeah. Well, no, not really. It's no big deal. It's just…"

"What is it?"

"I got a call today from my old teammate, Lucy Jane. We've known each other since we were kids, and she and I were on the D team together." Karla's voice cracked. "My dad never liked her. He thought she was a poor sport. She'd ski off the course if she missed a gate, stuff like that. But she was always nice to me."

"Is she still on the D team?" Ty asked.

"She just got called up to the B team."

"Oh, wow. That's big?"

"Uh-huh. I'm not jealous, but I can't help but wonder, what if, you know?"

Ty nodded. "Yeah, you wonder if you could have made the team. I mean, if you'd been able to keep at it for another year."

Karla gave her a pained look and nodded. "Don't get me wrong, Lucy Jane's an amazing skier and she deserves to be on the team. It's just, I used to be able to beat her. The real difference between us is, she came from money."

"Oh, Karla. I'm so sorry."

"It's okay. I try not to dwell on it, but getting the call from her today, it was like a kick in the stomach."

Ty rested her hand on the small of Karla's back and rubbed gently. "I'm here to listen if you want to talk more about it."

She gave Ty a weak smile. "Thanks, Ty. Maybe later. I don't want to be Debbie Downer at Teresa's birthday party." Karla's posture straightened. "What do you say we get some food? There's a major spread in the dining room. You've got to try the salmon cucumber boats. They're delicious."

"I'm up for that," Ty replied. "I'm so hungry I think I could eat my hand."

They loaded up their plates and perched on the edge of the stone fireplace in the family room. When they were done eating, Ty set her plate aside and rested her hand on Karla's knee.

Karla slid her arm over Ty's shoulders and asked, "So, what else do you have going on this weekend?"

"Studying, what else?" Ty said. "Oh, but I'm having dinner with my best friend Sarah tomorrow night. She's coming to Denver for some work thing. I haven't seen her in forever."

"Ooh, aren't you two cute," Val crowed as she walked up.

Ty expected Karla to pull her arm away, but she didn't flinch.

"Quite a party you've got going on here, Val," Ty said.

"It sure is," Karla said with a laugh. "I saw a few women doing tequila shots earlier."

Val rolled her eyes. "I should have known better than to bring out the hard stuff." She pointed toward a petite young woman passed out in a chair near the kitchen. "I'm afraid one of our classmates had a bit too much to drink."

"Uh-oh," Karla said. "I'd be happy to give her a lift home if you want. She certainly doesn't look like she's in any shape to drive."

"Are you sure?" Val asked. "That would be a huge help. If you don't mind?"

"Don't mind at all. I should head out anyway," Karla said. "I've got to get up early tomorrow. Hoping to get in a run before I hit the books."

When Val walked over to see if she could rouse the petite woman, Karla turned to Ty. "Sorry we didn't get more time together tonight. Any chance you'd join me for a run in the morning?"

Ty gave her a thumbs up. "Sure, I'd love to. What time?"

"Say, nine a.m.? Maybe I could come by your place and we could do a couple of laps in City Park?"

"Why don't you bring a change of clothes? You can shower at my place and we can study together for a little bit before you head to school."

"Hmmm, good plan. I'm meeting some people to work on a group project, but not until later in the day."

They hugged goodbye. "See you in the morning," Ty said.

She watched Karla and Val help the overserved woman out of the chair. No question, Karla was a saint for offering to drive her home.

* * *

Ty groaned when her alarm blasted her out of a deep sleep at eight the next morning. Her bed was warm, and she had no interest in getting out of it anytime soon. But then she remembered. Karla. Running. She rubbed her eyes and kicked off her heavy down comforter.

After she brushed her teeth and got dressed, she went downstairs to make coffee. She ripped open a banana and nibbled on it while she watched the rich dark liquid fill the coffeepot. Coffee in hand, she nestled into an overstuffed chair in the family room.

It suddenly dawned on her that the house was a total disaster area. She didn't have much time. Karla would be arriving any minute. She set down her coffee and made a mad dash through the house, picking up magazines, dirty dishes, take-away containers, and various articles of clothing that were strewn about. In general, she was a fairly neat person, but she'd been so busy lately, and although she'd meant to hire a housekeeper, she hadn't gotten around to it. It was funny in a way. All her life she'd dreamed of being able to afford a cleaning woman, and here she was with all the money in the world, yet she still didn't have one. It struck her as odd she hadn't made it a priority.

As she was plumping the cushions on the couch, the doorbell rang. She ran to open the front door.

Karla was on her front stoop bouncing from foot to foot and vigorously rubbing her hands together. Black running tights covered her strong legs, and she had a bright blue running jacket zipped all the way to her chin. A dark brown ponytail poked out the back of her knit cap.

"Brrrr, it's chilly out there," Karla said when she stepped inside.

"Are we nuts to run when it's this cold?" Ty asked.

"Nah, I've run in weather much colder than this. It'll be invigorating."

"Invigorating, my ass." Ty reached into her front hall closet to grab a fleece vest to wear over her windbreaker.

Karla shrugged off the small duffel bag on her shoulder and dropped it to the floor near the staircase. "I brought a change of clothes, like you suggested."

"Oh, good." Ty zipped up her fleece and pulled a thin wool cap over her head. "Ready?"

Karla nodded, and they headed out the door. Given how cold it was, they ran, rather than walked, the few blocks to the park.

"How far do you want to go?" Ty asked.

"Are you up for five?"

"I think so. As long as you don't run too fast. Otherwise, I'm going to stop and make you do pushups."

"Oh, aren't you the funny one so early in the morning," Karla said with a laugh.

By the time they finished the first lap of the park, Ty was already sweating. She shed her fleece vest and hung it on a nearby tree. When Karla's watch chirped to indicate they'd hit five miles, Ty stopped in her tracks. When she bent forward to catch her breath, Karla rubbed her back.

"You okay there?"

"Yeah, I think I'll live," Ty said as she stood back up. She let out a laugh when she looked at Karla. Her cheeks were barely flushed. "How is it," Ty said, "we run five miles and I'm a slobbering, sweaty mess, but you look like you just took your dog for a stroll around the block?"

Karla smirked. "You're not really slobbering. I'd classify it more as panting."

"Bite me, Rehn." Ty pulled her vest down from the tree. "You hungry?"

"Starving."

"There's this deli on the way home. They have awesome breakfast burritos."

"Sold."

When they got back home, Ty poured two cups of coffee and handed one to Karla. "You ready to hit the shower? I don't know about you, but I'm starting to get that post-run chill."

Karla nodded and carried her coffee into the front hall to get her duffel. Ty led her upstairs and paused at the door to the guest room bath.

"There are fresh towels under the sink."

"Super, thanks," Karla said. "I won't be long."

"No rush. I'm going to jump in the shower too." Ty blushed. "The one in my room."

This elicited a raised eyebrow from Karla.

Ty's groin pulsed at the thought of lathering up Karla's breasts, but Karla said she wanted to take it slow, and Ty needed to respect that. She turned on her heel and fled before she changed her mind.

When Ty got back downstairs after showering, Karla was hovered over her computer in the family room. She had on glasses and she looked all studious.

Ty plopped down on the leather chair across from her. "Looks like you've already cracked the books." She laughed. "My dad always used to say that. Doesn't really make a lot of sense anymore, huh? Given that everything's on the computer."

Karla looked up at her and smiled. "I knew what you meant."

Ty pulled her laptop out of her bag and fired it up. For the next few hours, they sat together and studied. Occasionally, Ty peeked over the top her screen and snuck a glance at Karla. Her brow was furrowed, and she nibbled on her bottom lip as she read. There was a pen tucked behind her right ear and every once in a while, she'd pull it out and scribble a note on the legal pad next to her.

Karla looked up from her computer and caught Ty watching her. She smiled softly and went back to work. The simple expression made Ty feel all warm inside. It also served to ruin her concentration.

"You up for a break?" she asked. "I could use a little snack?"

Karla shut her laptop and stretched in her chair. "Sure, a break would be good."

Ty's cupboards were pretty bare, but she did have a good supply of her favorite snack. Pretzel sticks and cream cheese. Armed with the bag of pretzels and a small tub of cream cheese, she walked back into the family room and set the food down. Karla eyed her with a raised eyebrow when she jabbed a few pretzel sticks into the cream cheese.

"What in God's name are you eating?"

"Pretzels and cream cheese. It's an East Coast thing. You wouldn't understand."

Karla gave her a skeptical look.

"What? It's good."

Karla reached for the bag of pretzels. "I'll try anything once." She dipped a handful of the small salty sticks into the cream cheese and nodded approvingly after she popped them into her mouth.

"Pretty good, eh?"

"Hmmm, not bad."

Ty laughed when Karla went in for a second round. She took a swig from her water bottle and asked, "Do you want to come to Steamboat with me next weekend?"

Karla's eyes went wide, but she didn't respond right away.

"No problem if you can't. I mean, I totally understand if you've got other plans or whatever."

Karla shook her head and said, "I don't, and I'd love to come."

"Sweet," Ty replied. She barely managed to refrain from pumping her hand into the air.

"Val said your place there is amazing. I can't wait to see it."

"Um, yeah, about my house…" Ty's jubilation morphed to panic. The moment Karla saw the house, it would become extremely evident she had gobs of money. She knew that if she and Karla continued down the path they were on, she'd eventually have to come clean, but she wasn't ready to, not yet. The last thing she wanted was to scare Karla off before their relationship even got off the ground. Ty swallowed hard. "The house, it actually belongs to my brother. I'm kinda like a caretaker since he lives so far away."

She regretted the words as soon as they were out of her mouth, but she was too chickenshit to take them back.

"Oh," Karla said. "Lucky you."

Ty didn't feel so lucky right at that moment. She couldn't look Karla in the eye. She reached for another handful of pretzels, but her phone vibrated before she made it to the cream cheese. It was a text from Sarah.

Hey girl. Just landed. Can't wait to see you.

Ty set down her phone and picked at a loose thread on her chair. "That's my friend Sarah. I think I mentioned last night she was coming to town."

"Yeah, you did. That's great. Are you excited to see her?"

"Big time."

Karla looked at her watch. "Shoot, I didn't realize how late it was. I should probably get up to campus." She gathered up her stuff and stuffed it in her bag.

"Thanks for keeping me company today," Ty said as they walked to the front door.

Karla reached over and tucked a loose strand of hair behind Ty's ear. "It was my pleasure, even though you serve weird snacks."

"It's not weird."

"Is so." Karla slipped a hand around Ty's waist and placed a few soft kisses on her lips. She pulled back slightly, then leaned in for one more kiss before reaching for the door and stepping outside. She looked back over her shoulder. "Bye, Ty."

Ty waved goodbye, closed the door, and leaned her forehead against it. She pinched her eyes shut. The woman of her dreams had just walked out the door. And she'd just told her a big fat lie.

CHAPTER THIRTY-FIVE

Sarah was sitting in the lobby of her hotel when Ty walked in.

She jumped to her feet and pulled Ty into a tight hug. "It's soooo good to see you."

Ty faked a cough. "You're crushing me."

Sarah released Ty from her arms. "Smartass."

Ty kissed her on the cheek. "It's good to see you too."

Sarah took a step back and gave Ty a once over. "You look great. Apparently, Colorado suits you." She tugged at Ty's sweater. "Nice threads. Never thought I'd see you sporting designer clothes." She pulled back the collar of Ty's sweater. "Oooh, Burberry. *Fawncy*."

Ty was wearing the cashmere sweater she'd bought before her date with Karla. "Um, thanks. It's new."

"No shit. You never owned anything half that nice when you lived in Asheville."

"It's like one of the very few things I've bought for myself, you know, since—"

"Since you became obscenely rich?"

Ty's eyes darted around the lobby. "Shhh."

"Your paranoia hasn't dissipated, huh?"

"No, not that much." Ty shifted gears. "So, where do you want to go for dinner?" Knowing Sarah, she'd probably already researched all the restaurants within a five-mile radius of the hotel.

"The concierge suggested a tapas place a few blocks from here."

"Yum, that sounds perfect."

The restaurant had a horseshoe-shaped light wood bar and exposed brick walls with houseplants sprouting out of them. They took a seat at the bar and ordered an array of small plates to share and a bottle of Rioja wine.

After the waiter poured their wine, Sarah raised her glass. "To good friends."

"To good friends." Ty took a sip and asked, "How's the new job?"

"It's going really well. I'm up for a promotion. If I get it, I'll start traveling more internationally."

Ty brought her glass up for another toast. "Go you."

"What about you?" Sarah asked. "How are things with *the skier*?"

Ever since Ty had met Karla, she'd been blathering to Sarah about her.

"Karla." Ty grinned when she spoke her name. "She's good. We're going to go up to Steamboat together next weekend."

"You really like her, huh?"

Ty nodded slowly. "Yeah, I do. It's different with her. And we got to be pretty close friends before, you know, we got together."

Sarah patted her hand. "My sweet Ty."

Ty took another sip of wine and peered at her friend over the rim of her glass.

"I will *never* fall in love again," Sarah teased, mimicking the words Ty had spoken in the dark days after Rosie dumped her.

Ty rolled her eyes. "I know, I know." She punched Sarah playfully in the arm.

Sarah feigned injury. "Ow."

"Whatever. You were right, you know?"

"About what?"

"I was so vulnerable when I met Rosie. I got so caught up in her because I was desperate. Desperate for a place to throw my anchor after my parents died and Reed moved to Vietnam. Rosie was strong, and she made me feel safe. She said all the right things, even if she didn't mean them, but I didn't know that then. She was so charismatic and charming. I guess I got sucked in."

Sarah squeezed her hand but didn't say anything.

"God, when she dumped me for that totally hot PhD student, I literally thought I was going to die. You tried to tell me that one day the sun would shine in my world again, but I didn't believe you." Ty chuckled. "You know what's funny?"

"What?"

"Since I moved back here, I've barely thought about Rosie at all. Looking back, I think I was more infatuated with her than *in love* with her. And there were some red flags. I just chose to ignore them. Sometimes, she could be extremely possessive and controlling."

"If you want to know the truth, I never really liked her."

The waiter set down a plate of mini stuffed peppers. Ty grabbed one and slipped it into her mouth.

"Why didn't you say something?" she asked when he was gone.

"I don't know. You were so into her and you seemed happy."

"I thought I was, but now, being with Karla, it's so much better."

"How so?" Sarah asked.

"For one, I can't imagine Karla ever being controlling or manipulative. I don't think it's in her nature. She listens to me when I talk, and she seems to really care about what I have to say. She's incredibly driven—she never would have made the US Ski Team if she wasn't—but she's gentle and kind, too. I don't know. Being with her is just easy."

Sarah twisted her glass and watched the wine swirl around in it. "Have you told Karla about Lionball?"

Ty nudged one of the olives on her plate with her finger. "No, not yet. She sort of has an aversion to rich people."

"What do you mean?"

Ty explained about why Karla had had to walk away from skiing. "And the town where she grew up is super expensive because out-of-towners have driven up the cost of living."

"And you're worried about how she'll react when she finds out about you?"

"Uh-huh. And, well, it's still early days for us. We aren't exactly at the point of sharing credit scores and bank account balances."

"Fair enough, but that's still a pretty big piece of information to keep from her. Plus, she's got to at least have a clue."

"What's that supposed to mean?"

"Well, your clothes for one." Sarah reached up and wound a strand of Ty's hair around her finger. "And it looks like you got your hair cut and highlighted at a high-end salon, and—"

"You only notice those things because you knew me before I won the lottery."

"Maybe, but you said Karla grew up around rich people. I'm sure she knows an expensive sweater when she sees one."

"It's possible."

"What about your car? A lot of other college students driving around in brand-new Teslas?"

"A few."

"Bullshit. Okay then, what about your house in Steamboat? From the pictures you've sent, it looks amazing. And I know what you paid for it. Karla will definitely know you're loaded when she sees it."

"Yeah, about that." Ty went back to playing finger hockey with her olives. "I might've fibbed a little. I told Karla the house belonged to Reed."

Sarah's wineglass hit the bar with a thud. Her eyes bore into Ty. "Please tell me you're kidding?"

Ty shook her head and looked down at her hands.

"Oh, Ty. That's not good, not good at all."

"I know. I'm a fucking idiot."

"It's just not like you. Shit, we've been friends since elementary school, and I can't think of a single time you've told a lie."

Ty mumbled into her glass. "Until now."

"You are one of the most honest people I know, Ty. It's one of the things I love most about you."

Ty felt the blood rush to her face. She wanted to lash out at Sarah. "It was only a little lie. She probably won't even remember."

Sarah set her napkin on the bar. "Look at me, Ty."

Ty slowly lifted her head to meet Sarah's gaze.

"There's nothing little about it. And that's no way to start a relationship with someone."

She knew Sarah was right. "I panicked and the words just slipped out. I'm petrified she'll lose all respect for me if she finds out I'm stinking rich."

"I'd be a hell of a lot more worried that she'll lose respect for you when she finds out you outright lied to her. You need to fix it."

Ty wanted to crawl under the bar and hide. "I'll come clean to her soon. I promise."

CHAPTER THIRTY-SIX

Late the next afternoon, Ty spotted Karla outside the coffee shop on campus. As usual, Ty's heart rate picked up at the sight of her, but today, clammy hands were another side effect. After dinner with Sarah, she'd been determined to set things straight with Karla. Tell her the truth about her house. Now, seeing Karla, her resolve weakened. There was no telling how she'd react when she found out Ty was a lie-telling multimillionaire. She took a deep breath and marched forward.

Before she closed the gap between them, her cell phone rang. Ty glanced at the caller ID. It was Reed. It had been a while since they'd talked and she should pick up, but she was afraid that if she didn't talk to Karla now, she'd lose her nerve.

She stuffed the phone back in her pocket and smiled up at Karla, "Hey."

"Hey." Karla leaned forward and brushed her lips against Ty's cheek.

A quiver shot through Ty's body and her cheek burned where Karla had touched her. But her delight was instantly replaced by trepidation. What if, after she spilled the beans, she never got to feel those lips against her skin again. She twirled her hair.

"Um, do you have a sec? I was hoping we could talk."

"Everything okay, Ty? You seem so serious."

"Yeah, yeah, everything's fine. I've just got something on my mind."

Karla nodded toward an empty table inside the coffee shop. "Let me grab a cup of coffee and we can sit there."

"Sure, okay."

"Can I get you anything?"

"A skinny latte would be great, thanks. I'll go grab the table." While Ty waited for Karla, she pulled out her phone to text her brother, but a text came in from him before she finished typing.

Aunt Paisley died this morning. Call me.

Karla sat down across from her and slid the latte across the table. "So, what is it you wanted to talk about?"

Ty looked up from her phone. "I'm sorry, I need a second. I have to call my brother." She got up and walked outside.

Reed picked up on the second ring. "I assume you got my message about Aunt Paisley?"

"Yes, oh my God, what happened?"

"Fluke accident. She went to go get cigarettes during a severe thunderstorm, and apparently, a tree fell on her car."

Aunt Paisley had been a chain smoker for most of her adult life. Nothing came between her and her *smokey treats*, as she liked to call them. Ty hadn't seen her aunt more than once or twice since her parents died, but evidently not much had changed. Against doctor's orders, she was still lighting up.

"Shit. Have you talked Garth?" Ty asked.

"Yeah, he called me. That's how I found out she'd died. I guess he tried to call you first but got a wrong number."

Ty felt a pang of guilt. "Oh, he probably doesn't have a current number for me." She didn't have to spell it out for Reed. He knew Garth had sniffed around after the Lionball drawing. Garth may be family, but her brother didn't trust the guy either.

"Anyway," Reed said, "even though she wasn't exactly the epitome of health, her death was a bit sudden. They haven't made arrangements yet, but Garth said they'd probably have a service at the small church in town this Friday."

Ty knew the church well. It was in her hometown, and her family had been faithful members of its flock for years. "Are you going to go?"

Reed didn't respond right away. "I wish we could, but it's a long way to travel…"

"I understand," Ty said. Right now, she wished she lived in Vietnam too. It was the perfect excuse not to attend. "Gosh, I'll feel bad if I don't go. We weren't all that close, but she *was* Mom's sister."

"I wouldn't begrudge you if you didn't go," Reed said. "You know I've never trusted Garth. He's out for no one but himself. I doubt even his own mother's funeral would trump his ulterior motives."

"I know. I'm just torn. We have such a small family."

"Why don't you call Garth and see if you can find out more about the services? See what kind of vibe you get from him."

They hung up, and Ty called Garth. It meant he'd have her new number, but the poor guy had just lost his mother. It was a time for compassion, not cynicism. However, about two minutes into the call, she changed her tune. Garth seemed more concerned about where Ty was than about his dearly departed mother. Cynicism won out. Decision made. She wasn't going to the funeral. She didn't want to risk it.

When Ty got off the phone with Garth, she called Reed back. He fully supported her decision not to attend her aunt's funeral. A card and flowers would have to suffice, and once the family specified where donations could be made in Aunt Paisley's memory, Ty would make a generous contribution.

By the time she walked back into the coffee shop, Ty's resolve to tell Karla the truth had all but evaporated, but it didn't matter anyway. Karla was no longer sitting alone. Cyndi and Dipti had joined her at the table.

Karla was in mid-sentence, but she paused and looked up at Ty. "Everything okay?"

Ty forced a smile. "Yeah. Just some stuff with my family. I'll give you the scoop later."

"I'm afraid your latte is cold by now."

"That's okay. I need to get some caffeine in me." Ty sat down. "Sorry, I didn't mean to interrupt."

Karla waved her hand. "That's okay. I was telling these guys about my stupid car. It was making this weird noise, so I took it into the shop. The mechanic just called, and I guess there's something seriously wrong with my brakes."

"Oh, that sucks," Ty said. "Did he tell you how much it would cost to fix?"

"He wasn't sure, but he gave me an estimate of seventeen hundred bucks."

Ty let out a low whistle. "Shit."

"I know."

"Do you trust the guy?" Dipti asked. "Maybe he's trying to rip you off."

Karla shrugged. "He seemed honest enough, and Val recommended him. I just don't know where I'm going to come up with that kind of money, but I don't have time to worry about it right now. I've got to get to class."

After Karla left, Ty got an idea. She excused herself and walked back outside to call Val. She wanted to find out the name of the shop where Karla had taken her car.

"It's called Zeek's Autobody," Val said. "Why? You having car troubles too? Zeek's old school. Not sure he'd know what to do with a Tesla."

"I just want to ask him a question. Hey, and do me a favor. Don't tell Karla I asked you the name of the shop, okay?"

"Um, okay."

Ty's next phone call was to Zeek. She gave him her credit card number and told him, no matter how much the repair was, to charge Karla a hundred bucks and put the balance on her card. She made it clear that under no circumstances should Zeek share the details of this arrangement with Karla.

If Zeek was surprised by the request, he didn't say so. He probably didn't give a crap who covered the bill as long as he got paid.

Ty whistled as she pulled out of her parking spot on campus. Covering Karla's car repair made her feel a teeny tiny bit better about the lie she'd told the day before. On her way home, she made a quick pit stop at the stationery store to buy a condolence card for Garth.

When she got home, she wrote what she thought was a heartfelt message and addressed the envelope to Garth but opted to omit her return address. Garth having her new phone number made her nervous enough. She certainly didn't want him to know where she lived.

* * *

Karla bounded up to her at the gym the following evening. "Hey, Ty."

"You seem to be in good spirits."

"I am. Remember that car repair I told you about yesterday?"

"Of course."

"Well, I got all stressed out for nothing. It only ended up costing me a hundred bucks."

"Wow, that's great."

"I know. I guess once Zeek took a closer look, the problem wasn't as bad as he first thought."

It felt wonderful. To know that the broad smile on Karla's face was a result of something Ty had done. She'd made Karla happy. Not only that, she'd removed a big stress—having to come up with $1,700 she didn't have—from Karla's life.

Ty smiled back at her. "Lucky you. In the history of car repairs, I don't think a mechanic has ever uttered those words: 'it was less than I estimated.'"

Karla laughed. "I know, right? I owe Val big time for suggesting the shop."

"I'd say."

Karla nodded toward the locker room. "We should probably head in and change. Otherwise, we'll be late meeting Val and Teresa for dinner."

Ty followed Karla into the women's locker room and set her gym bag and yoga mat on the carpet-covered bench that ran between the row of lockers.

"Oh, shoot," she said when she unzipped her duffel.

"What's wrong," Karla asked.

Ty pulled the condolence card out of her bag and held it up for Karla to see. "It's for my cousin Garth. I forgot to mail it today."

"I can take it if you want. I've got to go to the post office tomorrow to mail my dad's birthday gift."

"That would be great, thanks. It's bad enough I'm not going to my aunt's funeral. I'd look like a real jerk if I didn't at least mail a card."

CHAPTER THIRTY-SEVEN

After their morning class on Friday, Ty and Karla climbed in the Tesla and headed for Steamboat. Usually Ty stayed on I-70 until she got to Silverthorne, but she was bored of going that way. Instead, she decided to take the "scenic" route and hopped off I-70 much earlier. Highway 40 took them past Winter Park and through the metropolis of Kremmling. It took a bit longer, but it was a beautiful sunny day, and they would still get to Steamboat well before dinner time.

"I haven't been to Steamboat in a few weeks," Ty said as they descended Rabbit Ears Pass, "so any food in the fridge is probably way past its due date. A trip to the grocery store on our way up to my, uh, the house would probably be well advised."

"Sounds like a plan," Karla said. "I want to cook you dinner one night. Is there a grill at the house?"

"Yep, there's one out on the front deck. It's got all these fancy dials. Maybe you can figure out what they all do."

"Hmm, okay. I need to decide what to make." Karla furrowed her brow and twisted her lips into a pucker as she thought. "Is the kitchen pretty well stocked? I mean, is there a whisk, a grater, a sauté pan, stuff like that?"

Ty nodded. Karla was seriously going to shit when she saw her kitchen. Reed's kitchen, she reminded herself. The previous owner must have liked to cook. He'd left behind a full set of All-Clad pots and pans and every cooking gadget imaginable. Since she'd bought the place, they'd gone woefully underutilized.

Thirty minutes later, they were roaming the aisles of the grocery store. Ty leaned over the cart and nudged it along as Karla tossed items in. Coffee and stuff for breakfast, premade steak and veggie kebabs for dinner that night, and all the ingredients Karla needed for dinner the following evening. After a sweep through the cheese department, they went to check out.

Karla whipped out her credit card, but Ty insisted she put it away, saying, "You're my guest for the weekend."

Karla pointed to the liquor store adjacent to the grocery store as they were wheeling their overloaded cart out to the car. "What about wine and beer?"

"All set in that department. There's plenty at the house."

A gasp escaped Karla's mouth when they pulled into Ty's driveway. "Holy shit, Ty. Is this your brother's house?"

Ty swallowed hard and cringed slightly. She was such a chickenshit. "Yep."

"This place is incredible. Val told me it was nice, but still, I envisioned a sweet condo or something. I certainly didn't expect something quite this grand. I know how much these slope-side homes cost. Your brother sure is generous to let you use the place."

Ty unlocked the front door and ushered Karla inside. The interior lights clicked on.

Karla's eyes roamed the foyer. "Your brother has great taste in art."

When they stepped into the kitchen, Karla said, "Ha. Yeah, I think this kitchen will do." She set her bags on the island and ran her hand over the concrete countertops. "Wow."

Ty nibbled on her bottom lip. "Want to see your room?" They'd only shared a few kisses, and as much as she wanted Karla in her bed, she didn't want to assume anything. She'd just have to wait and see where the weekend led.

"Okay, sure."

Ty couldn't read her expression. Was she relieved or disappointed by the prospect of having her own room?

"I could get used to this view," Karla said when they entered the largest of the house's three guest rooms, the one with windows overlooking the slopes.

As they toured the rest of the house, Karla peppered her with questions. Each time Ty answered her, she was digging herself deeper and deeper into a hole. A hole she was starting to think she may never climb out of. Once or twice, the truth was right on the tip of her tongue, but she couldn't muster the courage to push the words out.

"Want a beer?" she asked when they returned to the kitchen.

"Sure, thanks." Karla took a swig of her beer and looked around. "So where's this grill you were talking about?"

Ty pointed outside. While Karla inspected the grill, she set the kabobs they'd bought out on a platter and carried it out to the deck.

There wasn't a cloud in the sky and the temperature was dropping quickly.

Karla crossed her arms and vigorously rubbed them with her hands. "It'll take the grill a bit to warm up. I think I'm going to go in and grab a jacket."

Ty followed her inside and pulled a parka out of the closet near the front door. She held it up for Karla. "Here, you can wear this."

Karla eyed the jacket. "Is that your brother's?"

"No, it's my friend Scotty's. He lent it…" Ty caught herself. If her brother owned the house, one would assume he'd have his own ski clothes. "Um, I mean, yes, it's Reed's but he won't mind if you wear it."

Karla slipped on the jacket and ran her hand over the outside. "Sweet threads. Your brother must be a real fashion plate."

Ty cringed. Her lie was taking on a life of itself. "How about we get those kabobs on the grill?"

After dinner, Karla asked, "Have you seen the weather forecast for the weekend?"

"I checked it earlier. It's supposed to be sunny tomorrow, but we might get dumped on tomorrow night."

"Wow, it would be kick-ass to get another powder day."

"It sure would," Ty said. She reached for the bottle of wine. "Another splash?"

Karla held up her glass and nodded.

Ty topped off both their glasses. "Do you want to see something really cool?"

She'd intentionally left the observatory off their earlier tour of the house. She wanted Karla to see it for the first time when it was dark outside.

Karla picked her glass up off the counter. "Sure."

"Follow me." Ty reached for her hand and led her over to the right side of the fireplace, stopped in front of the silver button, and pressed it with great fanfare.

"No way! How cool is that?" Karla said when the wall slid open to reveal the passage to the spiral staircase. "It's so James Bond-y."

In the absence of sunlight from the skylight above, the passageway was dark save for the LED lights embedded in the steps of the staircase. They wound their way up the stairs, and when they reached the landing, Ty pressed the second silver button to reveal the observatory. The soft accents lights illuminating the bookshelves didn't give off much light, but it was perfect that way. It meant they could see the incredible night sky.

With her neck craned toward the stars, Karla said, "Holy fucking shit. It's so beautiful." She lowered her head and looked at Ty. Gesticulating with her hands she said, "I realize I've dropped the f-bomb like twenty times since I stepped foot in the house, but I can't help it. It's so unbelievable."

Ty nodded but didn't reply. She pushed away the guilt and tried to take solace in the fact that she'd come by her wealth from sheer luck, not by growing up rich and having a trust fund. Even though she had a massive bank account, she was just like Karla. Her family had also had to scrape by when she was growing up.

She looked out the windows. The trees were heavy with snow, and although the light from the nearly full moon made it a bit harder to see the stars, it made the snow-covered slopes sparkle.

"They should open the resort for night skiing when there's a full moon," Ty said with a chuckle.

"Ha, I know, right? It's amazing how bright it is."

Ty set her wineglass down on the small wooden coffee table. It, and the accompanying loveseat, were one of the few purchases she'd made since buying the house. It had meant removing one of the leather chairs, but it was totally the right call. The room had become her little nest.

"You want to look through the telescope?"

Karla set her wineglass down next to Ty's on the table. "Nah, I like soaking in the whole vast sky."

Ty stood beside her and snaked an arm around her waist. They stood in silence for a few minutes, enjoying the breathtaking view. Eventually, Karla turned and rested her arms on Ty's shoulders, bringing their lips inches apart. Ty looked into her beautiful dark eyes and leaned forward to place a tender kiss on her lips. After a few gentle kisses, Karla paused and smiled against Ty's lips.

"Being with you…" she kissed Ty softly, "…makes me really happy."

A burst of heat flared in Ty's chest. "Is that a fact? Well, it just so happens that being with you makes me really happy too."

She gripped Karla's waist and kissed her deeply. Their bodies melted into one another as the kiss grew more passionate. It provoked a carnal lust in Ty that was so strong, her body trembled as the heat between her legs spread through her body.

When they came up for air, Karla whispered, "I want you, Ty." After another hungry kiss, she tugged Ty's sweater over her head and tossed it aside.

A groan escaped Ty's lips as Karla traced long fingers over the silk of her bra, causing her nipples to press against the fabric. Karla gave her a knowing smile and reached back to release Ty's bra. "So beautiful," Karla said as she ran her fingers over the newly exposed skin. She captured one breast in her mouth, sucking it gently and circling it with her tongue before moving to the other one.

Karla gently pushed Ty down on the couch and straddled her. She bent forward and resumed teasing Ty's nipples with her mouth. Ty squirmed beneath her and the throbbing between her legs reached a boiling point. In two frantic movements, Karla shed her sweater and bra. When she leaned forward again, her large breasts hovered just inches from Ty's.

Ty needed to touch them. She cupped them with her hands, sighing at the feel of the warm, soft skin. Karla arched back, inviting Ty to stroke her.

One of Karla's hands fumbled with the buttons on Ty's jeans and when the last button popped free, Ty lifted up and pushed them down, allowing Karla to slide a hand between her legs.

"Oh, so wet," Karla moaned.

Using her tongue and fingers, Ty teased Karla's breasts while Karla gently rubbed her throbbing clit. Strong fingers slipped inside her, exploring tentatively at first, but gradually pushing deeper and harder. It didn't take long. Ty cried out as she came hard against Karla's hand.

Karla stared into Ty's eyes as she eased her hand out and traced Ty's thigh with moist fingers.

Ty kissed her softly on the lips before shifting to move above her. "How is it that you're still wearing pants?"

She made quick work of the buttons on Karla's pants and tugged them down over her hips. Karla shimmied out of her jeans and kicked them off.

Ty ran a finger around the band of Karla's silk underwear before trickling fingers over the wet spot between her legs. She grazed Karla's breasts with her own and dipped inside her panties. Karla's stomach tensed at Ty's touch.

"I want to taste you," Ty said, her voice hoarse with lust.

Without a word, Karla shimmied out of her panties and guided Ty down toward her swollen clit. With each swipe of her tongue, Karla cried out, "Yes, yes…" She gripped Ty's hair and held her head firmly in place until her hips bucked up. When she collapsed back onto the couch, Ty crawled up next to her and nestled her head against Karla's chest.

Warm arms snaked around her and Karla kissed her softly on the lips. "Mmmm, that felt good."

Ty nodded in agreement and pulled their bodies closer together. Satiated and laying in Karla's arms, joy burst through her. She closed her eyes and felt them moisten. For a brief second, she considered telling Karla. Telling her that she loved her. There was no doubt in her mind that it was true, but it was too soon. That, and…She still hadn't come clean about the house. She vowed to tell the truth soon—very soon.

CHAPTER THIRTY-EIGHT

The sun woke Karla early the next morning. At some point during the night, she and Ty had migrated from the couch in the observatory to the master bedroom. A naked Ty was sprawled across the bed. Her hand was curled into a fist and tucked under her cheek like a small pillow. She took deep breaths in and sputtered the air back out through a small gap between her lips. It was like a dainty snore. Her long eyelashes fluttered slightly, and she rolled over onto her back.

Karla scooted next to her and ran a finger down her arm. "Morning," she whispered.

Ty's eyes remained closed, but she greeted Karla with a smile. "Morning."

Karla peppered Ty's shoulder and neck with feather-light kisses. When Ty's eyes opened, she held Karla's gaze before kissing her tenderly on the lips. The tender kisses became more urgent, and Karla's body reacted immediately. She reached for Ty's hand and brought it between her legs. As Ty stroked her, she slipped her finger into Ty's folds, and within minutes they both cried out. Karla pulled Ty tight against her and dozed off again.

When she woke next, Ty was still sleeping soundly. Karla crawled out of bed and crept down to the guest room, smiling when she eyed the perfectly made bed in the middle of the room. She hoped it would look the same way the next morning, too—unslept in. She rummaged through her duffel and dug out ski socks, fleece pants, and a long-sleeved thermal top.

Once she was dressed, she went into the kitchen to make coffee. She stretched like a cat as the coffeepot churned to life, slowly filling the kitchen with the aroma of the Costa Rican roast. Her body felt looser than it had in ages. No doubt thanks to yoga, but the release she'd experienced under Ty's touch probably also had something to do with it. She and Dana had had sex, a lot of it. They'd been like wild animals in the bedroom. It hadn't been like that with Ty. The sex had been amazing, but it had been more…She struggled to come up with the right word. Sensual, maybe. The sex felt like it had a purpose, one beyond the need to please each other.

When the coffeepot chirped, it snapped Karla from her thoughts. She pulled two mugs from the cupboard, filled them, and carried them back upstairs. Ty hadn't moved.

"Time to get up, sleepy head," Karla said softly as she sat on the edge of the bed.

Ty stirred and looked up at her. "Hey."

Karla looked into her beautiful blue eyes. "Hey." She held up the two steaming mugs. "I brought you some coffee."

Ty propped herself up on a pillow and accepted one of the mugs. "Thanks."

Karla nodded toward the windows. "It looks like it's going to be beautiful day."

Ty leaned forward to peek around her. "Mm-hmm. Sure does. I can't wait to get out there. I love skiing with you."

Karla placed a hand on her leg. "And I love skiing with you. You're an incredible skier. You're not afraid of anything." She pulled back the sheets. "Come on. Feet on floor. Time to rock 'n' roll."

Ty kissed her forehead. "Okay, give me sec to get ready. I'll be right down."

After they each polished off a giant bowl of oatmeal, they strapped on their skis and scooted down the hill in Ty's front yard to the slopes. Given that it was a fairly warm day, they headed straight to the top of the mountain. As she flew down the slope, Karla hummed to herself. She was insanely happy. The fresh air, the crisp snow, and having Ty chase her down the mountain. It didn't get any better than this. The sky was bluer, and the sun was brighter. Each time they rode the chairlift, they snuggled together. Even when there were other people on the lift with them, Karla didn't hesitate to throw her arm over Ty's shoulders.

They managed to get in ten runs before breaking for lunch and a cold beer at one of the lodges on the mountain. Although the sun had begun to sink toward the horizon, it was still fairly warm. They sat in two of the colorful Adirondack chairs scattered in the snow on the back side of the lodge.

When they were done eating, Karla reached for Ty's hand, rested her head on the back of the chair, and closed her eyes. The warm sun felt wonderful on her skin and she was about to nod off to sleep when Ty squeezed her hand and said, "We'd better get going."

Karla's eyes fluttered open and she squinted at her surroundings. Ty was right. Few people were left lounging around them, and the lifts would close soon. They ambled over to the nearly empty ski rack. Karla shivered as she clicked into her skis. By now, the sun hung low in the sky and the temperature had dropped significantly. She tugged at the zipper of her coat, pulling it tight around her neck before she took off down the mountain.

By the time they got back to Ty's brother's house, their teeth were chattering. She looked at Ty and they both said "hot tub" in unison. Within a minute, they'd stripped out of their ski clothes and were immersed in the steaming water.

Ty wiggled herself behind Karla and snaked her arms around her torso. Karla let out a long, contented sigh and rested her head back on Ty's shoulder. They sat there and let the water do its magic, warming their bodies and soothing their muscles. After a while, Ty loosened her grip and kneaded Karla's neck and shoulders.

"Are you thinking what I'm thinking?" Karla asked.

"I think so," Ty replied. "Bed, now."

They ran naked through the house and up the stairs. Karla pulled back the plump down comforter and they tumbled onto the cool, dry sheets. Their lips came together, and their hands roamed each other's bodies. Karla let out a loud cry when she came and collapsed on top of Ty.

Ty rolled them over so she was on top. She placed a light kiss on Karla's lips and said, "How come I can't seem to get enough of you?"

Karla replied with a kiss and wrapped her arms around Ty. They stayed like that for a long time and Karla wondered if Ty had fallen asleep.

"You awake?" she asked quietly.

"Hmm-mmm. Just content."

"You hungry?"

"For you, yes."

Karla kissed her on the nose. "I meant for dinner, silly."

Ty rolled off of her. "Yeah, I guess I could eat."

Karla swung her feet to floor. "I'm gonna jump in the shower before I start that dinner I promised you. Want to join me?"

"Is the Pope Catholic?"

Once they'd showered and dressed, they wandered down to the kitchen. Karla dug through the fridge and assembled all the ingredients for dinner—steak and veggie fajitas—on the counter.

"What can I do to help?" Ty asked.

Karla pointed to the pile of peppers and onions. "It would be great if you could cut those into thin slices." Karla opened the fridge again and opened and closed the various compartments. "Hmmm, that's weird. I could have sworn we bought flour tortillas, but I don't see them anywhere."

"The cashier at the grocery store was a bit of a flake. Maybe they never made it into the bags. Can we get by without them?"

Karla shook her head. "They're kind of a vital component to the meal." She looked at her watch. "It's still pretty early. I'm gonna run down to City Market real quick."

"Want me to come with you?"

"Nah, why don't you stay here and get started on the chopping?"

"Okay." Ty pointed toward the foyer. "The keys to the Tesla are in a bowl near the front door."

"You sure you don't mind me driving it?"

"Not at all."

Karla grabbed her backpack, bound down the front steps of the house, and slid behind the wheel of Ty's car. *Shit, this is a nice ride*. Once she figured out how to get the thing started, she zoomed off to the store.

"That'll be three dollars and eighty-nine cents," the same flaky cashier said when she reached the checkout.

Karla reached into the outside pocket of her backpack to get her wallet, but it wasn't there. That was odd. She always left it in the same spot. She set her backpack on the conveyer belt and rummaged through it, eliciting an eye roll from the woman behind her.

"Ah, phew," she said when she felt her wallet at the bottom of the bag. "Ah, darn it," she mumbled when her hand touched the sympathy card for Ty's cousin. The one she'd told Ty she'd mail earlier in the week.

When she left the store, Karla spotted a row of blue mailboxes across the strip mall from the grocery store. She steered the Tesla in that direction and slipped the card through the slot of one of them. She felt like a shit for forgetting to mail the card, but only a few days had passed, so hopefully no harm was done.

CHAPTER THIRTY-NINE

The next morning, Ty snapped awake when Karla leapt out of bed. The weather forecasters had been right. They'd gotten dumped on overnight.

"Powder day!" Karla squealed. "Hurry, let's get out there."

Ty scrambled out of bed. Half asleep, she tugged on her ski clothes, and twenty minutes later they were out the door.

As the saying goes, the early bird gets the worm. They caught one of the first gondolas up the mountain and each nibbled on a protein bar during the thirteen-minute ride to mid-mountain. The gondola swept them into the offload station and swung as it slowed. As soon as the doors to their little capsule slid open, Ty and Karla were off in a dash.

It had stopped snowing and the sun was now out. Ty shielded her eyes when they stepped out into the morning air. According to a chalk board propped up against a nearby ski rack, fifteen inches had fallen overnight. A snowcat had cleared the area near the gondola, leaving corduroy-like lines in its wake. The snow crunched under their boots as they maneuvered away from the gondola station. They dropped their skis on the fresh snow and clipped in. Seconds later, they were off, both impatient to dip their skis into untouched powder.

"Fresh tracks, baby," Karla yelled over her shoulder. And like that, she was out of sight. She disappeared over the lip of one of their favorite runs. Ty pushed hard off her poles and dropped in behind her, sinking into the fresh snow. Within an instant, powder sprayed up in her face and she grinned like a kid as her skis bounced through the snow.

After half a dozen runs on the marked trails, Karla said, "What do you say we head into the trees? Bet we can still find a few pockets of untouched powder."

Ty clinked her poles together. "Lead the way."

And once again Karla was off, like she'd been shot from a cannon.

Steamboat was known for its 'Champagne' powder—light and fluffy—and although the snow was thigh deep, it was weightless against their legs. They sailed through the trees like they were in a wide-open meadow rather than a dense forest. About halfway down the run, Karla paused under a bare Aspen tree.

"Don't tell me you're stopping to catch your breath," Ty said with a laugh when she rounded a tree and stopped next to her.

Karla waved a gloved hand in the air and tilted her head upward. "Just stopping to soak it all in."

Ty looked up. A bright blue sky served as the background to long, thin branches coated with airy, glistening snow.

Karla used her ski pole to draw a line in a nearby patch of untouched snow. "And the skiing. Wow. I haven't had a day like this in I don't know how long."

"These are the days you live for," Ty said. She touched Karla's arm with her gloved hand. "And it's even better because I get to share it with you." Those words didn't even come close to expressing how Ty felt. There was so much emotion coursing through her, she was giddy.

Karla pulled off one of her gloves and ran a finger over Ty's lips. "I feel the same way, Ty."

Ty turned in her hand and kissed her palm. The moment was broken by the ding of her cell phone. She unzipped her coat pocket and tugged it out.

"It's a text from my friend Scotty," she said. "He wants to know if we can meet him and his husband James for lunch."

Karla pulled back the cuff of her coat and peeked at her watch. "Wow, I can't believe it's almost noon." She looked back up at Ty. "Sure."

"Great. I'd love for you to meet them. Scotty was my…" Ty once again had to catch herself midsentence. "Scotty sold my brother the house here in Steamboat. He and James have become good friends of mine. I mean, because, you know, I stay at Reed's house all the time. Anyway, I told him you and I would be in town this weekend."

If Karla sensed her sudden nervousness, she didn't show it. "I'd love to meet them."

"Okay. Let me text him back real quick." *Shit, shit, shit.* What if Scotty said something about the house being hers? She hammered off a text.

Rendezvous @ 12:30? BTW, Karla thinks the house belongs to my brother. Can you play along?

By the time Ty got her cell phone tucked back in her coat, Karla had already disappeared into the trees.

* * *

Ty waved when she spotted Scotty in the crowded lodge.

"Hey, girl," he said when they approached.

Ty pulled off her ski helmet and gave him a warm hug before turning to introduce Karla. "Where's James?" Ty asked once they were seated.

Scotty gestured toward a neighboring table. "Just saying a quick hello to a friend of ours."

Moments later, James came snaking his way back through the sea of tables. He ran up, gave her a quick kiss on the cheek, and shook Karla's hand.

"It's nice to meet you." He smiled mischievously. "We've heard *a lot* about you."

Ty blushed and gave Karla a sideways glance. "Okay, so maybe I've mentioned you once or twice."

James pointed back in the direction he'd come from. "You know that house on Slope Side Drive that's been for sale forever?" he asked Ty. "The one that's two doors down from you."

Ty clenched her jaw and shot Scotty a look. "Uh-huh."

"Our friend just went under contract to buy it," James continued. "Looks like you guys will be neigh—"

Scotty nudged him in the shoulder. "Why don't we go get something to eat?"

James gave him a confused look and Ty blurted, "Great idea. I'm starving."

She joined the food line with Scotty, leaving Karla and James to guard the table. While they waited to order, Scotty leaned down and whispered in Ty's ear, "What's the deal with pretending your brother owns the house?"

Ty's eyes darted around to make sure Karla wasn't in earshot. "I'll explain later." She pointed to the young man tossing vegetables in a wok behind the counter. "Oh, look, your favorite cook is on duty today."

Scotty bent around the woman in front of him to get a better view. "Mmm mmm, isn't he delicious…The way his muscles bulge when he works that wok."

When Ty and Scotty got back to the table, James and Karla were deep in conversation.

"What took you guys so long?" James asked.

"The wok guy made Scotty a special order," Ty said.

James laughed. "Oh, I bet he did."

CHAPTER FORTY

"*So*, how was the weekend in Steamboat?" Val asked.

Ty had just bitten into her double decker BLT. A smile crossed her face as she chewed. Once she'd swallowed, she said, "It was good."

"Just good?"

Ty tried for nonchalant. She shrugged one shoulder and said, "We had a nice time."

Val didn't say anything in response. She raised her eyebrows and pursed her lips.

"What's with the look?"

"Oh, I dunno. I can't help but notice…This is the second weekend you and Karla have spent *alone* together in less than a month."

"And your point is?"

"I'm just saying."

"Okay, fine. The weekend was *really* good."

"I gathered," Val said. "You've got that dreamy look again."

"Whatever."

"You look...relaxed. Like you—"

"Got laid."

Val cackled. "Yeah."

"Well, maybe I did."

Val patted Ty's arm in a motherly fashion and flashed her a big grin. "I knew it. I like you two together. I'm pulling for you."

"Thanks, I'm pulling for us too. I like her a whole lot."

"Duh. That's been glaringly obvious since the day you two met."

Ty hated that she was so transparent, but she knew that when it came to Karla, she was a lost cause. Val was right. She'd acted like a giddy teenager the first time she'd set eyes on Karla, and her behavior hadn't improved much since then.

She took another bite of her sandwich and thought back to the weekend in Steamboat. It had been perfect. Well, except for the fact that she hadn't come clean about owning the house. She briefly considered discussing her predicament with Val but decided against it. Val and Teresa knew it was *her* house, or probably assumed it was. Ty hadn't given them any reason to think otherwise. If they wondered how a twenty-something college student could afford such a place, they hadn't said anything. If Ty told Val about the corner she'd painted herself into, it would likely bring up a host of other questions. Questions Ty was not prepared to answer. And the whole topic would only highlight the fact Ty was wealthy when she was trying to pretend the opposite was true.

"Penny for your thoughts," Val said.

Ty shook her head. "Sorry, I've just got a lot on my mind."

Val snickered. "I bet you do. Anything to do with a tall, dark-haired beauty with thighs of steel?"

"Maybe," Ty said. She gritted her teeth as panic rushed over her. Panic about how Karla would react when she learned Ty had lied. She took another bite of her sandwich, hoping Val wouldn't notice the change in her demeanor.

* * *

That evening, Ty met Karla for what had become their usual Wednesday night yoga class. Although they'd exchanged a slew of text messages over the last two days, this was the first time Ty had seen her since they'd gotten back to Denver on Monday morning. She grinned when she spotted Karla standing near the front desk at the gym.

"Hey, you," Ty said as she walked up to greet her.

Karla gave her a little wave and leaned in to give her a quick peck on the cheek.

"It's good to see you."

"It's good to see you too. I've missed you."

Ty smiled up at her. "I've missed you too." *You're pretty much all I've thought about for the last two days.*

The guy at the front desk was staring at them while they ogled each other like love-struck teenagers. Ty subtly nodded toward him and Karla rolled her eyes as she pulled her gym pass out of her pack. They hurried off toward the locker room to change for their ninety-minute fundamentals class.

After class, Karla asked, "Wanna come back to my place for dinner? I've got stuff to make stir-fry, and Cyndi and the kids are out of town."

Ty dabbed her face with a towel and said, "Yeah, I'd love to."

After a quick shower, she followed Karla back to her house. She sipped a beer and watched in awe as Karla fastidiously chopped vegetables for dinner.

"Aren't you afraid you're going to cut yourself?"

"Nah, I'm a master chef," Karla said with a smirk. She poured a little olive oil in a wok. Once it crackled, she tossed in the veggies and swirled them around like someone on *Top Chef.* Just before she pulled the wok from the flame, she threw in some diced tofu and turned off the stove.

They took their plates into Karla's small living area and settled into the couch in front of the TV. Karla grabbed the remote. "Whatcha feel like watching?"

"I love action movies. What about *Oceans 8* or something like that?"

Karla laughed. "Action? I was thinking something along the line of *Bridget Jones's Diary.*"

"Oh, God, are you kidding me?"

"What?" Karla poked Ty teasingly in the chest. "Come on, it's a classic."

Ty rolled her eyes. "Whatever. Drama city."

They finally settled on a light romantic comedy—*Overboard* with Goldie Hawn and Kurt Russell. After Karla stabbed the play button on the remote, she grabbed a blanket from a nearby chair and draped it over them. Ty cuddled up against her but sat upright moments later when it became obvious that they both knew practically every line in the movie by heart.

After they recited, "Listen to me, medical people," in unison, they fell back against the couch giggling.

When the credits scrolled, Ty sat up abruptly, worried she'd overstayed her welcome. "Well, I should probably head out."

"Stay?"

Ty looked over at Karla and their eyes locked. "Really?"

Karla nodded.

"Okay. I'd like that."

Karla stood, refolded the blanket, and returned it to its chair. They switched off lights as they made their way to Karla's bedroom.

"You want a toothbrush?" Karla asked.

"Sure, thanks."

Karla stepped into the bathroom, opened a drawer in the vanity, and pulled out an unopened toothbrush. They stood together in front of the mirror and brushed their teeth like it was something they'd done together a thousand times before. Ty's stomach did a flip flop, like she'd just jumped out of an airplane. Once again, she was struck by how incredibly easy it was to be with Karla.

Without saying a word, Karla dug into her dresser and came out with a pair of boxers and an old T-shirt with the words *Atomic Skis* printed across the front. She handed the clothes to Ty and reached under her pillow to pull out a similar outfit for herself.

Ty shed her clothes on a nearby chair. Although the evening thus far—save an occasional peck on the lips during the movie—had been completely innocent, Ty's erect nipples brushed against the T-shirt when she tugged it down over her body. It sent a small shock to her groin. She pulled back the covers and slipped into bed next to Karla.

Karla clicked off the bedside lamp and inched over next to Ty. She pulled Ty into her arms, brushed a hand over her cheek, and placed a soft kiss on her lips.

"It's nice to have you in my bed," she said.

"It's nice to be here," Ty said and pulled her into another kiss.

Before long, two sets of boxers and T-shirts were in a heap on the floor.

* * *

Ty watched Karla as she poured them each an overflowing bowl of Wheaties the next morning. She knew she had a silly grin on her face, but she didn't care.

"What's with the goofy look?" Karla asked as she pulled the milk from the fridge.

Ty looked down at her cereal and shrugged. "It's just...being with you...It makes me feel really good inside."

Karla pushed the fridge closed with her hip. "Is that a fact? Cuz it just so happens, you make me feel really good inside too."

"I do?"

"Uh-huh. Super warm and fuzzy."

Ty cleared her throat. "This is probably a dorky question, but are we, you know...girlfriends?" She felt a bit like she was in the seventh grade, but she didn't know how else to ask for what she wanted.

Karla sat down on the stool next to her and took her hand. "That's not a dorky question. I take it you're asking if we can, um, be exclusive?"

Ty swallowed hard and nodded.

Karla took her hand. "I'm not someone who sleeps around. Aside from a few flings when I was on the circuit, I've always been a one-woman kind of girl. With you, I wouldn't have it any other way." Karla shifted in her seat and curled her long legs around the front legs of the stool. "I really, really like you, Ty. Our relationship, although still somewhat new, is vital to me." Her face lit up and she said, "So, the answer to your question is an unequivocal yes."

A wave of euphoria slammed Ty. She knew she was in love. Had been for a while. There was no question about that. She'd never in her life had feelings this intense for someone—not even close. She jumped up from her seat threw her arms around Karla.

Karla laughed and peppered her face with soft kisses. "So, I guess you liked my answer, huh?"

Ty grinned. "You could say that."

Karla took both Ty's hands in her own. "I'd be crazy not to want to be with you, Ty. You're beautiful, kind, honest, and smart."

The only word Ty heard was *honest*. Her elation was instantly supplanted by guilt. She hadn't been honest with Karla, and she hated herself for it. She shuddered. When Karla learned the truth, she might walk away, leaving Ty's heart in a million pieces.

CHAPTER FORTY-ONE

As spring quarter chugged along, Ty and Karla fell into an easy routine—go to class, go to the gym, make dinner together, and fall into bed. With each passing day, Ty fell more and more in love, but she also fell deeper into the hole of deceit. Her heart and her brain were at constant war. The longer she misled Karla, the worse it would be when she finally told her the truth.

She'd begun having a hard time sleeping. She was so incredibly happy and so incredibly tormented at the same time. Repeated conversations with Sarah on the matter hadn't helped. Sarah grew more frustrated with Ty each time they talked. She was beside herself that Ty still hadn't been honest with Karla, not only about the house but about her financial situation in general.

"When does ski season end?" Val asked one day when the three of them were having lunch on campus.

"It depends on the resort," Karla answered. "Some places, like Arapahoe Basin, stay open until early June, but most of the big resorts in Colorado usually close in mid-April."

"I think Steamboat closes April tenth," Ty added.

"Will you use your house much over the summer, Ty?" Val asked.

"Um, yeah, probably. In fact, even though I love to ski, I think I might prefer Steamboat in the summertime. Everything is green, there's a ton of hiking and mountain biking, and the town should be a lot less crowded than it is in the wintertime."

Karla nodded. "I'd have to agree with you on that. I always loved the summers in Jackson."

"Have you ever considered renting out the place in Steamboat?" Val asked. "I mean, I know with school and everything, you aren't able to get there as much as you'd like."

Ty's heart rate picked up and she practically had to gasp for air. How the fuck was she supposed to answer that question? She took a sip of water. "I, um…" Her mind raced. She'd led Val to believe the truth, that she owned the house. But Karla thought it was her brother's place. She looked down at the paper napkin in her lap. She'd scrunched it into a ball. "I'd hate to see the place rented out," she said and laughed nervously. "Someone might trash it."

"You have a valid point," Karla said, "but, given how little he uses it, I can't believe your brother hasn't at least entertained the idea of renting it out. Don't get me wrong, it's certainly nice of him to let you—"

Val's brow furrowed and she cocked her head toward Ty. "Brother?" she asked. "I didn't realize your brother owned the place. I thought it was yours."

Ty wanted to crawl under the table. *This is what happens when you lie. It catches up with you. It always catches up with you.* She stared back at Val and blinked a few times. She had to make a split-second decision. Perpetuate the lie or set the record straight.

She opened her mouth to speak, but before she got the chance, a voice called from across the room, "Hey, guys. Coming to class?"

Ty looked up. Dipti was waving at them from the doorway.

Karla looked at her watch and nodded toward Val. "We better go."

Val popped the last of her Reuben into her mouth, took a gulp of water, and she and Karla stood to leave.

"Catch you later, Ty," Karla leaned down and gave Ty a peck on the lips before they hurried off to class.

"See ya," Ty croaked.

As soon as they were gone, she collapsed back into her chair. That was a close call. A *very* close call. She decided then she had no choice. She couldn't wait any longer; she had to tell Karla the truth. She crumpled up the paper from her sandwich and flicked it around the table like a soccer ball. She needed a plan.

A lightbulb went off in her head. She'd take Karla on a little weekend getaway and break the news to her then. She pulled her laptop out of her bag, opened her browser, and typed *romantic getaway*. She clicked on a link to *Travel + Leisure's* Top 50 Best Romantic Getaways.

New York City was first on the list. Ty immediately dismissed that as an option. She wanted to go somewhere relaxing, not bustling. Second was Grenada, Spain. Too far away. Third was Namibia. Ty laughed. Yeah, right. She was going to whisk Karla off to Namibia for a long weekend. It would probably take them three days just to get there. She needed to find something a bit closer to home. She opened Google Maps and scanned the region around Colorado. Bingo! Moab, Utah. That was it. Moab was only four or five hours by car, and it had some of the best mountain biking and hiking in the US. Ty had been there once when she was in college the first time around and loved it.

* * *

"So," Ty said over dinner that night. "What do you think about a little road trip to Moab this weekend?"

Karla set down her fork. "God, Ty. I'd love that, but I don't think I can swing it. Money's pretty tight right now."

"What if it didn't cost you anything?"

Karla threw her head back and laughed. "Ha. Yeah, wouldn't that be nice."

"I mean it. My treat."

Karla set her elbow on the table and rested her head in her hand. "That's too generous. I couldn't accept such a—"

Ty reached across the table and laid a hand on Karla's arm. "I've got some savings. Please. This is something I really want to do."

Karla stood up and started to clear the table. "It wouldn't feel right. I've got this thing about paying my own way. If I can't afford it, I don't do it. Period."

"You've got a birthday coming up, don't you?" Ty asked.

"I do, but…"

"But what? Consider it my birthday gift to you."

After a few more rounds of back and forth, Karla finally relented.

"Okay, but only if we stay somewhere cheap, and I'm driving. I doubt there's any place in Moab to charge that Tesla of yours, and even if there is, you don't have a bike rack."

"Deal." The tension in Ty's back and shoulders dissipated ever so slightly. She'd take Karla out to a nice dinner the last night they were in Moab and tell her about the Lionball. After this weekend, there would be no more secrets between them.

CHAPTER FORTY-TWO

Karla inspected the bike rack for the twentieth time, jiggling the bikes to make sure they were secure. "Okay, all set. You ready to hit the road?"

"Yep," Ty said as she loaded the last of her bags into Karla's car.

Ty played DJ as Karla drove along I-70 toward Moab. They sang along to the radio while they sped along the interstate. As they belted out John Denver's "Take Me Home, Country Roads," Karla felt all warm inside. Although she'd protested about Ty footing the bill for a weekend away, she had to admit, she was really looking forward to it. A whole weekend alone together in the great outdoors.

The sun was just about to set when they pulled up to the hotel in Moab. The sky looked like an inverted ocean swell of pink and purple. Karla offloaded the bikes while Ty checked in. The hotel was a bit nicer than she'd expected, but she wasn't going to give Ty grief about it now. What would be the point? The reservation was probably nonrefundable, and she didn't want the weekend to start off on a sour note.

Once they'd unpacked, they made the short walk into the center of town to have dinner at a little Mexican place the clerk at the hotel had recommended. The patrons in the restaurant were a mix of hearty looking athletic types with sun-kissed faces and slightly doughier, although no less cheerful, car tourists—people who drive up to a scenic vista, snap a few photos, and hop back in the car. They were likely making a pit stop in Moab on their way either to or from one of the nearby national parks.

After sharing a massive portion of steak and veggie fajitas for two, polishing off a mound of chips and salsa, and downing a couple of rocks margaritas, they strolled back to the hotel to rest up for the next day.

The next morning, they set off for Canyonlands National Park to do a hike Karla had read about and suggested they try. After multiple stops along the way to take pictures, it was practically noon by the time they reached the trailhead. Fortunately, it was still spring in the desert, so it wasn't too hot yet, and there was a steady breeze.

"You think we can do the whole ten mile-loop before it gets dark?" Ty asked as they loaded up their packs.

"I do. As long as we keep up a good pace."

Ty pulled a baseball cap on her head. "Are we talking a Karla super-athlete pace, or your run of the mill power walk?"

Karla responded with a chuckle and started down the trail.

Massive red-and-white-banded rocks lined either side of the trail as they wove through one narrow canyon after another. After one particularly grueling climb, they came across a long slickrock bench.

"You up for a quick break?" Ty asked.

Karla responded by plunking herself down on a portion of the bench that was shaded by a nearby rock formation.

Ty sat next to her and used a bandana to wipe the sweat off her forehead. "You got any of those dried apricots left?"

Karla foraged in her pack for her snack bag and tossed it to Ty. She leaned back on her palms and sighed when they pressed against the cool, smooth rock.

"What a relief to be out of the sun for a little bit."

"Roger that," Ty said. "Want some more sunscreen?"

Karla nodded and Ty squeezed a dollop of SPF 50 onto her palm. Once they were sufficiently lubed, they set off to finish the hike. The last few miles of the trail required them to scramble over a lot of large rocks, causing their pace to slow considerably. The sun was low in the sky when they neared the end of the loop.

Karla stopped abruptly when they were about a quarter mile from the parking lot and pointed up to a rocky ledge hanging high above the trail.

"Want to clamber up there and watch the sun set?"

"Sure, that'd be awesome," Ty said. She reached back and tapped the side of her pack. "I've got a flashlight in my bag in case we need help finding our way back to the car in the dark."

Karla laughed. "My little Girl Scout." With that, she turned and started to scale the rocks up to the perch.

Ty scrambled up behind her. "Wait up."

When they reached the top, they sat on the edge of a long, thin rock, their feet dangling below them. Karla took in their surroundings. The sky was bursting with deep shades of purple and pink, just like it had the night before, and jagged red rocks sprinkled the horizon as far as the eye could see. There was not another soul around, and the only sound was the light wind sweeping over the landscape. Their perch was only about thirty feet off the ground, but it felt like they were much higher. Like they were floating above the rocky desert landscape.

Karla nudged Ty with her shoulder. "It's like we're on a magic carpet ride."

"Why don't you tell your dreams to me," Ty sang, quoting the famous song by Steppenwolf. She scooted closer to Karla and reached for her hand.

They sat in silence and watched the sun creep lower and lower in the sky. It was one of life's perfect moments, and Karla wished she could freeze it in time. Ty squeezed her hand as if she'd been reading her mind. She'd never felt as connected to another human being, and she couldn't imagine sharing this moment with anyone but Ty. Karla gasped audibly as a surge of emotion crashed over her. It was so intense, it was like she'd had the wind knocked out of her.

"Ty," she said.

Ty glanced over at her. "Uh-huh?"

The sun was just about to dip below the horizon, and she could barely make out Ty's face in the fading light. Karla reached up and brushed a strand of hair out of Ty's face and trailed a thumb over her cheek. Their eyes locked. A lump formed in Karla's throat.

She took a deep breath and whispered, "I love you Ty…I mean, I'm completely and totally head over heels in love with you."

Ty kissed her softly on the lips and when she pulled back, she croaked, "I happen to be completely and totally head over heels in love with you too."

"You are?"

"Mm-hmm. I think I've been in love with you since the day we met."

Karla was too overwhelmed to speak. She'd never felt like this in her life. Not even close. She draped an arm over Ty's shoulders, and as they sat together in silence and watched the sun disappear, a warm tear slid down her cheek. When Karla looked over at Ty, she was crying too.

Karla pulled her into a hug and said, "I don't think I've ever been this happy."

* * *

Ty flopped onto the bed in their hotel room as soon as she'd toweled off from her shower. Her eyes were heavy, and within a few minutes, she drifted to sleep. The long hike in the hot sun and the intensely emotional end to the day had rendered her fuel tank empty. Sometime late, she awoke to soft kisses on her neck and face. When her eyes fluttered open, Karla's big brown eyes were looking into hers.

Ty let out a soft sigh. "What time is it?"

"Almost nine o'clock."

"Did you fall asleep too?"

Karla shook her head. "No, I've just been watching my beautiful girlfriend sleep...and drool."

Ty instinctively reached to wipe her face. There was no evidence of drool. "Smart ass," she said and rolled over on top of Karla. She kissed the tip of her nose.

Karla rolled them over again, so she was on top, and kissed Ty deeply, igniting a fire inside her body.

Ty slid a hand under Karla's T-shirt. "Oh, no bra. *Sexy.*"

She cupped one of Karla's ample breasts, causing her nipple to harden. Ty flipped them over once again so she straddled Karla's waist. She wiggled Karla's shirt over her head and attacked her nipples hungrily. One of Karla's hands traced her torso, from her shoulders down to her hips, and slipped between her legs. Karla gently teased her center before gliding inside of her. Ty rode her hand hard until she climaxed and collapsed on top of her.

Ty laughed at herself. "God, I can't believe how quickly I came."

"I love touching you, Ty. You get so wet. You're like silk."

Ty began to knead Karla's breasts. "I love touching you too." Karla writhed beneath her when Ty captured one of her breasts with her mouth. "And I love how your tits are so sensitive."

"Touch me, please."

Ty circled the waistband of Karla's shorts and tugged them over her hips. After only a few caresses, Karla's legs tightened around her hand. Moments later, her body convulsed before going still. Karla closed her eyes and her head sunk into the pillow.

She opened one eye and said, "Guess we both needed that." Her eye fell closed again and she muttered, "You know just how I like it."

"Your amazing body is serious motivation." Ty lay down next to her and said a silent prayer.

Please don't let my dishonesty destroy what we have. I promise, I'll make things right tomorrow.

CHAPTER FORTY-THREE

Just after sunrise the next morning, they set off for a mountain bike ride. Like many of the rides in and around Moab, the one they'd chosen was a series of steep climbs and descents over smooth red rocks. Although the ride was only twelve miles, it was likely to take them over three hours to crisscross its challenging terrain.

Ty had to get off her bike and walk on more than one occasion, and she looked on with envy while Karla sailed up even the most difficult sections of the trail.

"You make it look so easy," Ty said when they stopped for a water break. "Are you sure you don't have an electric bike?"

"Very funny," Karla said. She patted one of her muscular thighs. "Remember, I spent half my childhood doing leg presses and wall sits."

Ty winked at Karla. "You don't have to remind me you have legs of steel."

The sun was high in the sky by the time they got back to the car, and Ty's bike jersey was drenched in sweat. When she licked her lips, they tasted like salt. Karla pulled two Gatorades out of the car and handed one to her. It was warm, but she was too damn thirsty to care. She cracked it open and guzzled half the bottle.

When they were about halfway back to the hotel, Ty's phone rang. She patted the pockets of her bike shorts and peered into the cup holders in the center console.

"Shit, my phone must be in my backpack." She stretched her arm into the backseat. "I can't reach it."

"It's probably a telemarketer," Karla said.

Ty settled back into her seat. "You're right."

When her phone rang again thirty seconds later, she said, "I better check and see who it is." She unbuckled her seat belt, stretched back, and yanked her backpack into her lap. She managed to answer the call before it went to voice mail. "Hello…Oh, hi James. Is everything…Okay, Uh-huh…Oh, wow. How bad is it?" Ty's hand tightened around the phone and she pinched her eyes shut. As she listened to James explain what had happened, she gasped for air. Her mind filled with images of that horrible day when she'd laid her parents to rest. Their caskets closed because their mangled bodies were too gruesome to display. She heard herself say, "I'm in Moab. I'll get there as soon as I can."

Ty ended the call and collapsed back against her seat.

Karla eased the car to the side of the road. "What happened?" she asked.

"Scotty was in a car accident. He's in the hospital."

"Oh my God. How bad is it?"

"Pretty bad, I think. James sounded really shaken up."

They sped back to the hotel, showered, and checked out. About ten minutes outside of Moab, Ty remembered the dinner reservation she'd made at the nicest restaurant in Moab for that evening. Tonight was the night she'd planned tell Karla the truth. The best-laid plans…Unfortunately, that conversation would have to wait. It certainly wasn't one she wanted to have in the car while they hightailed it to Steamboat. She called the restaurant and cancelled the reservation and then called James back.

"Karla and I are on our way," she said when he answered the phone. "We'll probably be there around six."

* * *

They drove straight to the hospital in Steamboat. Scotty was conscious, but he looked horrible. His face was covered in bruises and cuts, and his head was sheathed in gauze. According to James, he'd fractured a few ribs, suffered a concussion, and broken both legs. Major injuries but nothing life-threatening.

It probably hadn't been necessary for them to cut their Moab trip short and rush to Steamboat, but James was still extremely rattled, and Ty was happy she was there to offer her support. And just laying eyes on Scotty did wonders to calm her. She hadn't realized just how panicked she'd been since getting the call from James.

As they left the hospital, Karla curled her arm around Ty's waist. "When you heard Scotty had been in a car accident, it triggered something, didn't it?"

Ty leaned into her. "All I could think about were my parents and the day they died."

Karla kissed the top of her head. "We did the right thing coming straight here."

Ty stopped and pulled Kalra into her arms. "Thank you for being the sweetest, most thoughtful girlfriend in the world."

From the hospital, they drove to Ty's house in Steamboat. It was too late to drive back to Denver and Ty wanted to check in on Scotty again tomorrow.

While Karla washed down their dust-covered mountain bikes in the garage, Ty pulled some pot pies out of the freezer and turned on the oven. While she waited for it to preheat, she pulled out her laptop and scanned the news headlines. A loud knock at her front door startled her. Ty wasn't expecting anyone. She padded over to the front door, and as soon as she disengaged the lock, whoever was on the other side shoved it open, nearly knocking Ty to the ground. She stumbled backward.

"Surprise," a male voice said.

Ty looked up. Her cousin Garth was standing in the open doorway. His hair was matted and greasy, the stubble on his chin was way past the point of a five o'clock shadow, and his eyeglasses were askew.

"What the hell are you doing here?" she asked.

He skipped the pleasantries and pushed past her into the house. "Nice digs, Ty."

"Um, thanks," she stuttered. How the hell had he gotten her address?

He scanned the living room and kitchen before his beady eyes fell on her. "Guess the rumors were true, huh? You *did* win the fucking lottery." He picked a decorative glass bowl off a nearby shelf and smashed in on the floor. "Funny, I don't remember you sharing that little detail, you greedy little bitch."

Ty thoughts immediately went to Karla down in the basement. Should she shout out and warn her? Tell her to call the police? Or was it better not to let Garth know someone else was in the house? She slid behind the far side of the kitchen island and eyed the wooden block full of chef-quality kitchen knives, but she didn't want to resort to that quite yet. Instead, she figured her best tactic was to keep him talking. Maybe Karla would overhear them and call for help.

"What do you want, Garth?"

He moved toward her. "Money. In case you forgot, I'm your first cousin."

Ty laughed nervously. "Good one, Garth. Of course I didn't forget."

"Yet, you skipped town right after you won the lottery…"

The last thing Ty wanted to do was confirm she *had* actually won. "How did you find me?"

"It wasn't too difficult," he said with a cackle. "I got your sympathy note when Mother passed."

"I see," Ty said, wondering how that had led him to her. She was certain she hadn't included a return address.

"The envelope was postmarked in Steamboat Springs."

Ty's mind raced. She couldn't remember where she'd mailed the card.

Garth yanked open the fridge, pulled out a beer, and tugged the top off with his teeth.

"I did a little digging," he said after he spit the bottle cap out on the floor. It rolled along the tile floor and came to a stop near Ty's feet. "Turns out the LLC—Merce the Nurse LLC—that claimed the big Lionball prize in North Carolina last spring… just so happened to purchase an expensive home in Steamboat Springs a few months later." He tapped a finger on his head. "I'm a smart guy. I connected the dots."

Ty took a few steps back toward the sliding glass doors that led outside to the deck. Out of the corner of her eye, she saw her phone sitting on the edge of the counter. She lunged for it, but Garth was too quick. He beat her to it and flung it across the room.

"What's going on?" Karla asked as she ascended the stairs from the basement. "Oh, my God. Is that a gun?"

Ty's eyes flew to Garth. He was holding a small black handgun, and it was pointed at her. She ducked below the kitchen counter and screamed, "Karla, run! Call the police."

Garth fired a shot. It ricocheted off the pans hanging over the stove. Ty needed to get to Karla. Make sure she was okay. She duck-walked around to the edge of the kitchen island. Garth was standing at the top of the stairs that led to the basement and he was swinging the gun from side to side. In one movement, she sprung to her feet and lunged in his direction, hitting him hard and sending him tumbling down the stairs.

He hit the basement floor with a thud and yelled, "Fuck you, bitch."

He slowly got to his feet and aimed the gun back up the stairs.

Ty scrambled into the foyer and called out for Karla. There was no answer. She opened the front door and stepped outside. Karla was probably trapped in the basement. Ty needed to find her.

Her socked feet were like sponges on the moist spring ground. She tried to run toward the garage but slipped and her ass hit the muddy ground hard. She peeled off her socks, stood, and took off down the slope toward Karla's car. The garage door was open, and their mountain bikes were leaning against the wall inside. The door on the far-right side of the garage led into the basement via the equipment room. Ty pulled it open and stepped into the dark room.

"Karla?" she called out.

"Over here. What the hell is—"

A large bang sounded from the game room in the basement and they heard Garth shake the handle on the door to the equipment room. It was locked, and he cursed when it didn't open. His fist pounded on the door.

"I know you're in there."

Ty pulled Karla toward the garage, but they weren't fast enough. Garth shot open the door and burst into the room. Karla grabbed a pair of skis—still wrapped in cellophane and not yet mounted with bindings—off a nearby rack and swung them in the air. They made a loud *whack* when they came into contact with Garth's forehead. He dropped to the ground, and Karla was on him in an instant. She jammed her knee into his back and pinned his arms to the ground.

"Call the police!" Karla yelled.

"My phone's upstairs," Ty said.

"Go get it."

"Are you sure?"

Garth fought against Karla, but he was no match for her strength. "Yes, I've got him," she said. "Hurry."

* * *

Later that night, after the police had taken Garth away, Karla and Ty sat in the living room of her house. She looked down at her hands and back up at Karla.

"I guess I have some explaining to do?"

Karla didn't say anything in response. She just nodded.

Ty took a minute to gather her thoughts. She'd rehearsed what she wanted to say to Karla, but it was an explanation she'd expected to give over a nice dinner in Moab. The circumstances were now a whole lot different.

"I lied to you," Ty blurted. She waved a hand across the room. "This house is mine. I own it. Not my brother."

Karla's eyes narrowed. "I don't understand."

"I'm rich, Karla. Like crazy rich. I won the lottery. A massive Lionball jackpot." Ty rambled off some of the details, eager to lay it all out. "I've kept it from you. I know it was a stupid thing to do, and I hate that I lied to—"

Karla laughed. It wasn't a nice laugh. "Were you afraid I'd want you for your money?"

Ty shook her head vigorously. "God no, just the opposite. I thought you *wouldn't* want me because of my money. You said rich people—"

Karla stood and paced around the room. "That didn't give you an excuse to lie to me." She let out a long breath. "Makes me wonder, what else haven't you told me?"

Ty wiped a tear from her cheek with the sleeve of her shirt. "Nothing. I swear. I don't usually make a habit of lying."

"Well you could have fooled me." Karla stormed toward the front door and grabbed for the handle. "I'm leaving."

"Wait, please. Can we talk about this?"

Karla shook her head and walked out the door.

Ty jumped off the couch and ran after her. "Please, Karla. I love you."

Karla looked back at her. Tears were streaming down her face. "I love you too, but that doesn't change the fact you lied." She shook her head in dismay. "I sure can pick 'em. First Dana and now you."

Ty didn't know what to say. Karla was right. She'd lied to her just like Dana. She stood in the doorway and watched Karla back down the driveway and disappear down the street. She closed the door, climbed the stairs to her room, and crawled into bed.

CHAPTER FORTY-FOUR

When Ty woke up late the next morning, the sheets were knotted around her legs. She kicked herself free and stared at the ceiling. The events of the previous day came rushing back, and she placed a hand over her heart and closed her eyes. She felt like a hollowed-out pumpkin. She grabbed the pillow from Karla's side of the bed and hugged it with all her might. It only made her feel worse.

She didn't even know where Karla had gone. Back home to Denver? It had been late when she'd left. The road between Steamboat and I-70 would have been dark and desolate. Ty had tried to reach her a dozen times the night before but the calls had all gone unanswered.

She snatched her phone off the night table and stabbed Karla's number. The call went to voice mail. She tried again. Same result.

"Fuuuuck."

She slapped her phone back down on the table and pulled the covers over her head. It was hard to breathe, but she didn't care. She deserved to suffocate.

It took the ringing of her phone to pull her from her dark cocoon. She threw off the covers and sat on the edge of her bed. James's name flashed on the screen. Ty slumped forward. Not only was she a rotten girlfriend, she was a shitty friend. She should have gone to see Scotty at the hospital first thing that morning.

"Hi, James. How's Scotty doing?"

"He just went into surgery. For his left leg. He probably won't be out for a few hours."

Ty's guilt-o-meter inched up a few notches. All the more reason she should've gone down to see him that morning.

"Oh, gosh, okay." Ty looked at her watch. "I'll come down around two then?"

"Okay," James said. "That should be good."

Ty ended the call and padded into the bathroom. When she flicked on the light, her reflection in the mirror caused her to recoil. Her eyes were bloodshot and puffy. There was dried blood on her lower lip, probably from nibbling it obsessively during the night, and her hair was matted against her head.

"Nice."

As she brushed her teeth, it occurred to her that she didn't have a car—Karla had been her ride. She slapped her hand on the vanity.

"Fucking A. Goddammit."

She pushed away the fact that she had class at eight a.m. the next morning, in Denver. That was the least of her worries right now.

She spit out her toothpaste and leaned her elbows on the vanity, then hung her head and began to cry. Eventually her legs gave out and she slumped to the floor. Her body convulsed against the furry bathmat as she sobbed. Just over a year ago, she'd been a bartender, struggling to scrape together enough money to pay her rent each month. And now, she had all the money in the world, but she didn't have the one thing she really wanted. Karla. And why? Because she'd been a moronic twit and lied to her. The prospect of losing her for good sent Ty into another fit of sobbing.

She eventually scraped herself off the floor and climbed back in bed. She needed to talk to Sarah. Maybe she'd know how to fix the mess Ty had gotten herself into.

"Hey, sweetie," Sarah said when she answered the phone.

The sound of her voice was enough to set Ty off crying again.

"What's wrong?"

"Kawa weft," she said through her tears.

"Tell me what happened."

"Howd on." Ty yanked a tissue from the box on her nightstand and blew her nose. She took a few calming breaths. Her lips still trembled, but the crying stopped. "Garth showed up at my house in Steamboat last night," she said finally. "He wanted money."

"Garth as in your crazy ass cousin?"

"Uh-huh. He threatened me with a gun."

"What? Oh, my God. Are you all right?"

"Yes, thanks to Karla. She smacked him in the head with a pair of skis and pinned him to the ground."

"Holy shit."

"I know. She's so fucking brave." Ty's eyes welled up with tears again, and she gasped for breath.

"It's okay. Take your time," Sarah said softly.

"I called the police while Karla held him down," Ty said finally. "They took him away."

"Thank God. Is he still in jail?"

"Yeah. Apparently, there was an outstanding warrant for his arrest. He probably won't see the light of day for a very long time."

"How the hell did he find you?"

"You know how my aunt died a few weeks ago?"

"Of course. And you were afraid to attend the funeral because of Garth."

"Right, but I sent him a note with my condolences. I didn't include a return address but the enveloped was postmarked in Steamboat"—Ty skipped over the fact that Karla had forgotten to mail it from Denver—"and he did some sleuthing. Traced

the LLC that claimed the Lionball prize in North Carolina to a
home purchase in Steamboat…"

"Wow."

"Wow is right. I should have been more careful."

"Have you told Reed what happened?" Sarah asked.

"Yeah. I called him right after the police took Garth away."
Ty paused for a moment. It was hard to believe the whole
incident with Garth had actually happened. That it wasn't just
a bad dream. Especially the mess with Karla in the aftermath.

"Ty, you there?"

"Uh-huh, sorry. The last twenty-four hours of my life have
been—"

"Fucking hell?"

"And I haven't even told you the worst of it."

"Shit, there's more?"

"I hadn't yet told Karla about the house and Lionball and
all that."

"Ty. Really?"

"I'd planned to tell her this weekend." Ty gave Sarah a quick
overview of the weekend in Moab and having to leave to come
to Steamboat.

"Is Scotty okay?"

"No, not really. I mean, he'll recover, eventually, but his
injuries are pretty bad. He's in surgery now. He broke both of
his legs, one more badly than the other."

"So, when Garth showed up at your house, it let the cat out
of the bag?"

"Essentially," Ty said. "Once the police left with Garth, I
told Karla everything. Admitted I'd lied about the house in
Steamboat belonging to my brother, all of it."

"And how'd she take it?"

"Not well. Not well at all." The tears started again. "She was
really upset, and she stormed out."

"I can't say I blame her."

Ty reached for another tissue and blubbered into the phone.
"What if she never wants to speak to me again?" Ty blew her

nose. "I wish I'd never won the stupid lottery. Because of it, I may have lost Karla, the love of my life."

Sarah's response was stern. "No, Ty, if you lost her, it's because you lied."

CHAPTER FORTY-FIVE

As Ty drove over the pass out of Steamboat the following Wednesday, Pink's "What about Us?" came on the radio. She cried as she sang along.

What about love? What about trust?

What about us?

Aside from visiting Scotty at the hospital, she'd spent the last few days holed up in her house. She'd skipped all of her classes and eaten no fewer than four pints of Ben and Jerry's Chocolate Chip Cookie Dough ice cream. And last night, Karla had finally answered one of her calls. They hadn't talked for long, but they'd agreed to meet so they could talk about what had happened. Ty had danced around her house after they'd gotten off the phone. She knew there were no guarantees that Karla would forgive her, but she took the fact that she was willing to talk as a good sign.

When she walked into Bella's Coffee House a few hours later, she spotted Karla sitting in a leather chair in the back corner. At the sight of her, Ty's stomach churned with a mix of anxiety, fear, and hope. When she approached, Karla stood and greeted her with a stiff hug.

"I miss you," Ty said into her neck.

Karla pulled back. Her beautiful brown eyes lacked their usual sparkle. "I miss you too," she said softly.

Ty wiped a tear from her cheek and sat down in the chair across from her. "Thanks for saving my life."

The smallest smile crept across Karla's face. "You're welcome."

"You were so brave."

"I don't know about that," Karla said. "I was pretty terrified."

"So was I. There was no telling what Garth was capable of. He's deranged."

"Clearly. I'm just glad no one got hurt."

Ty nodded. *That is, unless you factor in my broken heart.*

"So, you wanted to talk?" Karla asked matter-of-factly.

Ty stared at her while she tried to conjure up the lines she'd rehearsed. Karla's lips were pursed in a straight line, forming neither a frown nor a smile. Her strong shoulders sagged uncharacteristically.

"I'm sorry," Ty said finally. "Sorry I lied to you. Sorry for everything." She paused and took a deep breath. "I'd like a chance to try and explain why I did what I did. I know it won't excuse my behavior, but I hope you'll hear me out anyway."

Karla sat up taller in her chair, but her expression didn't change. "Okay."

"All right, here goes." Ty looked Karla straight in the eye. "I lied to you about the house in Steamboat belonging to my brother because I wanted something with you so badly...I was so afraid that if you knew the truth, that I had a lot of money, I'd never get to be with you. And once I lied to you about the house, I knew I'd only made things worse. Dug myself deeper into a hole. I got pulled under by the tide of dishonesty. I didn't work hard enough fight it. I let it carry me out to sea."

Karla looked unmoved.

"And as time went on, as we grew closer and became a couple, I was petrified that if you knew the truth, you wouldn't want to be with me. Being with you, being in love with you. I don't even have words to describe how incredible it is."

Karla's lips curled into the faintest smile but then quickly resumed their neutral position.

Ty unzipped her fleece vest and tugged it off. "Is it hot in here or is it just me?"

"It's just you."

Ty threw her vest over the back of the chair and said, "I know I was a total idiot."

"I'm the one who was an idiot," Karla replied, "for not figuring it out on my own."

"Figuring what out on your own?"

"That you weren't who you pretended to be."

Karla's words stung. Ty pinched the bridge of her nose and took a deep breath. "I wasn't pretending to be anything I'm not."

"That's not true," Karla bit back. She leaned forward in her chair and pointed a finger a Ty. "You listened to me talk about how I had to walk away from skiing because of money and you acted like you understood what it was like to be in my shoes."

"Because I do," Ty said more loudly than she intended. "Before I won the lottery, I was barely making ends meet, and growing up, money was always tight." She reached for Karla's hand and gripped it tightly. "I don't have any other secrets. Everything else I've told you about myself is true."

Karla pulled her hand away. "How do I know that? How do I know what's true and what's not?"

"You just have to believe me, which I know, after what I did, is asking a lot. The fear of losing you was so intense. I've lost so much over the last few years, with my parents being snatched away from me and then my brother moving to Vietnam so soon after that. I didn't think my heart could survive being split in two again, and it caused me to do the worst thing to you. To lie to you. I've never felt as strongly for anyone as I do for you, Karla, not even close. I'm begging you. Please give me another chance."

Karla bit her lip and looked up at the ceiling. When she looked back down, her eyes had regained the slightest bit of their glimmer.

"I love you, Ty. So much." She paused to wipe a tear from her cheek. "But I cannot stand it when people are dishonest."

An ache stabbed Ty's heart. She bowed her head and clenched her hands. "I know," she whispered.

"When Dana lied to me it hurt, a lot, but I didn't care for her the way I do for you. When I drove away from your house the other night, the pain was so crushing, I thought I might die of a broken heart."

Ty felt like she'd been kicked in the stomach. Tears streamed down her face as she spoke. "I hate that I made you feel that way. I love you, so much." She reached for Karla's hand again. "Is there any way you can ever forgive me?"

Karla didn't respond right away. She leaned back in her chair and looked back up at the ceiling. When she lowered her head, she said, "I need a little time."

The tiniest sliver of hope slid into Ty's heart. "I understand. Take as much time as you need. I'll wait as long as you need."

"Maybe we could have lunch together tomorrow?" Karla suggested.

Ty smiled and nodded eagerly. "Lunch? I can do lunch."

Karla stood and gathered her coat. "I'll see you then." With that, she turned and walked toward the door of the coffee shop.

Ty watched her go.

Please, please. Let everything be okay.

CHAPTER FORTY-SIX

They met for lunch the next day, and the next, and the next. Gradually, the casual touches and lingering gazes returned. Although the fateful night in Steamboat had been one of the worst nights of Ty's life, second only to the night her parents had died, one good thing had come out of it. The truth had been exposed. Now, everything was out in the open. To Ty that was extremely liberating. As she worked to regain Karla's trust, she was able to give her full self to Karla in a way she hadn't been doing before *the incident*, as she like to call the night Garth showed up. Even though their relationship was still somewhat tenuous, she felt an even stronger connection to Karla than she had before. Not surprisingly, her feelings for Karla only intensified. Saving their relationship was all that mattered.

One day, as they were making their way to class, Karla reached over and took Ty's hand. Neither of them said a word. They just walked across campus hand in hand. Ty wanted to skip. To her, it was a strong signal. Their relationship had been transferred out of the ICU. It was still fragile, there was no doubt about that, but its condition was no longer critical.

Before they parted for their respective classes, Karla asked, "Are you up for a run tomorrow?"

Ty tripped on the steps up the building and dropped her backpack.

"Yes, definitely," she said as she bent to pick up her bag.

For the next few weeks, it continued like that. They had lunch together, ran together, and even started having an occasional dinner together, but Karla slept at her house and Ty slept at hers. There was nothing beyond a goodbye hug here and a hello kiss—on the cheek—there.

One afternoon, Ty sat in the courtyard on campus talking to Sarah on the phone while she waited for Karla to show up for their standing lunch date.

When she saw Karla walking toward her, Ty said, "Hey, Sar. I need to go. Karla just got here."

"Let me talk to her," Sarah said.

"What?"

"I want to talk to Karla."

"Um, okay. Hold on." Ty pulled the phone away from her ear and gave Karla a one-armed hug. "I'm on the phone with Sarah. She wants to talk to you."

"To me?" Karla asked

Ty handed her the phone. "Uh-huh."

With her brow furrowed, Karla raised the phone to her ear. "Hello, this is Karla."

Although she wanted to stay and listen, Ty made a quick lap around the courtyard to give them a little privacy.

When she circled back, Karla was ending the call. She smiled and handed Ty back her phone.

"Everything okay?" Ty asked.

"Yep."

Ty shuffled her feet. "What did Sarah have to say?"

The smile on Karla's face grew larger. "She said you were a dumb shit for lying to me, but that you have a heart of gold."

"Really?"

"Really."

"That sounds like something Sarah would say," Ty said with a laugh.

Karla pulled her into a tight hug. "I told her I agreed with her on both counts."

Ty's heart pounded in her chest. "You did?"

"Uh-huh."

That night, after dinner at Ty's house, Karla took her hand and silently led her upstairs to the bedroom. The room was dark except for a small white nightlight in the corner. Karla stopped short of the bed and placed a series of tender kisses on Ty's lips, causing her skin to prickle all over. When Karla pulled back, Ty could just make out the soft features of her face in the dimly lit room. She held Ty's gaze and they shared a smile, but neither of them uttered a word. Karla gave her one last kiss before turning her attention to Ty's shirt.

Karla caressed each button with her thumb before she slipped it free and paused briefly before moving onto the next one. Her pace drove Ty wild with anticipation. When she released the last button, she slid the shirt off Ty's body and dropped it to the floor. Karla unlatched her bra and sent it in the same direction as the shirt. Ty arched her back, beckoning Karla to touch her. Instead, Karla directed her hand to the zipper of Ty's jeans. Only once Ty was completely naked did Karla touch her. Ty's stomach tensed as strong fingers moved over its surface. Karla's hands smoothed over her bare breasts. Ty's head fell back, and she arched again. Karla's fingers trickled up and down her arm before sliding around her waist.

"You are," Karla whispered, pausing to kiss Ty's right shoulder and then her left, "so beautiful."

A cocktail of arousal, love, and happiness poured through Ty. It was intoxicating. Like she'd just rounded the top of a rollercoaster and was dropping down the other side. She pulled Karla into her arms and moaned in frustration when she realized she was still fully clothed. She kissed Karla softly on the lips and tugged at her sweater.

"Off," she commanded.

Karla pulled her sweater over her head and reached back to unlatch her bra. As soon as her breasts sprung free, Ty reached up to cup them in her hands.

"I've missed you guys," she whispered.

Karla let out a soft laugh and eyed Ty as she bent to capture one of her hard nipples with her mouth. Ty sucked hard and Karla moaned. Together they fumbled with the buttons of Karla's jeans, and once they were loose, Ty tugged them and her silk panties to the floor.

Ty stood back and raked her eyes over Karla's naked body. She ran a hand over Karla's hard ass and down over her strong thighs. This time, when she pulled Karla into her arms, Ty's skin sizzled. Karla's breasts pushed against hers and their hips thrust together.

When Karla's lips crushed against hers, Ty's legs went weak and she collapsed into Karla's arms. Karla pulled back slightly.

She smiled into Ty's lips and asked, "You okay there?"

Ty nodded. "Just happy." She started to cry. She felt Karla's finger wipe a tear from her cheek, and when Ty looked into her eyes, she saw that Karla was crying too. She pulled Karla into her arms and hugged her with all of her might. "I cannot imagine my life without you."

Karla nuzzled her head against Ty's neck. "I can't imagine my life without you either."

They stood there like that for a long time, their naked bodies wrapped tightly together.

Eventually, they fell to the bed together, and in an instant Karla's lips were on her. She kissed hungrily, and the fire between Ty's legs reignited with a vengeance.

Ty circled each of Karla's breasts with her finger before moving her hand over her firm stomach and along the inside of her thighs.

"Touch me, Ty," Karla pleaded.

Her breathing deepened when Ty's fingers danced over her mound and glided between her folds. Karla swung one of her strong legs over Ty's torso and squeezed her tightly as she came. When the leg went limp, Karla whispered, "Get up here."

She greeted Ty with another passionate kiss and caressed her breasts. When she pulled her lips from Ty's, she drew them down along her shoulders, her chest, her stomach, leaving light kisses in her wake. When Karla's mouth found its target, Ty hissed. A few swipes of Karla's tongue were enough to push her over the edge and she cried out when she came. Karla kissed the inside of both her thighs before crawling back up beside her. Ty wept silently as she fell asleep in Karla's arms. At that moment, she doubted there was a happier person on the planet than her.

CHAPTER FORTY-SEVEN

As she looked around Val and Teresa's family room, Ty's heart swelled. A big banner with the words "Congratulations Ty!" hung over the kitchen island, a massive sheet cake with "You Go Grad" occupied much of the dining room table, and a dozen helium balloons bounced against the ceiling. She'd earned her degree a few weeks earlier and had just gotten word she'd passed the nursing exam.

Most importantly though, the room was filled with lots of laughing people. All the friends Ty had made since moving back to Denver. Even James and Scotty had come in from Steamboat for the party. Scotty was still in a wheelchair, but he looked as dapper as ever. Sarah hadn't been able to make it because she was traveling for work, but she'd promised to visit soon so she could congratulate Ty in person.

As Ty thought back to when her parents had died and how far she'd come since then, her eyes moistened.

Karla walked up beside her, and when she noticed the tears in Ty's eyes, she rubbed her back. "What's wrong?"

Ty shook her head. "Nothing's wrong. Just the opposite. Everything is perfect. I think I'm overwhelmed by it all." Ty grabbed a *Happy Graduation* napkin off the table and dabbed her eyes. "There was a time when I thought my dream of becoming a nurse was lost forever. I stopped believing in myself." She waved her hand across the room. "Yet, here I am, nursing degree in hand and surrounded by all these loving, caring people."

Karla wrapped an arm over her shoulders and kissed her on the forehead. "You should be really proud of yourself. I know I am."

Ty leaned into Karla and smiled. She wasn't a terribly vain person, but she was proud of herself too. After winning the lottery, she could have squandered the opportunity to turn her life around, but she hadn't. Instead, she'd perused her dream, and she'd found Karla. Kind, smart, sexy, and strong Karla. It was as if she'd won the jackpot twice in one year.

She turned in Karla's embrace and said, "I was going to wait and tell you this tonight…"

"What, baby?"

"I got a call just before the party. It was the Hartford Clinic," Ty said.

"And? What did they say?"

"I got the job. I start work in two weeks."

A huge smile lit up Karla's face and she snaked her strong arms around Ty's waist. "Holy shit! That's fantastic news. Congratulations. I knew you'd get it."

"Thanks. I'm so freaking excited." Ty looked around to make sure no one else was in ear shot and said, "After they offered me the job, the issue of salary came up. And well, I insisted they pay me a dollar a year." She grinned. "You know, since I don't really need the money."

"How'd they react when you told them that?" Karla asked with a chuckle.

"There was silence on the other end of the line. I think the woman thought I was kidding. I assured her I most certainly was not."

"Ha, I bet she was downright giddy when realized you were serious."

"To put it mildly," Ty said. "The clinic relies on grants and private donations for most of its funding, and I get the sense they're barely scraping by. Having an RN who's willing to work full time for basically free will make a real difference to their bottom line."

"I bet it will." Karla dropped one arm from Ty's hip, grabbed a chip from the wicker bowl on the nearby table, and popped it into her mouth. "It'll also make a real difference to the patients who rely on the clinic. From what I've heard, most of them live below the poverty line and many of them don't have health insurance."

"That's true and that's the main reason why I want to work there, but it's not just that. I like that the Hartford Clinic is staffed by nurse practitioners, not doctors. The concept makes a lot of sense."

"And nurse practitioners are a lot cheaper than doctors."

"That's for sure, but the care they can provide is pretty similar to that of a physician."

"So is your goal to eventually become an NP?" Karla asked.

"Yeah, definitely. A bunch of RNs *work* at the clinic, but if I want to play a major role there, and I most certainly do, I'll need to earn a graduate degree in nursing. My plan is to work at the clinic as an RN for a year or so and then apply to grad school."

"That means," Karla said and gave her a soft kiss on the lips, "you should finish grad school about the same time I finish my undergrad. The timing will be perfect."

A lump formed in Ty's throat and she about melted right there in Val and Tereasa's living room. Karla's words meant she was thinking about the future, a future where the two of them were together.

"I love you," Ty whispered.

"I love you too, Ty." Karla slid a hand into Ty's and placed another soft kiss on her lips.

There was a commotion in the kitchen, and Ty looked up to see Sarah walk into the room. She burst out crying. If the day hadn't been perfect before, it certainly was now.

"Surprise!" Sarah said. "What, aren't you happy to see me?"

"Come here, you big dope," Ty said and pulled her into her arms. When she stepped back, she wiped tears from her eyes and looked at Karla. "You had something to do with this, didn't you?"

Karla shared a look with Sarah. "I might have."

CHAPTER FORTY-EIGHT

A few weeks later, Ty put in a call to Kate and Derek. The annual fundraising gala for the Hartford Clinic was in early September, and Ty wanted to make a significant donation before then. She asked Kate to do a little research on the clinic's financial situation.

Kate called her back a few days later. "The clinic's finances are extremely tight, but they appear to be well managed."

"Thanks for doing the due diligence."

"Not a problem," Kate said. "Have you thought about how much you'd like to donate, Ty?"

"I'm thinking three million dollars." Ty wasn't sure she'd ever get used to talking about such large dollar figures like they were nothing.

"Based on my conversation with their director of development, a donation of that size would have a real impact on the clinic," Kate said.

"I hope to give them more in the future," Ty said, "but that feels like a good place to start."

"Since this is the first of what are likely to be numerous charitable donations, we suggest setting up some sort of charitable account. We'll fund the account with stocks and other assets that have appreciated. This way you get to double dip on the tax benefits. You'll avoid capital gains *and* get a sizable tax deduction for the donation."

"Okay," Ty replied somewhat hesitantly because she wasn't totally following.

Kate patiently explained the tax benefits of setting up the charitable account and funding her donations from that rather than just donating cash.

"Do whatever you need to do," Ty said.

"Okay," Kate said. "We'll work to get everything arranged and reach out to the Hartford Clinic to figure out the logistics."

Before they ended the call, Ty said, "It's absolutely *imperative* that the donation be made anonymously."

"Understood. That shouldn't be a problem," Kate replied.

That night, Ty relayed her conversation with Kate to Karla as they readied for a run around the park.

"Shit, she seems so damn smart. You're lucky to have her."

"I know, right? I called Kate the day after I won the lottery. It was one of the smartest decisions I've ever made."

Karla gave her a sweet smile. "Ty, you really have handled all of this extremely well. You should be crazy proud of yourself. It's obvious you have a good head on your shoulders."

"Coming from you, that means a lot."

"Thanks," Karla said, "but I think you're selling yourself short. You're incredibly resilient."

Ty gave her a goofy grin. "How did I get so lucky to have the most amazing girlfriend in the whole world?"

Karla gave her a quick kiss on the cheek. "Catch me if you can," she yelled, and took off running down the bike path.

God, I love that woman, Ty though as she hurried after her, giggling like a little girl.

* * *

The clinic's fundraising gala was held at an old warehouse turned trendy event space. Flowers seemed to cover every surface. There was a cocktail reception followed by a sit-down dinner. When Karla and Ty stepped inside, a smiling young woman greeted them at the check-in table.

"May I have your names please?"

"Margaret MacIntyre and Karla Rehn," Ty said.

Karla smirked when Ty uttered her full legal name. Ty had told her a hundred times just how much she despised it.

The young woman scanned the list in front of her. "You're at table seven," she said and handed them each a small card with a number etched on it.

Ty took Karla's arm and proudly led her into the cocktail reception. When a waiter walked by with a tray of white wine, they each grabbed a glass.

"We should look for Val and Teresa," Ty said. She'd bought a whole table at the gala and had invited Val and Teresa and a few of their other friends to join them for the evening.

The warehouse was teeming with people, but they eventually spotted Val and Teresa on the far side of the room. Val was wearing a black cocktail dress, and Teresa had on a stylish, Hillary Clinton-esque pantsuit.

Val let out a whistle when they approached. "Look at you *sexy* ladies. You both look amazing. I don't think I've ever seen either one of you in a dress, let alone heels," she said with a loud chuckle.

"And you're one to talk, Miss Tomboy," Ty said, waving her hand in Val's direction.

"You both look incredible. You clean up good," Karla said.

They eventually made their way into the dining room to find table number seven.

"What are these?" Teresa asked, picking a cardboard paddle up off the table.

"Oh, there's a live auction during dessert," Val explained. "I read about it in the gala program. Those must be our bidding paddles."

Wait staff appeared and set a salad in front of each person. As soon as they disappeared, a petite man approached their table.

He had a bottle of white wine in one hand and a bottle of red in the other. He introduced himself as Enrique and proceeded to circle the table, filling everyone's glasses. Over the course of dinner, Enrique ensured their wine glasses never went empty.

"They certainly are pouring the wine freely," Dipti remarked after Enrique made one of his many rounds.

"They want to get you liquored up before the auction. The idea is to bid high and bid often," Teresa said with a belly laugh.

As if on cue, the president of the clinic's board of directors approached the podium. "May I please have your attention," his voice boomed.

The chatter in the room quieted. He thanked everyone for coming to the gala and gave a short history of the Hartford Clinic. He paused briefly as the clinic's director of development joined him up on stage. The only noise in the room was the tinkling of forks against dessert plates.

"As you know," the man continued, "we have an amazing live auction planned for you tonight, but first, I have a major financial announcement!"

The clinking of forks ceased abruptly.

Ty shifted uncomfortably in her seat and held her breath as she waited for him to continue. Karla reached under the table and clasped her hand.

The director of development stepped to the microphone and cleared her throat. "The clinic has received an extraordinarily generous donation in the amount of three…million…dollars!"

The crowd erupted in applause.

When the applause began to subside, she said, "The donation has come to us anonymously and with no strings attached. These funds will have a *substantial* impact on the clinic and all of the people we serve."

Applause roared through the room again. Everyone seemed to be eyeing their neighbor, wondering who the anonymous donor was.

"That's fantastic news!" Val said.

"Truly fantastic," others at the table echoed.

"Holy shit!" Teresa hollered.

Of course, none of them, except Karla, had a clue the donor sat among them. Ty had known the announcement was coming. Kate had told her the clinic wanted to announce it at the gala. Still, she broke into tears. She dabbed her eyes with her dinner napkin.

"Sorry, I'm just so happy for the clinic," she said to her friends around the table. "You all know how deeply I believe in it."

Enrique appeared to top off their wineglasses as the auctioneer ambled up to the stage to begin the silent auction. As he explained the bidding procedure, attendants scurried around the room distributing pamphlets detailing the lots that would be up for bid. Ty took a deep breath as the auctioneer began the bidding for the first lot. The noise in the room disappeared.

She closed her eyes and reflected on how much she had to be thankful for. She had the most wonderful, kind, understanding, and beautiful partner in Karla. She was on her way to a rewarding career in nursing. She had wonderful friends, and she was starting to use her financial resources to help others. If her parents were alive, she knew they'd be so proud of her. And Merce the Nurse was probably smiling down at her, too.

Bella Books, Inc.

Women. Books. Even Better Together.

P.O. Box 10543
Tallahassee, FL 32302

Phone: 800-729-4992
www.bellabooks.com